YOU CAN TRUST SOME ALIENS

(Book Two of the Trust Series)

To start at the beginning of the Series,
please read: ***Can You Trust an Alien?***

K.S. Riggin

Table of Contents

Chapter One: Alien Husband

I was desperate to catch a glimpse of a Natharan, but I couldn't see a thing. I bit my tongue to keep from yelling out my frustration. I measured the seconds that passed by the beating of my speeding heart.

Yet, not more than a minute could it have been before the police forced the media back, and the cameras were swinging once again at me. Then, for the first time, I saw a Natharan.

As if someone had suddenly rammed his fist into my middle, all the breath in me exhaled.

The being I saw, the Natharan, was like all the beauty you expect to see when you reach Heaven. It wasn't like seeing an angel. One supposed that angels would be beautiful but untouchable, so clean and white and shining with the light of Heaven. The sight of them would almost overpower you with their brightness.

This personage was every bit as beautiful as an angel, but not in that same blinding way. He shone in a shimmer of greens, the color of leaves in spring when they are fresh and pure, and a quiet breeze strikes up so that the leaves flutter about and sparkle with their underside, like silver coins, flashing in the sunlight.

The leaves were his skin, and they, like tiny flower petals of individual shimmers, ran up his neck, almost into his face. His face, a smooth-skinned green, was exotically beautiful, with features similar to a human's but balanced exactly perfectly. His cheekbones were high and exquisite. It was as though an artist had carved them in spring-green marble to blend with his full lips that smiled an angel's smile of perfect peace.

This Natharan had the golden hair that Cegan had spoken of. It was shiny as bullion and, just as he'd said, the exact color of the metal. His hair stood upright, down the middle of his head, spiking up at least four inches and the same distance in width. The eyes of the alien, green as a cat's eyes with diamond centers, were looking at me, but I was frozen, staring at his great height, a full seven feet, with an additional four or five inches of hair.

The Natharan was wearing Earth clothing, a sleeveless blue vest, dark blue trousers, and mint-green jogging shoes. The shoes, for some reason, brought a smile to my face.

Once more, my eyes traveled upwards. Even at a second glance, I didn't know whether to bow or fall to the ground in worship at his beauty. I'd forgotten my husband, forgotten why I was there. I only knew that it would be wondrous to touch the being that I saw before me.

Then I heard him speak, and the spell was broken. I recognized the voice as Cegan. "Kira," he said. "Speak to me so I will know you."

I couldn't move, but I could talk. "Cegan, why didn't you tell me? Why would you not give me the chance to prepare? I thought I was ready for anything, but not this. Not you. You're like an angel, a huge, green angel."

He walked towards me, his eyes never leaving mine. "Kira, I am only Cegan, your husband. Know my soul as I know yours." He stopped two yards away from me. It was not close enough, and yet, for a moment, I wanted only to retreat.

"Kira, will you come to me?"

"She'll do no such thing. This has gone far enough." My father had found his tongue.

I'd forgotten there were others in the world. As if waking from sleep, I realized that flashes were going off, and there was a crowd of people all around.

"I would guess you are Kira's father. Forgive me for not greeting you, Mr. Stevens." Cegan spoke these words to my father, but his eyes never left mine.

"Damn right, I am, and there's not going to be any marriage between you two."

For the first time, Cegan's eyes moved from mine. I gasped with the pain the loss brought me. But Cegan was not upset. He smiled down at my father. "You are too late, Mr. Stevens. All the laws of Earth and Natharan tie Kira and me together. I will honor you, Mr. Stevens, as I honor your daughter. Shall we shake on it?"

Cegan moved forward, stretched out his hand, and took my father's before I think Dad even realized what he was doing. Then, my father was like someone hypnotized. His words of protest sputtered. He, like I, stared up at the green angel before us.

But when the hands were pulling apart, the handshake ending, Dad gripped Cegan's hand with his other to hold it locked in his. Looking deeply into Cegan's eyes, my father said, "Please, I ask you. Don't take Kira as your wife yet. Do you understand what I mean? Don't physically possess her. Wait a day. I beg of you. Give her time."

Once more, Cegan's eyes were on mine. I felt warm as if I were lying at just the right temperature of bath water. Cegan blinked and smiled down at me. "I will honor your request," he told my father, yet his eyes never relinquished mine.

The males' handshake ended, and Cegan turned his full attention back to me. Once more, I could hardly breathe, yet the feel of it was heaven. Cegan stretched out his hand. His palm was open, waiting for mine. "Will you come to me?"

"No, Kira," Joe yelled. "Don't go any closer."

I hardly heard Joe. My hand moved to touch Cegan's without my willing it. I took a step forward.

Joe caught my elbow and attempted to pull me back.

"Let me go," I said. "This is what I want."

I felt Joe's hand releasing me. Perhaps the others pulled him back. I don't know. Like a sleepwalker, I moved towards my husband until I stood so close I almost touched the greenness of his chest. Would I hear choirs of angels singing or trumpets announcing his presence if I leaned against him and listened to his heart?

The hand not holding onto me rose up to touch my cheek. "As usual, you have many protectors, Siren."

"I do not need them."

"I know. You have told me. Are you not afraid of me?" he asked, caressing my skin softly, hesitantly.

How could I speak with that finger teasing me with the daintiness of a butterfly's wings? I breathed in the scent of him. My voice whispered, "You are my husband, Cegan. How could I fear you?"

I could see that I'd amazed him. His facial gestures were not unlike ours. The corner of his mouth lifted, and he smiled down at me. "And if I ask you to go with me into the ship?" His fingers had stopped their feathery stroking as if waiting for my reply.

Did he not see how I could barely breathe from wanting to touch him? I longed only to feel his lips on mine and his fingers once again touching my cheek. "I will be happy no matter where we are if we are together," I said in a breathless whisper.

They were the words I'd said to him over the transystem. I saw that he recognized them and was pleased.

He raised my hand and touched his lips to it. "Ah, Siren, you have sung to me, and I have come."

He raised his eyes from mine then and stared out at the crowd a moment. The police and the black-and-red officials from SpacePort were holding the people back, but the chanting was in full force: "Alien-lover, alien bride; Terran traitor, where's your pride?"

The man with the loud speaker was still speaking on sin, asking how I could fornicate with an alien beast. Picket signs were waving back and forth to catch the attention of the cameras: "Kira Stevens, First Space Whore," proclaimed the one in front. Another said, "Aren't Earth Men good enough?"

Cegan's eyes moved back down to mine. "It distresses me that your innocence has been breached. My inability to protect you is a great pain inside me. If only . . ."

"You have done nothing to cause this. And I am not an innocent to be protected."

"My Kira," he said, smiling more broadly.

Then I saw his teeth. There were so many of them, large and smooth-edged, so different from ours. I pulled back suddenly.

"I have frightened you. How?"

He was holding his hands up. It was like the Cedtarant greeting. Should I touch my fingertips to his? I looked up at his eyes. His brow was wrinkled, his eyes narrowed. "I will not hurt you, Kira. Not ever."

I looked up at the ship. It was so huge. The copper trimmings on the black, smudgy metal no longer glowed in a friendly manner. It was an ugly ship. I shuddered.

"Your ship is so big," I said, needing to speak, not knowing what to say.

"All Natharan trader ships are, Kira. It would be quieter inside, but if it frightens you, we do not need to go there yet."

I took a deep breath. My legs were trembling. Could I enter that monstrosity? I wanted to hang back, to plead for time, but everyone was watching. I closed my eyes. *I will see only Cegan's soul. I will trust him. Please, God, help me to trust him.*

I took a step towards my husband and joined my hand to his.

"Kira, don't go with him!" my father cried out.

"We can't protect you if you go inside the ship," Joe said.

I jerked back. Instantly, Cegan's fingers released my hand.

I glanced at my father. He had not moved, but there were worry lines all over his face. "Kira, you don't know that alien. You don't know what he'll do to you once he gets you inside his ship."

Joe was standing beside my father. His face was white. His eyes were full of misery. The others were there, too: Terry, Juan, and Dave. They were all shaking their heads, telling me not to go.

I looked away from them and up at my husband's face. The green of his skin was jarring. His eyes were strange and frightening. How could I go with him? My father and the others were right. I didn't know this person. He was beautiful, eerily beautiful, but who was he really? He wasn't Terran. He wasn't one of us.

"Do you not remember the chord of shared memories that has woven us together, Kira?" Cegan's soft voice began to speak. "Do you not remember how we talked for so many hours about Trust, Truth, Integrity, and the meaning of life?

"Kira, my Siren, remember how our voices called to each other across the endless night, and we traversed space? Your laughter was the song of the night for me. Will you laugh for me again? Will I hear it when your fears are soothed?

"Kira, remember the day you married me, and we sat there with space between us, and yet our hands touched?"

His eyes were heartbreaking. I could read them. I could understand what they were telling me. And his words were thoughts that we had shared all those days between us.

"I remember, Cegan. I remember. I told you I wouldn't be afraid, but I am, Cegan. I don't know why, but I am."

"I will give you time, my Siren, all the time you need. Remember my promise?"

My hand stretched out once more to Cegan's. He let me take his, yet his fingers did not move to enfold mine. I stared down, waiting, but still he didn't move.

I drew another step closer until my other hand could touch his chest. Once more, I began to breathe in his sweet, fragrant odor. I curled the fingers of my right hand, entwining mine with his.

Why was it always me who hesitated? A flash of anger goaded my words. "You could force me to go with you, couldn't you, Cegan? You could pick me up and carry me into your ship before anyone could interfere. You could do that, couldn't you?"

Cegan remained silent. His eyes studied me, but their sadness did not change.

I knew my anger was irrational. Yet I needed to hear from him. "Please, answer me."

"I am Natharan, Kira. We do not force others. Have I misunderstood your question? If you wish me to pick you up, I will do so, but I think it will frighten your father and the others who watch."

It was such a Cegan reply. How could I have doubted him?

"Oh, Cegan. I'm sorry. I don't know why I said that. Let's go to your ship. I'm ready."

Cegan tilted his head slightly. His brow was still wrinkled. He was not smiling. "You are sure?"

I nodded my head. "Yes, I want to."

We had not gone three steps before my father called out again. "Kira!"

Cegan did not wait for me to stop this time. At my father's plea, he halted and paused so I could speak.

I did not let go of my husband's hand, but I turned towards my father. "Dad, I love you, but I'm going with Cegan. He's my husband, and I trust him."

"Don't trust him," Joe urged.

"Take care of my father, please, Joe. And thank you for being here and for protecting us. Juan, Terry, Dave, and Joe, I will be OK."

I tugged at Cegan's hand, and we walked forward. Neither of us spoke for those few steps. Then, as we reached the ship, Cegan said something in words I couldn't understand. I turned to question him, but the ship's door was sliding open, and then a ramp was rippling down.

"You closed it?"

"It was better that way."

Cegan stepped onto the ramp, and I followed him. There were only three steps to climb, yet each step brought me closer to entering the huge alien ship. We took the steps very slowly, step-by-step, side-by-side.

I think Cegan feared that at any moment, I would bolt away, and I prayed for my legs to support me. They were wobbly as if walking on stilts. At the top of the ramp, there was a raised threshold to cross. I lifted my right foot and stepped over it and into Cegan's ship.

Chapter Two: Onboard an Alien Ship

"Wait," said a gravelly voice, urgent in its appeal. My left foot had joined the right, but I turned and looked back down. Cegan had not yet entered. He was still on the outward side of the ship's threshold. We stood like that, me inside and Cegan out there, our hands still entwined. We waited to hear what the official wanted.

"I am from the United Nations of Earth, Mars, Venus, and the four moon colonies," the man said. "We wish to welcome you. Please follow me. We have prepared a meeting for you."

Cegan's body blocked the doorway. I could not see the man, nor could I see Cegan's face, yet when my husband spoke I knew the sound of his amusement. "I thank you for your welcome," Cegan told the man, "but I will be too busy to talk with you until next week. I am in a honeymoon."

With that, Cegan turned, entered the ship, spoke in his strange language, and the door closed with a heavy thud.

Cegan had still not let go of my hand. He lifted it up and kissed my palm. "Why do you tremble?" he asked. "Have I frightened you again?"

I was inside an immense alien vessel with a huge green giant that had spiked golden hair. I thought I had a pretty good reason to be scared, but I took a deep breath and tried to relax.

Cegan had dropped my hand and was backing away from me. His brow was wrinkled in worry.

"It's not you, Cegan," I said quickly. My voice came out little more than a whisper. "It was the door. It sounded so final like it was bolted shut."

"You have only to ask me to open it, and I will do so."

I was losing my voice. I coughed and tried to clear it. "Open the door, please, Cegan."

The door unbuckled at the sound of Cegan's voice saying some word in what I presumed was the Natharan language. The door slid slowly open.

I stepped towards it. I could feel Cegan watching me. I turned to look at him. His strange, green cat-eyes looked dejected. The diamonds in the center had closed slightly as the door slid open. As strange as they looked, the pupils in his eyes reacted to light just like ours. The thought gave me some relief.

I was standing in the doorway, one foot outside on the ramp, one foot inside. I was once again breathing Earth air. The strange scent that I had only half-noticed dissipated. Had it been the odor of plastic or being cooped up in a recycled environment? It hadn't been an unpleasant odor, but . . .

I watched as Cegan's hands balled into fists. The length of his fingers curled up within his palm and made a huge fist. Through the opening of his vest, I could see his chest was flexed tight. His arms, covered in petals, bulged outward with muscles that widened as the fists developed. He was not purposely posing as a body builder would, but his muscles were as taut as an overarched bow.

Even the bones of Cegan's face were more strongly revealed. It was as if the smooth-skinned flesh of his face had drawn inward, yet not unpleasantly so. but, though his body was rigid, I felt no violence in him. His hands stayed at his side. He made no attempt to prevent me from exiting out the door.

Outside the ship, the crowd was hysterical. The ranting had continued or perhaps escalated as the door was once more opened. The reds-and-blacks were still holding the media away from the ship. I could see Juan and Terry. Their eyes were staring into mine as if questioning me about what I wanted.

"Alien whore, come out of that ship of sin. Come back to us."

I shuddered and looked back at Cegan. He had not moved. "You will let me leave if I want?"

Cegan's eyes darkened, green overshadowed by black. A muscle twitched near his cheekbone. "You are my wife, not my slave, Kira. Why would I stop you?"

"Because you want me to stay?" I whispered.

The smile crept from the corner of his mouth to his eyes. It was just as I'd pictured it.

"Of course, I want you to stay, Kira, but you are free to go if that is your wish."

Outside, the reporters' cameras were flashing. The chanters had not stopped. The preacher was still sermonizing about sin. I turned back and waved to the crowd, searching for my father and Joe and Dave. If they were there, I could not see them. I spoke down to the microphones and said, "I'm fine. Please tell my father that."

I turned around then and walked back to Cegan. "Thank you. You can close the door again now."

The moan of the reporters was cut off by the sound of the door bolting. Somehow, the noise didn't threaten me this time. I reached down and picked up Cegan's hand. "Thank you for being so patient."

"I would wait years for you if you needed them, Kira, but you have been very brave."

I wasn't feeling brave. My eyes flitted about the room we were in. White walls, white ceiling, white floor. Nothing broke up the monotony. What if the rest of the ship were like this?

"I will show you my quarters," Cegan said, "if it does not frighten you to go there with me? When the night comes, you may share the room with me, or you can have your own if you prefer."

I sighed. "I would like to see your room."

Cegan smiled. "I like your sigh. I like your laugh. The only thing I do not like are your tears. Your tears cause me pain in here." The hand holding mine touched his chest.

"I will try not to cry often," I said, smiling up at him.

We walked through a long corridor. It was all done in white. Everything was quiet. Where was everyone?

Cegan was looking down at me. As if he could read my thoughts, he said, "I have told the crew to stay away. I think that one Natharan is enough to shock you."

He was right. I was pretty close to emotional overload already, and a whole crew of seven-foot, four-inch Natharans with spikes of golden hair was more than I could take.

Cegan's chamber, or quarters, as he called it, was white with touches of muted charcoal. I wasn't overly enthusiastic about its blandness. There was certainly not much to see: four walls and a bed.

Cegan watched my eyes circling the room. "When you are silent, Kira, I assume you are thinking. What are you thinking now, Siren? That the room is too large or too small, that you've made a mistake?" He had brought my hand up to his lips. There were sweet shivers in the touch of his mouth. The sound of his kisses was like a human's.

"I'm just confused, Cegan. Nothing is the way I thought it would be." I was looking down at my hand, the one he'd kissed. It was buried now in the largeness of Cegan's green, five-fingered hand. I was struggling against panic at Cegan's hugeness, his aura of strength.

"Is that good or bad?" Cegan was asking me.

I swallowed and breathed deeply. I looked down at his mint-green jogging shoes, struggling to remember that this was Cegan, the one I loved. I was trembling all over. I knew it was silly. It had to be a kind of delayed shock or that fear you had when you faced a dark room. You knew no one was there, no monsters, no threat, but you stopped, and you didn't want to go in until the lights were on.

"Cegan," I said, and my voice, which used to be so loud and sure, came out in the shakiest squeak. I took another deep breath and forced my voice to be stronger. "I have no reason to be, Cegan, but I am so scared."

"I know you are, Kira. Your body shivers as if you were cold, but I do not think you are. How can I ease your fear?"

"Oh, Cegan. I'm sorry. You're wonderful, and I think I love you, but . . ."

His body stiffened. "You *think* you love me?" It was almost an accusation. I had wounded him, yet I had not meant to.

"Cegan, please hold me," I cried out. I had told him I would try not to cry, but I found that the tears were rolling down my cheeks.

"If you are sure you want me to," he told me stiffly. The pain of my rejection was in each word he spoke.

I nodded through my tears.

Cautiously, Cegan raised up his arms. For a moment, I felt his hesitation, as if he worried that his touch would send me running off, screaming in fear. Then, carefully, gently, his arms enfolded me.

Strangely, I was not frightened by the feel of his arms around me. I was soothed. I shut my eyes and leaned my head against his chest. I could hear the beating of his heart. Did it beat more quickly than ours, or was our embrace speeding up its beat?

I breathed in the smell of Cegan. He smelled like rain on cement. It was a pleasing smell. The scent made me smile. As if I were hearing the pattern of those first drops of rain, there was a familiarity to it. The sound of his heartbeat was the rain steadily playing its drumbeat on my roof, and the sound and the smell made me feel warm and safe.

I felt Cegan's hand timidly move upward. He was so unsure of me. Did he still fear I would back away from him now? Once more, I could feel the same spell I had felt when I first saw him. It was weaving itself around me, calming me, making me desire Cegan's touch.

Cegan's hand had reached its goal. His fingers were stroking my hair. What magic was in Cegan's fingers that stole all my concentration? It was too strong for me. I was afraid again. Why could I focus on nothing but his hand and the fingers that made me feel so limp and weak?

"Please talk to me," I begged.

His hand stilled. "I love you, Kira. I will not hurt you."

I sobbed once, trying to get my breath.

"It's all right, Kira. Keep your eyes closed and listen to my voice."

I said nothing. I couldn't understand this fear. I was doing everything I had promised not to do. It was Cegan. How could I be afraid?

"I like your father, Kira. He has strength and courage. You must have inherited those qualities from his genes."

I breathed in, trying to stop my tears, listening to Cegan's heartbeat.

"It was hard for him to watch his daughter leave with one he does not know and does not trust. I would like it if we went to visit him tomorrow."

Relief poured through me. It was like the end of the rollercoaster ride a friend had talked me into. I'd thought I would die. It had gone on for hours, although my friend assured me it was less than a minute.

"Yes, Cegan, I would like that."

"If you can direct me, I will take us there."

I sighed. "I'm sorry I cried. Do Natharan women cry so easily?"

Cegan's fingers were once again separating the strands of my hair. He stopped to look down at me. One finger lifted up my face so he could see my eyes. "Kira, I have no interest in what Natharan women do. My wife is from Earth. I am only interested in her."

At that moment, I met his eyes. Then I shut mine quickly and burrowed my face back into his chest. "I'm sorry," I said, crying again. "You are so patient. I didn't know I was such a coward."

"You are not a coward. You are quite daring, Kira. I knew that Terrans were xenophobic. I was prepared to encounter your fear."

"With my eyes closed, it is the same as when we talked on the transystem."

"No, it is better. I am touching you, Kira. It is much better now."

I opened my eyes. When I did, my eyes saw only the vest that Cegan wore. I stared at the buttons, counting them, examining them. Then, I braved what I had been afraid to ask. "Am I ugly to you?"

"Oh, Kira, no. You are my heart's desire. Do you not know that? Will you let me prove it to you?"

I gulped and stared at the tiny silver buttons that held my eyes. "I think so," I said.

"There is indecision in your voice. How hard I have worked to smooth that out, to ease your fear."

He picked me up, and my eyes were once more level with his face. I stared at him. I saw again how beautiful he was. But he was alien, different, and strange.

He read my eyes, and again, he repeated, "I will never hurt you, Kira."

His eyes were watching mine so intently that I knew he was waiting for a sign of whether to put me down or continue holding me. Timidly, I reached up and touched his face. The lines of his cheekbone were like finely chiseled stone, hard and solid, yet the skin that covered it was smooth. "Is it all right to touch you?"

"It pleasures me, Kira."

I dropped my hand as if he'd scolded me. "Why did you pick me up?"

"Was it wrong? I will put you down if you wish." He was smiling as he looked down at me. His teeth were white, even, and perfectly spaced in double rows.

"I am heavy for you to stand holding me."

His smile grew even fuller. "Kira, I could hold you for one of your hours, and you would still not be heavy. I like holding you up close to me if it does not frighten you."

I did not like feeling like a sack of grain he liked to hold. "Cegan, I would rather stand or sit. Could we sit down somewhere?"

His mouth curled upwards. "I understand. I know you value your independence. I shall carry you to the bed platform if you will permit it?"

The platform was higher than a normal bed. It was about four feet off the ground. Cegan placed me down on it, and then he stretched out beside me with a space between us. I admired the feel of the platform's soft, padded fur. "It feels like my cat," I told Cegan as I ran my hand over the softness of its surface.

Cegan's eyes were smiling into mine, but I could tell he wasn't thinking about cats or the texture of the platform. His hand took mine and moved it to trace the muscles in his face. "I will not hurt you, Kira. Touch me. My hands will stay at my side."

I slid my hand further up his face. I could feel the hard bones beneath his skin. The lashes above and under his eyes were golden like his hair. I touched his brow. He had no eyebrows, not even fine individual hairs. The skin of his skull was like a beaded purse I'd had one time, smooth like the tiniest pebbles rounded by a flow of running water yet all knitted closely together.

Cegan's eyes encouraged me. I let my hand touch his golden hair. It felt like a bristly horse's mane cut short and growing out. I sat up on my knees and looked to see what Cegan's hair did in the back. The stripe of gold, like a Mohawk, continued down until it reached his neck, where it fell downwards. In the back, it reminded me of Daniel Boone's old raccoon hats.

"Is it like a tail?" I asked and then felt stupid.

Cegan smiled and nodded. His hand reached out to touch my hair. "It is not at all like yours. Is that what frightens you?"

I sat back down and looked into Cegan's eyes. They were strange eyes but not cold. They held as much expression as a human's. "You are not as frightening sitting down."

Cegan's mouth bobbed up at the sides. His eyes glittered like the stars in the night. "Must I always sit?"

I knew he was teasing me. I laughed. "You didn't tell me you were so tall. You said the same size as a Terran. You're gigantic!"

"And you are small. Would you love me if only I were your height?"

"You are teasing me again. It is in your voice, and your eyes are sparkling."

"You have not touched my lips," Cegan said, and his smile changed in some way.

I reached up to touch them, to trace their feel.

"Do you fear me still?"

I started to speak, but his lips were joining mine. It was only the briefest touch, and then he drew back, away from me.

I shook my head. I felt no fear. I wanted to kiss him again. I waited, and, once more, he leaned towards me. This time, when I felt him pull back, my arms went around his neck, and I held him against me. Slowly, I felt Cegan's arms gather me closer.

I don't know if all Natharans kiss like Terrans, but Cegan knew exactly what he was doing, and I wished for him never to stop. But he did. I moaned in protest when he pulled away.

His eyes studied mine a moment. Then he leaned forward to plant tiny kisses across my nose and cheeks. "Kira," he said, caressing my face with his long green fingers. "I would like to see all of you. Will you allow that?"

"Yes, I want you now while I can't think. Please."

I believe Cegan grunted at my words. It was a very human sound. Then he rolled over, away from me.

"Kira," he said, not looking at me. "I made a pledge to your father. I will not go back on it."

"What pledge?" I could barely remember our words outside the ship. Our meeting was a hundred years ago.

"I will not consummate our marriage today, Kira. It is what I promised your father."

I sat up. "Why? Why did you agree to that? You're my husband. Why shouldn't we . . ."

"Kira, my Siren," he said. He seized my hand and teased me with tiny kisses all across its palm. "It pleases me that you are ready so soon." His tongue took over, and the warmth of its touch on my palm was driving me crazy. I groaned.

"I did not expect you to be this adaptable. I was not sure you would ever . . ."

Again, I groaned. I could not take what he was doing to me. "Stop it, Cegan. Please. I can't endure this."

His lips were once more on mine. He gently forced me down onto my back. "Don't fret, my Siren. There are other ways to become acquainted. I will not leave you disappointed, my lovely wife."

I found Cegan's "other ways" enjoyable, but when our heat had dissipated and I was able to think rationally again, I was very irritated with my father's interference. It was long past time for the warden to retire!

Chapter Three: Getting to Know an Alien

We did not leave Cegan's quarters all that day. At times, we broke for refreshments. Cegan had a machine that dispensed bottles of water and energy bars. He assured me that neither would harm me if I took the pill he handed me. I swallowed it down without a qualm. I no longer had any fears about Cegan's words. He had been right about absolutely everything so far.

The energy bars were delicious. They tasted just like chocolate candy bars. Cegan explained how he had modeled them for me after human candy bars but had included all the essential vitamins and nutrients that I needed for my health.

"You could sell these and make a lot of money," I told him. "They are a lot better than any health bars I've ever tasted!"

Cegan only smiled and continued eating his own brand of the bar, which had no lovely chocolate smell and looked like something that could have been an early failure in energy bar experimentation. He swore to me that it was to his liking.

The water we drank came in blue plastic bottles. At least, that's what Cegan told me the bottles were made of, but the plastic felt more like glass, and it clinked when I clicked my fingernails against it. And it had the strangest top to it. There was nothing to open, even when it was first dispensed from the machine. Yet when I tipped the bottle upside down, the liquid flowed easily into my mouth. When we finished drinking the water, Cegan took the bottles and tossed them back into another section of the wall panel. Cegan explained that everything aboard the ship was recycled.

"I don't suppose you'd let me have one of those bottles when we go to see Dad, would you?"

"Why, Kira?" he asked me, with a look that told me he was still analyzing my facial expressions.

"Dad could take it to a bottling company and get rich from its design!"

"Would that make you happy?"

"To be rich?" I stared at Cegan, wondering if we were in the middle of one of those communication breakdowns.

He was still studying my face, searching my eyes.

"Everybody wants to be rich, Cegan. Don't Natharans?"

"It is one of the areas in which our cultures differ, Kira. No Natharan is ever without his basic needs, but accumulation is not a goal."

"So why do Natharans work? Why do you journey to different worlds to trade?"

"It is the family business. It is the service that my family gives to Natharan."

"Do you have to do it? What would happen if you were lazy or didn't like to travel through space? What then?"

"I would choose another in my place, as I will do if the business does not suit you."

"Then what would you do? Wouldn't you have to work at something to earn your food and . . . everything else?"

"Ah, Kira. So many questions. It is much easier to satisfy you in other ways."

"Cegan . . ."

The next morning came too early. I was not ready to "rise and shine," as Dad always put it, but Cegan decided that we needed to get up. When I wouldn't budge or open my eyes, he lifted me out of bed and attempted to dress me in fresh clothing. He had a good memory, but the problems he had trying to put on my bra had me laughing.

The clothes, he told me, had come from his clothing machine. I guess he'd understood from my countless descriptions of what I wore to work that my preference was pantsuits. I felt safest in trousers rather than dresses or skirts.

The shipboard suit he handed me was likely a linen-blend, or its alien equivalent, with a two-button navy blazer and matching business slacks. The white blouse that accompanied the outfit had the texture of silk. I bet none of it was washable.

I have no idea how Cegan knew my size, but he even got the underthings right. Neither the bra nor panty was the slinky black lingerie that my friends wore on dates. I didn't wear that kind of thing. These were more in the vein of common sense but perfectly form fitting and comfortable.

Cegan looked a bit embarrassed at my questioning but said that the machine reproduced anything that was inserted into its open slot. That told me how the clothing fit, but not how he so precisely chose something exactly right.

I giggled with a bit of embarrassment, too, because a male buying such personal things for me felt awkward.

Cegan froze and stared down at me. I stopped laughing when I saw the expression on his face, but it was too late by then. He seized me in an embrace so full of longing and desperation I could barely breathe between his kisses. I think I came close to passing out before Cegan realized it.

"Forgive me," he said, holding me away from him.

"For what, Cegan? I could kill my father!"

"Kira! You would wish to . . . ?"

"No, of course not. It's just an expression."

"I am relieved. It is not one I have learned yet. Perhaps I should use the translator again."

"You're not using it? But you're speaking Engspan!"

Cegan reached out for my hand. As he held it, I studied his. His hand had none of the soft-petaled skin of his chest. It was bald green from the wrist down. Cegan's fingers were longer than a human's, and his fingernails were tapered more like claws but without any point at the end. He was caressing my hand with his fingers, but he was unaware of my inspection. I could see by the unfocused gaze of his eyes that he was pondering some thought.

"Cegan, you don't have to figure it out. If you ask me, I'll tell you."

The black diamond centers of his eyes narrowed as his eyes came back into focus. "You were surprised I had learned Engspan. Did you not accept my word?"

"Cegan, of course, I believed you. It is just that Terrans take years to learn a language. You only had weeks!"

"I see," he said, and his eyes softened. He reached out and curled a strand of my hair around his finger. He teased the curl and played with its springiness. I felt like purring. Even the touch of his fingertip on a lock of my hair made my body yearn for his kisses.

Cegan's eyes were smiling into mine. I knew he was aware of my thoughts, yet still, he played, his fingers caressing and amusing themselves. He leaned forward and lightly kissed my forehead. "Once we leave your Earth, I will show you how to learn more quickly, my Siren. It will take you only a few months to learn Natharan. And, as you become more experienced, languages will be learned even faster."

I was unsure about that. How could Cegan know? I hoped he would not be disappointed in me.

Much too early that morning, in my opinion, we returned to the outer door of the ship. Cegan wanted to show my government that I was unharmed. I doubted if anyone in the government cared, but I did want to reassure my father.

The door slid open. The crowds of protestors had vacated the area. With them gone, it was much quieter. But, the media was still about. The video cameras clicked, and the flashes blinded me. Like a single mass, the horde descended. I panicked and stepped backward, wanting only to return to the peace of Cegan's ship.

"Be brave, my Siren," Cegan whispered into my ear. His arms folded around my body, securing my back firmly against his chest. Once more, I was being a coward. I sighed and nodded, and Cegan's arms dropped back to his side, but I did not step away from him. The feel of his chest at my back was an anchor.

The microphones were shoved into my face. My eyes searched for someone I'd talked to before, but it was a crowd of strangers. A sudden flash blinded me. I blinked and grabbed Cegan's hand.

"Are you all right?" the nearest reporter asked.

"Did he treat you well?" another blurted out.

"Did he hurt you?" cried a third.

How could I answer them? Which question should I address?

"What's it like inside there?"

"How many aliens are there?"

"Are you hurt?"

What a stupid question, yet that man had asked it twice. I twisted my head and smiled up at Cegan. "I'm fine," I said.

"Were you held prisoner?"

It was a woman asking that. She had hair almost the same color as mine. I smiled at her. "No. Cegan opened the door to show me I was free to go. I was never a prisoner."

The mike moved to Cegan. "Were you prepared for Kira to walk out on you?"

"My wife is free to do as she wishes at any time," Cegan told them.

"That's easy to say here. What about when you get up in space? Is that when the game changes?"

It was an older man who'd said that, a man somewhere in his late forties. He had deep grooves in his forehead as if he were stressed about a good many things. His mouth was pulled down into what I bet was a permanent frown.

"Cegan isn't like that!" I told him angrily.

"Kira, do not allow them to upset you. Their words cannot provoke me, nor will their doubts dishonor me. I will answer the man if you like," Cegan said softly.

He waited for my nod and then spoke to the reporter, "Do you wish me to be a villain? Were you hoping I had mistreated my young bride?" Cegan's eyes moved on to search every face. There was suddenly a silence, and no one cared to break it.

Then, from a reporter in the back came a question, "Are humans ugly to you?"

Cegan smiled slightly, and the tension of the moment left. "I have met very few humans. I have not made up my mind yet."

"What about your wife?" the same fair-haired reporter shot out.

Cegan smiled more broadly. "My wife is very beautiful."

"What do you think, Ms. Stevens?" joked another. "Is your husband beautiful?"

I felt Cegan tense. How could he be concerned about that? I squeezed his hand and smiled at the reporter. "Cegan is beautiful inside and out."

A reporter in the back, who I couldn't see, yelled out, "It's the alien who should tell us about that. How was Kira on the inside? Was she good for you?"

It wasn't until one of the reporters turned around and slugged the man that I understood the meaning of his words. I turned my back to the reporters and pressed my face against Cegan's chest. Once more, his arms circled around me, holding me, stroking my hair. "There will be no more questions, Kira," Cegan said gently. The firmness in his voice was tinged with anger. It frightened me.

"You won't hurt them, Cegan, please."

"Natharans do not attack others. I have told you that, Kira," he whispered to me as his hand continued to stroke my hair.

"I'm so glad, Cegan. I wish that were true of Terrans."

Chapter Four: Alien Travel

For a moment more, Cegan held me in his arms. Then, gently, he pushed my chin up so his eyes could see into mine. "Kira, you must give me your trust once more."

Cegan had told me that so often. I nodded automatically, but I was expecting an explanation. He didn't give me one. His hand reached into the pocket of his vest, and then a haze of yellow began to envelop us. I pulled away slightly and looked up and around. In seconds, I couldn't see the reporters or even the ship behind us. It was strange and such an odd feeling to be so close to everyone yet sealed off from their sight.

The reporters buzzed with excitement. They were seeing something new. I could hear the clamor of their tone escalating, but as the haze grew thicker, their voices sounded far-off and hollow. It reminded me of the times when my friends and I had spoken through long water hoses and listened for the sound waves to travel through twenty feet of rubber tube. The cameras were still sporadically flashing their lights, but from inside the haze, the flashes flickered off and on in such a muted way that it felt like they came from a great distance.

"How did you do that?"

"It will not hurt you, Kira. Do not be afraid."

"I'm not afraid, but what is it?"

Cegan either didn't hear me, or he ignored my question. "Follow me," he ordered, and taking my hand, he began to walk upwards as if the air had steps.

"Cegan," I cried out and pulled back. "I don't understand. What are you doing? How can I follow you?"

"Trust me." Again, he held out his hand for me to take.

I reached out and took it, but I couldn't follow him. How could you climb what you couldn't see? When Cegan took another step upwards into the yellow air, I dropped his hand and backed away. He was standing in a yellow cloud. His head had completely disappeared. I was feeling panicked at his desertion and worried that he'd be offended that I hadn't trusted him enough to follow.

In a second, his head popped back below the cloud. "You do not trust me?" he asked.

"I do trust you, Cegan, but . . ."

"You are frightened. I will give you all the time you need. Do not be afraid, my Siren."

I shook my head. He didn't understand. I couldn't follow him, no matter how much trust I had.

Cegan walked back down the invisible steps. His hands cupped my head, and then, tilting it gently back, he kissed me on the brow. "Do not be distressed. It is not important, Kira."

His hand slipped under my legs, and he lifted me and carried me up the invisible stairs. I could feel his legs stretching upwards as he placed each foot on a higher step, yet I could see that there was nothing there. Coward that I was, I shut my eyes and clung.

At the top, about six feet off the ground, Cegan attempted to let my legs slide down to touch the floor. I was sure I was going to fall, and I hung onto his body, forgetting my pride. Still patient as always, Cegan left his arm about me, neither forcing me to touch my feet to the ground nor prying my fingers from their death grip on his waist. He said nothing and didn't move for several minutes, but I was humiliated by my fear.

At last, still clinging like a frightened child, I tentatively lowered one foot and touched the yellow cloud. There was solidity under my feet. I could see nothing but the yellow mist and, under that, a crowd of reporters staring up at us, their mouths agape. Yet I could feel a hard substance, like an invisible flooring beneath me.

I lowered both feet and stood on my own, but I didn't let go of Cegan. My legs were shaking, and I felt ill. I closed my eyes. "Please, put me down, Cegan. I can't bear this."

"It is only a machine that will transport us to your father's residence. You do not need to fear it."

"I can't help it. Can't we travel on the ground?"

"You must trust me, Kira. I will not permit you to fall."

"I trust you, I trust you, I trust you," I whispered, but I didn't open my eyes or let my hands relinquish their death grip on his waist.

He sighed. "All right, Kira. You do not need to look, but in what direction should I fly us to your father's residence?"

"Toward the mountains."

"West, then. To the North or the South?"

"A little north."

I felt the motion as we moved. We were going higher. That frightened me even more. Down below us, I heard the voices of the reporters. At first, they were loud in a far-off way, like they were in a tunnel calling out to me. Then the voices faded out as we rose up and flew away. Soon, I heard only the sound of the wind rustling and the already-familiar sound of Cegan's strong, firm heartbeat as I lay my head against his chest.

Cegan began to lecture me about compasses and degrees. I knew he was only trying to tease me into forgetting our flight, and I took it much longer than I normally would have. But at last, I protested.

"Cegan, I do know about all that, but you can't drive on the highway using degrees. You have to use left and right and exits that swing around in the opposite directions than you want to go. And nothing is direct. Streets curve and roll around hills, and there's uptown and downtown, but it's not because of altitude."

"Did you know that your hair is softer than the skin on your face? It feels like liquid streaming through my fingers," he told me.

"I thought we were discussing directions."

"We were. I am lowering us to the ground so you can offer some more of your left, right, uptown, and downtown instructions."

I didn't need to open my eyes to hear the amusement in his voice. When we reached the ground, he said, "Navigate for us, my Siren," I opened my eyes and saw the same twinkling in his eyes that I'd always pictured there. I reached up and tugged at his neck until he lowered his mouth to mine. I savored his lips. They were green, but they felt human.

When our lips parted, I looked around us. I had no idea where we were. Only the mountains, capped in gray and white wispy clouds, allowed me to sound knowledgeable.

"Due west," I said, hoping I was correct. "See that spot on the mountain where it's darker than the rest?"

Cegan followed my finger and nodded.

"My father's farm is directly in front of that."

"At what degree?" Cegan asked, smiling into my eyes.

"Until we get to the grain depot. That's a huge silver metal building with concrete cone-like projections at the sides, called grain elevators. Then, we turn right, go four miles, and my dad's farm house is the one with the red barn out back."

"I see." He knew enough about me not to bring up the degrees again.

Once more, I shut my eyes and tightened my grip, and, like an elevator going up at three times the speed it should, we regained our former altitude. My legs felt as shaky as the day I'd tried out for the school play. I pictured fainting off the edge of our transport and spiraling down into someone's back yard. Would I splat or plunk?

Cegan pulled me tighter against him. He was like a rock. He didn't even sway in the breeze of our passage.

"Tell me about your father's farm," Cegan ordered. "Did you grow up there?"

I knew that again, Cegan was trying to pull my mind away from being forty feet in the air, but he was right. It was good to think about something besides wondering what your body would look like when it fell. I pictured the farm. It was stability, almost like Cegan's hard, firm body.

I pictured its wooden frame, described the scarecrow I used to erect in the front every autumn and the snowman in the winter. I took in a breath. It was an unsure breath, scarcely hopeful. I tried again, longing to breathe in the farm smells: new-mown barley or oat hay, dirt being turned under a disk harrow, and the sweet odor of canning peaches.

I began to talk haltingly at first, searching for things Cegan could understand. Then the words poured out like grain from a silo. I told Cegan all about Powder, my horse. Dad had been the one to name him, saying he was like Powdered Dynamite, ready to explode with the tiniest provocation.

"To expand with force and rapidity?"

I stared for a moment at Cegan, forgetting my determination not to open my eyes. "What do you do, memorize dictionaries?" I laughed.

"I do not understand "explode." How does it relate to a horse, Kira?"

"When a horse explodes, it means he erupts into bucking and rearing, or he runs away, ignoring his rider, or usually all of those put together. Sometimes, the rider falls off. Some people think that's what the horse wants, but Powder isn't mean like that. He just gets excited and forgets to be a gentleman."

"You do not fall off of him?"

"Sure, I do. All riders fall off their horses. It's part of being a rider."

"It does not hurt you to fall?"

"Of course, it hurts! Jenna, one of the barrel racers I competed with, she fell off her horse, Ginger, and broke a leg and an arm. She was out the whole season. That's probably why I became the champion. She was pretty stiff competition!"

"What is barrel racing?

I tried to explain the concept. "It's a game of skill and time. The fastest rider wins."

I could tell Cegan was amused. "You ride in circles around a metal container?"

I guess it wasn't a skill that captains had a lot of use for, but at least it was one thing Cegan didn't know how to do.

"I see the silver building with the cones of concrete," Cegan said.

I looked down. "Oh, God!" I moaned, losing all the strength in my legs. I would have melted like a spring snowman if Cegan hadn't tightened his grip. "Put me down. Please, please," I cried.

"We are almost there, Kira. Another minute, and I will land us."

"I don't like this. I don't like heights. Cegan, please, please put us down, now!"

He lowered us slightly. I saw the white roof of the Smith's farmhouse. They were our closest neighbors.

"The red barn. Look for the red barn!"

"I see it," Cegan said.

"Hurry," I cried.

Then, it was like it must be on an elevator when the cable breaks. We were falling, plunging to the ground, as I'd somehow known we would. For a moment, a memory of sea eagles swooping from great heights to plummet into the ocean flashed into my brain. Then I remembered no more.

Chapter Five: The Alien and My Father

I woke to find Dad bending over me, concern and anger playing havoc with the muscles of his face.

"Dad?" For a moment, I thought I was nine and he was waking me for school. But the couch jarred me. I wouldn't be on the couch. Like watching lightning strike and waiting for its sound to catch up, the memories of the day rumbled in.

"Cegan!" I cried out.

"I am here," he said so calmly; it was as if my moment of doubt was without reason. I stretched out my hand to him and sighed at the feel of his fingers enfolding mine.

"I'm sorry I fainted, Cegan."

"It was my fault, Kira. You wanted to land so urgently that I misunderstood. I will go slower next time."

I shuddered at the thought of next time.

Cegan turned my hand over and began taking my pulse.

"You're a doctor now?" I laughed.

His brow lifted at the insincerity of my chuckle, but he ignored my words. Cegan turned to speak to my father. "She has had a slight shock. She will need to lie quietly for a while. Do you have a blanket to cover her?"

"Cegan, I'm fine," I said, sitting up.

Cegan's hand gently but firmly pushed me back down. "You do not trust my knowledge?"

"I trust you, but . . ."

"But you are stubborn. It is a trait I like in your species, but it is not always wise. Close your eyes, Kira. I will try something."

Darn him. It wasn't enough that he'd read American medical books. He'd read the Chinese ones, too. There was a pressure point Cegan touched that sent me right to sleep. I didn't even have a chance to argue.

Putting me into Napville also gave Cegan a chance to talk with my father, a discussion that it should have been my right to be present for. Apparently, Dad had simmered down when he'd seen I was OK. I think he must have been impressed with Cegan's medical knowledge.

From what I heard afterwards from Dad, the two of them mainly talked about my fear of heights. Dad told Cegan how I'd fallen from the tree out in back when I was five. I've heard the story so many times I have my father's lines down pat.

"That tree was probably twenty feet tall, and she was almost to the top when her mother and I saw her, but it was too late. Kira was already falling then. It must have been the sight of her body, flailing those skinny little arms of hers, that drew our eyes. Mother always said it was a miracle that saved her life. You don't fall from that height and live to talk about it, but Kira landed in the haystack.

"She plopped in and sank almost to the bottom. We had to dig her out, but when we got to her, there wasn't a broken bone in her body. Kira was covered in straw, like a scarecrow. Straw was in her hair, standing straight up, like the bristles on a porcupine, and she was itching all over because the straw had gotten under her clothes.

"Kira wanted to walk, and we let her. She was just as stubborn at five as she is now. We were watching her real good, not knowing whether she'd hit her head and might need to be checked out. She walked straight, though, just like always, except a little more steadied and slow. Then she stopped. Her eyes went up to the top of that tree, and she stood there staring like she was watching a bird in the tree. We looked up, and we couldn't see anything that would hold her all still and staring. Then Kira just crinkled up like an old foil ball.

"I picked her up and carried her inside. We laid her on that same couch she's sleeping on now and in minutes, she sat up and was eating a slice of watermelon and talking away like nothing ever happened.

"Mother wanted me to chop down that tree, but I didn't need to. Kira's been afraid of heights ever since that day. She'll climb up on that horse of hers, but she won't go any higher, not even on a ladder, and she won't stand close to a rail higher than the first floor.

"Kira got in trouble at school about it. I think it was the only time the principal ever called to complain about Kira. She was always a good student, and she never caused any trouble, except for one time, and that wasn't her fault. Those darned fools at that school were trying to get Kira to climb up the high dive. They said she had to jump off of it, or they wouldn't pass her in swimming class.

"Well, what the principal told me was that Kira just stood there looking at that swimming teacher for a moment, and when she saw that he wasn't going to accept "no," she turned her back on him and walked off.

"They tried to expel Kira for that. I told the principal that he'd better back off and let her be, and he better pass her in swimming, too. Kira can swim like a sea bass. She doesn't need any two-bit PE teacher telling her she's gotta go climbing up ladders to swim. It all sputtered out, and Kira took dance the next session instead of swimming. But it was all the craziest thing. A girl sure doesn't need to dive off a high dive to be a success in life."

I can picture them — Dad sitting there in the chair by the coffee pot that he can almost reach, but he always gets up to pour every time his mug is empty. Cegan was probably sitting across from him, wondering what he was doing on a planet he'd never been to before with his new wife asleep on the couch.

I don't know what else the two of them talked about, but I knew every word of the tree-climbing episode. Dad had told that story probably a hundred times while I was growing up, never varying a word. He just added on to it, like the part about the high dive. Poor Cegan. Like all sons-in-laws, he'll probably soon hate hearing about my growing up years.

When I woke up, Dad and Cegan were still "chewing the fat," to quote my dad. They were all chummy like Dad hadn't noticed Cegan was green and was planning to take me further away from the farm than the city, where Dad believes all the evil of the universe resides.

I was kind of "ticked off" at Cegan. It was a nasty trick he'd played on me. What had happened to the "anything you want, you are free to do" speech?

I went in to join them when I woke up. I glared at Cegan for his trickery, but he didn't seem to notice. He stood up, reached out for my hand, kissed it, and then turned it over to take my pulse.

I shot a worried glance at my father to see how he was taking everything, but he was beaming at Cegan.

"You are recovered now, Kira," Cegan told me. "Will you join us? I am trying to drink coffee. Would you like some?"

I had to laugh. It was just too weird! Cegan was playing host in my father's kitchen. I looked over at Dad to see if he was mad about it, but he wasn't saying anything. He was staring at Cegan with a strange look. My eyes returned to my husband. The muscles in Cegan's cheekbones were pulled tight with desire, and his eyes were focused only on me.

Dad's chair scooted back abruptly, with a screech of protest, but the sound couldn't take my eyes from Cegan's. I heard my father, but he belonged to a different world. He couldn't invade in that look passing between Cegan and me.

Dad jammed a coffee mug into my hand. My hand tightened around the handle without thought. "Kira, look at me," Dad demanded.

It was a painful wrench away from Paradise. I blinked and discovered the mug in my hand. Part of the coffee had spilled on the floor. I put the mug down on the table and turned to go get a paper towel.

"Sit down, Kira," my father ordered. "You, too, Cegan. My father's voice held anger. I sagged down into my chair. Next to me, Cegan sat, alert but unfazed by the tenseness in the air.

"Cegan, I like you," my father said. "I didn't think I would, but there's a feeling about you. I think you'd do the best you knew how for Kira, but what you two want to do is wrong."

I started to speak, but Dad cut me off.

"Kira, you listen. For once in your life, you're going to hear me out without an argument. Understand?"

I nodded. I picked up my mug and took a sip. The coffee was so hot it burned my mouth.

"Kira, I wish I could say that Cegan is a good man. I'd like nothing better than to approve of your choice of husband, but he isn't a man at all. Are you blind, child?

"Look at me, Kira. I have skin like yours and eyes that see the world like a human does. How does Cegan see things, Kira? Does he see red like you do? Maybe his red is blue. Does he hear, smell, and taste things the same as you? I doubt it. Even two humans can't tell a story the same way because their eyes and minds view it differently. How can you and Cegan hope to have a common ground on which to base your memories when everything your brain tells you is different than his?

"You take that Powder of yours. He sees a paper flying, and his brain reacts differently than yours. You see it as a piece of paper floating in the wind, while he thinks it's a monster or a ghost. I don't know what he thinks, Kira. That's what I'm trying to make you see. We see Powder's reaction to it. He wants to run away, so we assume that he believes it is dangerous. But we don't really know what that horse is thinking, do we? And you and Powder are closer in every cell of your body than you and Cegan. Isn't that true, Cegan?"

"At the molecular level of DNA, that is true," Cegan responded, watching me.

"See there, Kira?" my father said smugly.

I was getting angry now. Cegan had been so nice to Dad, and Dad was doing everything he could to tear us apart. "Stop it, Dad. I'm already married to Cegan. It's too late for anything you say to change that."

Dad stood up and walked over to the refrigerator. When he returned, there were papers in his hand that looked official. "It's not too late," he said. "This is an annulment of your marriage. The marriage was never consummated. You're not really married to Cegan, Kira."

I stood up so abruptly that my chair fell back over. I didn't care if it broke. "You can't do this, Dad. I'm an adult. You can't control my life anymore." I was so angry I wanted to throw something, but I burst into tears instead.

At once, Cegan's arms were around me, and he was standing beside me, kissing my forehead and saying, "It's all right. Trust me, Kira."

I looked up into his eyes. There was no anger there, only concern for me. "You don't understand. He's trying to . . ."

"I do understand, Kira, but you are my wife. There is no paper that can undo the pledge we made together. You are allowing your fears to crowd out the Truth again."

Cegan pulled up my chair and gently but firmly pushed me down into it. Then, he stood behind me, his hands resting on my shoulders.

"Kira," he said. I looked up, but his eyes were on my father. "Kira, I ask you to let me settle this without speaking. Will you have faith in me? Your anger will only enflame the words spoken. Will you trust me enough to be silent, no matter what is said?"

I took a breath and let it out slowly. Cegan, towering above me, looked down and nodded at me.

"Yes," I said, not daring to look at my father or the papers he held in his hands.

"Medical books, human physiology, psychology, philosophy — these are not the only books I read on my approach to Earth, Mr. Stevens," my husband said. "I am fully knowledgeable of the way your legal system works. I thought it wise to be especially cognizant of the various statutes concerning marriage.

"I honored your request, Mr. Stevens, because I thought it wise. An annulment can be granted for a wide range of reasons. I am also grateful that it leaves a door through which Kira can escape.

"I do not blame you for attempting to use your demand as the loophole for her freedom. Every father protects his child from whatever he fears will do her injury, and I suppose I am all your fears incarnate. However, Kira trusts you to be completely honest, and you have not given her all the facts. You see, Kira, this document requires my signature. Do you have a pen I can sign it with?" he asked my father.

Dad handed Cegan the pen and pushed the paper towards him.

I couldn't believe this. Cegan was going to go along with it? I sprang up and made a grab for the annulment paper, but my husband wouldn't allow me to reach it. "Sit down, Kira. I am not finished."

"Don't sign it, Cegan. Please don't," I cried.

"Trust," said Cegan's lips. His eyes were staring into mine. I knew what he wanted me to do, but I couldn't move. My hand was still stretched out in a silent plea, waiting for the paper to be placed into it.

Cegan lowered my hand. "Sit down, my love. Keep hold of your trust."

I fell into the chair and let my arms pillow my head on the table. My eyes were closed so I would not see Cegan destroy all our dreams with his name sprawled across the line, ending our marriage.

Having signed the paper, Cegan spoke then to my father. "Now, are you happy, Mr. Stevens? Or is there more you want? To make this legal, you need Kira's signature. Is that not true?"

I looked up, suddenly hopeful.

"Kira," my father whispered. "Kira, he's letting you go free. Sign it, daughter. Quickly!"

I stood up, but it was not my father I needed to speak with, but Cegan. "Why? Why did you sign it? Do you want to be free of me?"

"Never," he replied, kissing my hand.

"Then why did you sign it?"

My father kept urging, "Sign it, Kira. Hurry, girl." I ignored him. He was a moth flapping at the light bulb. He could not hurt me. Only Cegan had the power to do that.

"For the same reason I opened the door of the ship yesterday, I will keep opening doors for you until your fear has all been replaced with trust."

"I do trust you, Cegan. Do you still want me as your wife?"

"Always, my Siren, always."

I took the pen from Cegan's fingers and threw it across the room. For once in my life, when I aimed at the trashcan, I made a basket. The sound of the pen hitting the inside of the metal tin, then sliding down, needed no scoring bell. No cheerleaders gave a victory yell, but some games were won in silence.

I tore the paper out of Cegan's hand. My fingers boldly ripped it into shreds and continued until there was nothing but tiny pieces fluttering down through the cracks in my hand. I carried them to my father.

"Here, Dad. This is yours," I said. I opened my hands and watched the fall of paper fragments filling his. "I think Cegan and I should go now."

My father stood up and walked to the can. He flung the handful away. Some of them flew down to rest on the flooring. Some coated the sides of the garbage can, but my father didn't seem to notice.

"No," he said, turning back to us. "I tried. You can't blame a man for trying to do what he thinks is right. Cegan, you understand that, don't you?"

"I understand, Mr. Stevens."

Dad looked me in the eyes. "You are right, Kira. You have to live your life now. I can't make your decisions anymore. I guess all I can do is accept them and not let them poison our love.

"Please, don't go, both of you. I'd like you to spend the day, the week, the month, however long you have before you leave," my father said, his eyes teary but resigned.

Chapter Six: Inquisition of an Alien

My father might be defeated, but he wasn't down for the count. Having failed to convince us to scratch our plan, Dad prepared to get underway with his idea of a friendly, fatherly interrogation. He sat down with his coffee mug, took a sip, and then started in.

"Will you ever bring my daughter back, Cegan? After you go up there in space, will you bring my Kira home again? I mean, for visits."

I forgot I'd been angry with him a moment before. It suddenly hit me how much I'd miss my father and how far away Cegan and I would be going. I flung myself at Dad's back, slinging my arms around his neck. A hug, a kiss on the cheek, and an *I love you* poured out of me.

"Thank you, Dad. Thank you for understanding and for accepting this whole thing. I'll miss you so much, but I really love Cegan, and . . ."

For a moment, Dad's eyes met mine. He kissed me and hugged me sideways. Then, he motioned for me to sit down and turned to Cegan, waiting for the answer.

"Mr. Stevens . . ." Cegan began.

"Hank," my father interrupted.

"Hank, the distance between the planets I trade with often means that a journey is many months long. Your planet, Earth, is off my normal route. If Terrans wish to establish trade, it will make my travels here easier. I will try to return at least once every other year. I hope that will be enough to keep Kira from being too homesick."

"It is more than I had hoped for," my father said. "Thank you, Cegan. She and I've been awfully close since her mother passed away. It would kill me not to think you'd be bringing her back sometimes."

"My ship has many quarters," Cegan told him. "You are welcome to come with us at any time or always."

I went to my husband and wrapped my arms around his neck to bring his mouth down to mine. I did not allow the amusement in his face to stop my lips from touching his. "I love you," I said.

"How about some eggs? Scrambled, OK?" Dad said, already opening the refrigerator. "Kira, come fix some toast. Cegan, could you slice those peaches into a bowl?"

I unwrapped myself from Cegan. We smiled at each other before turning to our tasks. I stuck the bread into the toaster slots. Cegan was holding the basket of peaches like it was a baby he was afraid he might drop. I could tell he had no idea what to do.

I took the basket from him and set it down on the counter. I pared a peach, allowing the skin to form a long, slender ringlet. Then, I tossed the skin and the pit into the compost bin. I took the naked peach and sliced it up, dropping the segments into a large fruit bowl.

I handed the knife back to Cegan, then grabbed a platter and went back to the toaster to pop in two more pieces. Dad was busy cooking bacon and handling the eggs, so I set the table, put out jam and butter, and started another pot of coffee.

I was trying not to laugh over what Cegan was doing to the peaches. He was mashing them pretty badly, and peach juice was running down his arms. I hoped it wouldn't stain his scales or petals or whatever he called his skin.

I had a plate full of toast. Dad was serving up the bacon and eggs, and I turned to see if Cegan was done. The peaches were all sliced in the bowl, but the pits were piled in a miniature hill on the counter, and Cegan was trying to cut one open with the knife.

"You can't open up that peach pit, Cegan. Only nature can do that," Dad said. He scooped up the pile of pits and tossed them all into composter. "Better wash up. The way you are now, you'd stick to the chair."

Cegan ate everything like eating was a novelty. The fork ended in his mouth at times with nothing, but he took to its use quickly. He ate his eggs, broke his bacon into bits and left it there, sampled the peaches, and filled up on toast.

"What do you eat on the ship?" my father wanted to know as he bit into his toast. "Can Kira eat what you eat?"

"The ship will prepare whatever she wishes, and the Terran digestive system can adequately process the same things Natharans can. I have already started Kira on capsules of a neutralizer that will adapt her system to the minute bacteria found in Natharan foods. It is the same capsule I take for Earth foods.

My father paused. The final piece of the toast that Dad had been eating hung there in the air with its tiny beads of butter. "You are sure this capsule will not harm her? How have you tested it?" The question finished, Dad shoved the piece into his mouth and chewed, watching Cegan.

I had thought we'd already had this out. Dad had promised to accept, hadn't he? "Dad, you are doing it again. I trust Cegan's word."

Cegan turned to look at me. There was a smile on his face as his eyes met mine. "Thank you, Kira, but it's a fair question."

He turned back to my dad. "I have had my research verified by the computers on Natharan. I would not risk Kira's life to something I might have overlooked."

"I see. When did you do all this?"

"In my approach to Earth."

Cegan had finished. I wondered if he'd eaten enough to sustain his body. I passed him the platter of toast, but he shook his head.

"So there's been no long-term studies done?" my dad persisted.

Cegan gave Dad his full attention. "That would be illogical. Once the adaptation is made, the body assimilates the foreign food source in the same way it did previously with its natural food source. We Natharans have been using the neutralizer for centuries. And Terran traders who have voyaged far have used it for almost as long."

"So, Terrans have taken this capsule before?"

"Yes, but not for Natharan food sources."

"But it should be the same. Water, too?"

"Our water is refined far above any level of your acceptance. Kira could never be harmed from drinking anything onboard the ship, and in our visits to other planets, the neutralizer would again filter out anything harmful to her."

I passed Dad the platter of eggs and bacon, hoping to give him the idea that this was breakfast, not an inquisition.

"No, thanks, sweetie. I'm not done with what I have on my plate," Dad said.

Dad didn't get the idea. He kept right on drilling away. "What about radiation? I've heard it's all over space, and there's no atmosphere to protect a body from it."

I was glaring at Dad, and he wasn't even noticing. Cegan did. He placed his hand on mine and lightly shook his head at me. Cegan was still watching me as he answered Dad. "Our ships are shielded three times more powerfully than Terran ships. Kira is safer on my ship than she is in your house."

I sighed and stood up. Dad was still working on his eggs, but at this rate, he'd never finish them, and a hundred more questions would pop into his head until he found one that Cegan had to say, "I don't know."

"Are you finished?" I asked, scowling at my dad.

"Kira," Cegan admonished me. The voice was a warning, but such a gentle one my anger almost melted away. Did Cegan know what kind of power his voice had over me?

"Your father's questions are intelligent. I am glad he asks them. It is good for both you and Hank to hear my answers."

"He won't ever stop, Cegan," I said, but my protest was sputtering, dying like a tractor short on gasoline. I turned away, hiding my eyes from Cegan, hoping he wouldn't see how easy it was to bend my will to his.

I began to cart the dishes to the sink. Dad still didn't have a sterilizer. He didn't even have one of the old-fashioned dishwashers. He insisted on hand washing. I was glad. It gave me something to do other than stare at my husband with calf eyes, melting at a word from him or a smile.

I heard Cegan push back his chair. He was getting up with dishes in his hand to help, but Dad said, "Let her do it. Kira needs something to do with her hands, or she becomes restless."

Cegan sat back down. "Kira, I will assist if you wish."

I smiled and shook my head. Cegan was probably torn between pleasing my father and satisfying the requirements of a good husband in one of those women's lib books we'd discussed. He was trying so hard. Was this a Natharan characteristic, or only one of Cegan's?

Muffin came to the door, and I let her in. She pressed her furry head next to my legs and brushed against me. Her purr was loud enough for Cegan to hear. I could tell by the way he tilted his head slightly that he was listening to the cat. I picked Muffin up and carried her to Cegan. She stretched out her head and sniffed at Cegan's outstretched hand. For a moment, her ears went back, and she gave a half-meant growl low in her throat.

I showed Cegan how Muffin liked her head scratched. The cat was still not sure about Cegan, but she didn't struggle in my arms. She allowed his hand to pet her soft fur. I told Cegan to move his hand slowly under the cat's chin and rub her throat.

Cegan's hand moved down, rubbing gently, carefully. My legs felt like rubber. I had to reach out and grasp the table. For a moment, I was jealous of Muffin. I wanted to be the one Cegan was petting, his hands rubbing at my neck, caressing my body. I knew I could purr just as sweetly.

Cegan looked up. I saw in his eyes he had caught my need. The corner of his mouth curled, and the same look came back to his eyes as when I'd laughed earlier. His hands still soothed and gentled Muffin, but it was me he was touching.

"The dishes, Kira," Dad said suddenly. His voice startled me. I jumped sideways, like a horse shying. I had forgotten Dad was there. Only Cegan's hand shooting out to grab me saved me from slipping on the kitchen rug.

Cegan's eyes twinkled. The touch of his hand on my arm sent shivers through me. He smiled into my eyes, and the connection between us was as strong as before. But then he let go of my hand, and I turned around, feeling the brunt of my father's eyes.

The dishes had waited for me, but the water was now cold. I partially drained the sink and added hotter water, watching as the bubbles grew.

"What do Natharans wear?" my father was asking. "The women, I mean."

I turned to look at Cegan. Muffin had curled up in his lap. She was purring softly, contented with the Cegan's stability and warmth.

"Dresses, more or less like Earth's, a little longer, though, than the one Kira's wearing in that picture."

The dress in the photo was a simple, long-sleeved cotton knit. It wasn't a mini dress, just a school dress.

I suddenly wondered if Natharans were prudish about dress length. Would they be like the teachers in junior high who used to measure the length of our skirts? Would a too-short skirt be a detention error or a town pillory disgrace?

I turned back to my dishes. Soapy water from my hands had dripped onto the floor. I shot a glance at Dad. He was frowning at me. "The women don't ever wear pants?" Dad prodded, still questioning Cegan to death.

"No," Cegan said. I felt his eyes watching me. I followed his eyes to a stray bubble that had dropped onto my trouser leg and was sliding down. I flipped the soap bubble off.

My father's eyebrows shot up. "I feel a problem coming up," he said. Both Cegan and I turned to look at him. We thought he was worrying about something entirely different than what people wore on Natharan. Couldn't Dad feel the tension stretched between Cegan and me? The air was alive with desire. I could reach out my hand and feel it throbbing.

"Jeans," Dad said. "Kira always wants to wear jeans. I'm surprised she wore her business attire today."

Cegan's attention had not left my legs. Where the soap bubble had played, so did Cegan's eyes. "Kira will be allowed to wear her native costume. There will be no clothing restrictions on her."

How could Cegan's voice be so calm? How could he keep up this act of interest in my father's words? I could feel his eyes on my back then. He was examining my body, remembering how it looked, how it felt to his fingers and to his mouth.

I had finished washing, and even the frying pan now lay clean and shiny on the drying rack. I pulled out a dishtowel and began putting the silverware back in the drawer.

"What restrictions do you place on women?" Dad asked.

I turned to eye Cegan. I'd only meant to sweep a glance, but his eyes held mine. For a moment, I almost dropped the platter I'd just picked up to dry. I wrenched my eyes away from Cegan's to place the platter up on the cupboard shelf.

"Women have the same restrictions as men — the normal laws found in any society that chooses to group together."

My father rose. He wasn't going to argue the issue of women's rights with me in the room, but he thought the old ways were better, the woman in the kitchen and the man in the fields.

"I have to run over to Sutter to pick up a part for the tractor," he said. "You two need anything? Toothpaste, toothbrushes, condoms?"

I gasped, and Dad laughed as he tromped off.

"Wait," Cegan threw after him. "You'll need a xxxxxx."

Dad turned around and came back in. "I'll need a what?" he demanded.

"I placed a xxxxx field around the farm. You can drive through it with no problem. You probably will not even notice it, but without this xxxxxx, you will not be able to get back onto your farm again."

"You mean like a force field?" I asked.

"A force field might injure someone if they drove into it. This is different, Siren. It is more like the farm doesn't exist for those outside the xxxxx's protection."

Dad reached out for the device that Cegan handed him. "You think the reporters are in Roxanne, then?" he asked, studying the contraption and pointing to the button with a questioning look.

Cegan nodded. "It is always best to be cautious, Hank. Push that knob once at the point where your land begins and drive forward. Even if you are followed, the others cannot enter without the device in their hand. I trust you will not show or discuss this technology with others. That would, of course, endanger Kira."

"You don't have to tell me . . ."

"Maybe you better not go, Dad," I cried out.

"Rubbish, Kira. No crowd of reporters or a flock of crazies is going to stop me from going where I want to go. And thanks, Cegan. I'm relieved that you're so vigilant with my daughter."

Dad pivoted and walked away. He stopped once in the doorway and waved goodbye to us, calling back, "I'll be gone a couple of hours. Hope you kids can find something to do while I'm in town."

I started laughing, but Cegan didn't wait for me to stop. At the sound of the door closing behind Dad, Cegan seized me in his arms. His hands smoothed my hair back, and his lips pressed kisses across my face. I stood up on tiptoes, trying to reach his mouth, but Cegan was already sweeping me up into his arms and asking where to take me.

Cegan didn't give me any lectures about degrees north and south. Left at the first door seemed to do it. My clothes and Cegan's were piled on the floor before Dad's car crushed the gravel on his way out of the driveway, and then our mouths joined, and we were somehow falling on the bed.

Chapter Seven: Married Life with an Alien

Our union was perfect, as I knew it would be. The pain of my virginity was over in a moment, and the feel of Cegan inside me was an ecstasy of pleasure. I discovered that Natharans, in the midst of their lust, put out a scent like vanilla and spice. It was intoxicating, and I breathed it in as if I were starving for air. Then, my world exploded into a kaleidoscope of colors and patterns, and I heard Cegan's heavy exhale of relief.

If one could soar into Heaven without dying, I knew I'd just done so. Our racing hearts sang on as we lay spent, still clutching each other's bodies, not willing to tear our two separate selves apart.

But then Cegan breathed a sigh, half sob, and half moan, and rolled off to lie beside me. I sat up to look in his face. I expected to see rapture in his eyes, but Cegan's eyes looked back at me with only wretched misery.

"Cegan," I cried out, "What's wrong? Please tell me." He shut his eyes and lay still.

"Cegan, I've never made love before. Did I do it badly? Is that the problem?"

"Stop it, Kira," Cegan ordered me in a voice tinged with pain.

I felt sick. How could I have been so foolish as to think I could please Cegan? I had no experience, no clear idea about what it took to even please a Terran male. I couldn't take the agony of losing Cegan.

I bolted upwards. His arms seized me, pulled me back beside him, and locked me against the bed.

"Let me go," I cried out, but, in my humiliation, the sound was little louder than a whisper. It sounded like the voice of an overwrought child, whiny and weak.

Cegan's arm strung across me, pulled my mind away from the problem. His hold on me irritated me. With a burst of anger, I struggled against him, flailing about like a landlocked fish. I heard Cegan's voice entreating me to listen, but I ignored it. I could only focus on my need to be free, free to hide from my pain.

I stopped to catch my breath. I knew my battle hadn't taxed Cegan's strength. He'd used only one arm to defeat me, and that arm had not loosened an inch, no matter how hard I'd fought its hold on me. I gave way to tears. I wept as if my sobbing would carry away the devastation I'd seen on Cegan's face and the sickness I felt in my heart.

"Kira, no. Don't cry," he said. His arm freed me then, but I couldn't run off any longer. I was limp and broken.

He sat up. His hands pulled mine away from my face. Once more, I felt his right arm encircling me. Then, he pulled my body closer.

"Leave me alone," I snarled through my tears.

"Why do you fight me, Kira? I have been trying to explain."

"I won't listen," I cried out, not wanting to hear the pity in his voice when he told me why our marriage couldn't work.

"You will hear me out, my wife," Cegan ordered. The sternness of his voice drew my eyes. There was no softness in the lines of Cegan's face now. Where my hand had caressed him earlier, an unbending resolve warred with his beauty.

I sniffled and gulped a breath.

At once, Cegan's eyes were softening again. "Do not fear me, Kira. I will let you go after I see that you have considered my words."

I tossed my head, throwing my hair out of my face, then lifted my chin to glare at him. "I'm not afraid of you."

A smile peeked from the corner of Cegan's mouth, but it disappeared almost as quickly. "I am glad," he said. His hand lifted to stroke my hair. "Kira, this was all a misunderstanding. The fault is mine, not yours."

"Please don't say . . ."

"I am not finished, Kira." Again, the sternness in his eyes stunned me. The diamond pupils flashed like sharpened, black obsidian. I shut my mouth and swallowed further words of protest.

"I didn't know, Kira. There was no reason to suspect that you . . . You are young, but the data showed . . ."

"What?" I cried out, angry again. "The data didn't explain that we're incompatible? You said . . ."

My tears were flooding Cegan's green-petaled chest. I brushed at the wetness, but the tears had settled in, falling beneath the petals.

"Is that what you think?" Cegan stared down at me, stunned. "Is that why . . . ? Oh, Kira, no. Couldn't you tell? My love, we are so compatible the stars quivered in jealousy at our fire."

I stopped crying to look at Cegan. "We are compatible? But you didn't look like that. Your eyes were all full of grief and . . ."

"Oh, Kira, my sweet, lovely Siren, you are so much more than I ever hoped for. I never dared to dream that our joining could be that extraordinary."

Cegan's words stopped, and he shook his head at me as if he couldn't believe my doubts. He smiled down at me, his eyes no longer sharp, black obsidian. They were midnight skies with glittering stars.

He raised his hand to touch my cheek. One finger stretched out to caress my face. The touch of it on my lips made my body tingle. I breathed in sharply, amazed by his power.

Once more, Cegan's eyes changed. The glittering stars burned brighter, and his lips met mine. I was lost. My hands reached up to grasp at his neck, to hold him close.

I didn't understand what had passed between us, but I no longer cared. I'd never let go of Cegan, never release his lips to talk. I'd meld our bodies until he could never refuse me.

For a moment, all was sweet music and magic. But then Cegan's lips broke free from mine, and the strength in his arms forced my hands from his neck as easily as if I'd been a neck scarf he'd decided to remove. With the same fluid motion, Cegan brought my arms up above my head and held them there.

"Without the establishment of communication, misunderstandings develop. You must listen now so you understand why I am burdened by guilt."

The lavender walls of my childhood bedroom were swimming with tears. Horse trophies atop hanging shelves seemed to shift their position. Even the white, polka-dot lace curtains over the window were blurry. I closed my eyes.

I knew relationships were difficult. My friends swung in and out of them, high on hopes one day, crushed into smithereens the next. But I'd thought Cegan and I would be forever, not destroyed by our first time together in bed. I couldn't endure it. I needed to get away, to hide from the pain, to lick my wounds and . . .

"Let me go," I half-demanded, half-begged. My voice held little firmness. It didn't even sound like me.

Once more, my husband's eyes darkened. It was as if he looked inside me, searching through my thoughts. "I can see you are not frightened, Kira," he said. "You are only irritated by my dominance of strength."

I started to speak, but his spare hand closed my mouth as securely as his other still held my wrists. "It is not Natharan way to overpower another he whispered into my ear You have just cause for the anger that sparks in your eyes now. But, you do not have the training of a Natharan. You prolong the conflict with your angry rush of words. How can I get you to listen?"

Cegan removed his hand from my mouth and stared down at me in exasperation. His brow wrinkled up as if he was appalled by his own actions. "Forgive me, wife. That is no excuse. It is wrong of me to have treated you as I did. Only, I beg you to grant me your silence."

My anger disappeared as quickly as it had flared. I didn't appreciate Cegan's manhandling, but I did have to admit I hadn't given him a chance to speak.

We were lying on my childhood bed inside the room where I'd once dreamed and imagined what adulthood would bring. Had I just reverted back to that stubborn five-year-old in the story my father had told Cegan? Was I too much the child to hear what Cegan had to say?

I sighed and relaxed my battle.

When Cegan saw that I was yielding, he kissed my lips in several quick, short, but lovely contacts. "Thank you, Kira. If I release your arms, I fear you will wrap me in passion again. Then, I would not be able to explain. Forgive me if I do not release your wrists yet."

I sighed but nodded.

"You panicked when you read my unhappiness, Kira, but the fault was not in you. You have brought me great pleasure. Even when you rage, your eyes are dark and thunder-clouded, and your body is tossing about like stormy water, I am thrilled by it. Although it is foreign to all that I have known, it makes my life force throb. What powers do you have, Siren?

"But again, I stray from what I meant to say to you. My unhappiness, Kira, was because I promised that I would not hurt you, yet I did. When we joined our bodies, Kira, it caused you pain. That is why you saw the agony in my eyes. Natharans do not lie, Kira. We are honor-bound. That I should have lied to you, my little Siren. . . ."

Once more, his lips were on mine, yet still, he didn't loosen his hold on my wrists. Although my mind was fogging with lust, I was attempting to wiggle my hands free. I wanted so much to hold Cegan close, to touch his golden hair and the fine granular texture of his face.

Cegan kissed my ear, then whispered, "Natharan women do not have pain on first entrance as you Terran women do. I did not mean to be false with you."

"It doesn't matter, Cegan. Just, please, let me go."

Cegan lifted up, away from me. His eyes were puzzled. I realized that he had gone into one of his silence modes. I almost groaned with impatience. Instead, I sighed and watched the diamonds in Cegan's eyes grow fuzzy edged as he focused his understanding. It was a short meditation. He was back almost immediately.

I felt his grip lessen, and I started to move my hands, but the hold was immediately restored. "No," he said.

I thought, at first, that he was referring to my request, but that apparently was insignificant to his train of thought. Cegan resumed his speech once more. "It does matter, my love. You do not understand. To a Natharan, honor is of the highest importance."

Then, as if the rest of my words finally entered into his thoughts, he said, "Be patient, Kira. I know that you find my greater force to be an unfairness, but I have still not finished. I must explain, my little Earth Siren."

Cegan looked down at me as if he were waiting for my permission. I would have thought that with my arms over my head and my wrists prisoner to his grip, it was obvious I was a captive audience for his speech, no matter how long it took. However, I nodded my head for him to go on.

"It was my fault, Kira. I should have realized there was that possibility with you. I had read books that mentioned it, but you lived in the city. You said you dated many men. When you told me that, I assumed you mated with these men. I should have asked. If I had done so, I could have prepared you. I beg your forgiveness for my error in the falseness of my assumption, Kira, and for the lie I spoke."

Now, he wasn't the only exasperated one. "I don't understand what difference it makes. You didn't mean it as a lie."

"You cannot trust me, Kira, if my words to you are not accurate. I promised you I would never hurt you, and that was false."

"Cegan, I told you. It doesn't matter, and I do trust you. I knew that it might hurt the first time, but, Cegan, the pain was so brief, and the rest of it was wonderful."

Cegan froze and stared down at me. The diamonds in his eyes were once more sharp-edged and clear. They narrowed slightly as he considered me. What did he see peering into my soul?

"Would you let go of me now?" I asked.

Cegan released my arms and allowed me to circle his neck with them, but I knew he wasn't finished. He had that look on his face when he was sorting through words in his mind, seeking the ones he wanted that would tell me his thoughts.

His lips kissed my forehead. I used my hands to pull his lips downward where they belonged, but too quickly, he was lifting up and away from me.

Cegan captured my hand. He held it to his lips and kissed it. His touch was so delightful that he had gathered in my other hand before I was aware of it.

"My wife, you are a meadow, and I delight in the adventure of you."

Why was I a meadow? Why were my hands imprisoned again?

"I reached out at the sight of the most beautiful flower I had ever seen, Kira. Its fragrance was of freshness and spring. I bent down to savor its beauty. And another blossom further on drew me forward."

Why was he talking about flowers? I attempted to withdraw my hands. As before, Cegan seemed unaware of my struggle.

"Then I saw more clearly," he continued. "To my wonder, I discovered that you were alive with blossoms, and each one needed to be touched tenderly with fingers that caressed their velvety texture. That is you, my Siren, you with all the wondrous complexities that make you Kira."

I understood then. It was poetry, and with the words of it being uttered by his deep, melodious voice, the warmth inside me almost boiled over.

Cegan let go of my hands then and kissed me. It wasn't like before. Before, it had only been a taste of what could be between us.

Strangely, the kiss reminded me of a time when I was a young child. I'd gotten lost at the beach. There were people all around me, a crowd of them, but none of them had been my parents. I'd begun to weep in their midst. I'd felt so alone and frightened and utterly devastated by the knowledge of that aloneness.

Strangers crowded around me, coming closer, attempting to console me. Yet they'd only made me more fearful and even more distanced from all I'd ever known. Then my parents found me. Their arms encircled me, and they kept repeating, "It's OK now. You're safe."

Cegan's kisses were like what I'd felt at that moment with my parents' arms around me: the love, the sharing, and the absolute joy. It was the finding of something lost. The knowing that you belonged.

Our kisses continued. We rested awhile. We talked. The quiet was soothing, and in that calm, we healed and bonded.

After a time, we heard the outside door open and close. We knew my father had returned. I let my husband to the bathroom, and we showered together, exploring another kind of familiarity.

Afterward, poor Cegan had only the clothes he'd worn from his ship. I promised to try to find him others, but where could we find anything in his size? Nothing my father owned would fit him.

I got out my jeans and tee shirt and dressed as I always did on the farm. I was tucking in my shirt when Cegan turned to look at me. His face yellowed to a lime green, and he looked unwell. Like a fish out of water, he was gasping for air. I could tell he was trying to keep from saying what was bothering him. His eyes had gone fuzzy, diamonded again, and he would not look in my direction.

I moved close to him and rested my hands on his chest. "What is it, Cegan? Please tell me."

"It is a problem," he replied, and his petals yellowed even more.

"Please. Cegan. Talk to me."

His eyes were staring at my jeans. It was the look of a drunk with no money gazing into the window of a liquor store.

"The jeans?" I asked.

Cegan wouldn't meet my eyes. He dropped his gaze to the floor.

"Why, Cegan? Please tell me."

"It is difficult. Your planet has many customs I have read about. I have seen the cinema reels as well, but being here and involved with you as my wife will require adjustments.

"I have vowed to give you every freedom, Kira. But I do not know if . . . How can I ask you not to wear what is apparently normal for you to wear?"

I looked down. They were ordinary jeans, not tight or fancy, just farm-like. "Why is it a problem, Cegan? I don't understand."

Cegan took my hand and led me back to the bed. "Sit down, Kira."

I did, and Cegan tossed a pillow into my lap. Then he kneeled down in front of me. He picked up my hands, kissed each of them, and began to speak.

"Long ago, Kira, in your history, women wore dresses that disguised their gender with frills and fullness. Males still knew a woman's gender, but it was hidden, secretive. Then, here, in your country mainly, women began to dress like men, except in dressing so they were more openly women because every curve and hollow was displayed openly. Over time, your world has accepted this, but that is not the case elsewhere.

"It is not that I object to your costume . . . your jeans, but for a time, I will have difficulty keeping my thoughts on something other than your body. And, on the ship, the jeans would confuse the crew. They would think you were male and would . . ."

Cegan sighed. Had he always sighed so humanly, or was it something he'd picked up from being around us?

"I will not discuss the crew now, Kira. I will save that for another day, but I ask that you not wear those jeans onboard the ship, not outside my quarters. And when we visit other planets, Kira, there will also be an element of danger. The tight-fitting nature of what you are wearing would be a provocation, shall we say, to the males. I am extremely sorry to say this."

Once more, Cegan's brow was wrinkled with stress. His eyes brimmed with unhappiness. How could I argue? After all, I would be going to planets where everything was different. Giving up jeans was really only one minor adaptation. "It's all right, Cegan, I'll wear dresses when I need to."

Again, Cegan kissed the back of each hand. "It will honor me if you will do so, my wife."

"You'll still accept my wearing jeans here, though, right?"

"I do not forbid you to wear your native costume anywhere. I will not rob you of the independence your gender has fought so hard to obtain, but I must warn you that not all planets have the same viewpoints. It would be exhausting to untangle you from the constant lust your apparel would cause."

"So you will accept my wearing them here?" I repeated.

Cegan reached over and removed the pillow. "I will attempt not to notice."

We stood up and began to walk to the door, with Cegan behind me and his hands on my waist. I was in front of the door and wondering how liberated planets could be if they required dresses for a woman to be safe. Just as I reached out to unlock the door, Cegan suddenly swung me around. His hand reached down between my legs, and he groaned.

"I am Natharan, Kira, not a saint," he said, carrying me back to bed.

Chapter Eight: A Keg of Powder

The next time we finished showering, I folded my jeans and pulled on a dress. Sheepishly, Cegan kissed the top of my head.

My father was out feeding the chickens when we found him. He turned and looked at me. Apparently, he was satisfied that I was okay. He went back to tossing the grain. "I thought you'd be wanting to ride Powder," was all he said.

"I do," I agreed. "Maybe later."

I gave Cegan a tour of the place, saving my horse for last. My husband was not afraid of any of the animals, not even the horse. I was surprised. Most city people were skittish around farm animals and downright uneasy as a thief next to a guard dog when they got up close to a horse. I guess you couldn't group an alien with city people.

Powder, at first, shied at Cegan's outstretched hand, but my horse pretended to be afraid of everything. Blowing heavy snorts of false challenge, Powder finally calmed down enough to take the carrot from Cegan's fingers. Then he stood sniffing at Cegan, mashing the carrot with his giant yellow teeth.

"You do not wish to ride your horse because of the pain I caused you?" Cegan asked with a wounded look.

"Cegan, no. Forget that," I said. I shot a glance at him. My husband was looking very guilty. I was lucky he hadn't worried about hurting me on our second round. He'd been a little too overwhelmed by lust then for thinking.

The wrinkled brow was back. I realized that Cegan was still fretting over it.

"Cegan, I'm not riding Powder because I'm not wearing jeans. Bare legs get chapped. It's kind of hard to ride in a dress." I lifted up my dress slightly to crouch down in a riding position with my legs spread apart so Cegan would understand.

Immediately, the shade of Cegan's face started to yellow. He may have seen what I was trying to show him, but his brain had only focused on one thing. I scrambled to the other side of Powder and started brushing.

Cegan left for a moment. When he returned, he had another currycomb. We groomed Powder together, and I talked about horses. I told Cegan how I used to dream about getting a young colt and training him from scratch.

"From scratch? I do not understand this, Kira."

"It means from the beginning," I told him, concealing my smile.

"Training a colt from scratch is enjoyable to you then?" he asked.

"Incredibly so! It would have been a lot of fun."

I showed Cegan how to clean Powder's hooves. My husband told me he was impressed that a twelve hundred pound animal would lift up its feet at the command of a girl weighing scarcely over a hundred. "Your pet is large but docile," Cegan said.

I laughed, forgetting the effect it had on Cegan. He paled only slightly, but he held out his hand for the brush I was holding. Taking it from me, he returned it to the tack room. "Even in a dress, you destroy my serenity," he called back over his shoulder.

"Well, you shouldn't have called Powder docile!" I threw back at him.

I lay my head on Powder's big, strong neck. I loved the smell of horses, warm and musky. I inhaled. Powder stood perfectly still, enjoying the feel of me.

Cegan crept up behind. His arms wrapped me in green silk, anchoring me to Powder. "I do not understand," he said. "Your Powder is as docile as your Muffin."

I turned to see if Cegan was kidding. When I saw he believed it, I wiggled underneath his arms and ran back to the house to scoot into my jeans and boots. I knew it looked silly, but I left the dress on over my jeans.

In a minute, I was back and saddling up Powder. Cegan moved away to go sit on a bale of hay and watch. I saw the double row of teeth in his wide grin as he scanned my outfit, but he didn't say anything.

Powder knew the moment he saw the saddle that we were doing barrels. It was a special lightweight saddle. I never took him out on trails in it. He tossed his head and pawed with his hooves until he'd made deep grooves in the dirt. I placed the bit into his mouth, threw the reins over his head, and then I was up in the saddle, my second home. God, did it feel good!

Without saying a word to Cegan, I scooted Powder backward, opened the gate, stepped him sideways to close it, and we were in the arena. Powder was as skittish as a young colt. His nostrils flared red, and there was a bounce in his legs as if he had all four feet on a trampoline.

I warmed him up, at as close to a walk as I could get him, and then we jogged a bit until I felt his muscles start to untighten. An easy lope, with a stiff-legged buck here and there, then an out and out gallop, just to get the sass out of him. Powder reared up when I stopped him, and I heard Cegan yell out, "OK, Kira, he's not docile!"

Dad shushed my husband, but I'd heard the worry in Cegan's voice. I didn't need to see his face. I should have paused to reassure him or smiled at least, but my mind and Powder's were on the same focus. The barrels were in front of us. When I said, "Go," that's when you saw why Powder deserved to be called Powdered Dynamite!

"Go," I yelled, and we were off. It was serious business then. There were no bucks or shying. Powder's ears followed each barrel, and we swayed inwards together. I loved the feeling of the power beneath me and the communication of our shared goal. I leaned forward, almost over his neck, as we galloped all out to the fence. Then, rocking backward in a sliding stop, half-rear, half-sitting on haunches buckled underneath him, we came within an inch of the fence, throwing dirt up to the highest bar.

As I turned Powder around, Cegan was already opening the gate and walking towards me, yelling, "Get off, Kira. Get down." Cegan's whole body was tinged in blue. He looked even sicker in blue than in yellow.

I threw my leg over the saddle horn and slid off, dangling the reins to the ground. Powder was breathing hard and needed walking, but he wasn't as bad off as my husband. Cegan didn't wait for me to reach him. Two steps, and he covered the distance between us. His arms surrounded me in a bear hug that pulled me straight up off the ground. "We've got things we need to discuss, Kira, and the first one is that you're not going near that horse again," he ordered.

His words set me off like a firecracker, but I don't think Cegan was even aware I was fighting him. "Dad!" I cried out.

"I'll walk Powder until he's dry. Don't worry," Dad called after me, but at that moment, I hadn't been thinking about Powder.

Cegan carried me to my room and tossed me onto the bed. "What was that all about?" he said. "You almost rammed that fence. Were you trying to kill yourself?"

"That was barrel racing! I didn't almost ram the fence. That's the way it's supposed to be done," I yelled back.

Cegan stood there staring at me like he wasn't sure he knew me. I realized he was thinking, trying to sort out what he'd seen with what I'd just said.

"Cegan, I wasn't in danger. I've done that hundreds of times. I've won trophies and belt buckles, doing exactly what I did out there, in the arena."

Cegan scooped me up into another bear hug, then kissed every inch of my face. "Kira," he said. "I never felt fear until today when you rode that horse. I never wanted to cause anyone pain until I picked you up in that arena and wanted to spank your bottom until you could not sit on that beast again. And I never knew how consuming love was until I thought you'd go flying into that fence and the wall beyond it. I thought I would lose you forever."

He kissed my lips, but it wasn't a sharing. It was an assault, a demand I couldn't refuse. And when he broke away to stare at me, I didn't attempt to fight his withdrawal from me. I knew I didn't have the strength.

"Kira, in one day, you have robbed me of my Natharan tranquility and turned me into a Terran madman."

"I love you," I said, and then cautiously, I wrapped my arms around his neck, unsure what he would allow. He said nothing. His eyes watched me. I couldn't read his expression.

He was still sitting on the bed, stiff and formal. I sat up and pushed hard at his chest. Cegan's eyes held a spark of amusement then. He let me push him down onto his back. I followed, stretching out my body beside him. I kissed Cegan long and hard. My anger was forgotten. I wanted to erase all the hurt and the pain from his mind. I slid my body up on top of Cegan, and the passion that swept us along in its force carried us away.

Afterward, there was apology after apology on both sides. Cegan was afraid I'd lost my trust in him. I kept trying to tell him how I trusted him more because he'd shown how much he cared.

"But I made demands on you, Kira after I told you I'd never forbid you to do anything. During the very first full day, we were together, I found there were two things sliding between us."

"Cegan, do you remember how you understood my father's interference? You said it was only because he loves me. Wasn't it the same with you?" My hand was caressing the soft, downy petals of Cegan's chest. He stopped me.

"Kira, if I ask you not to ride that horse again, will you promise not to?"

I sat up. "No, Cegan. I will ride again no matter what you say."

He sat up. His eyes flared. Then he took a long breath and let it out slowly. "We Natharans have been conditioned for a thousand of your years not to explode into anger. Yet, you have the power to make me need to take a calming breath." He was silent then and thoughtful.

I said nothing, either. I wouldn't back down. He needed to know that now.

He stared down at me for a long time. At last, his hand rose up to touch my hair. He brushed a lock of it back with his fingers and then gave me the merest touch of a kiss on my lips. "It is wrong for me to forbid you," he said. "You will ride Powder because it is your right, Kira. But do not ask me to watch you again. That I cannot do."

I should have let it go at that. Cegan had given in to me, but there was a testing between us. Neither of us knew quite what the other would do. "My father watches me, Cegan. He trusts in my ability," I said.

It was the turning point. With my words, a sly smile appeared in the corner of Cegan's mouth. "I noticed that your father's hair is entirely white, Kira. Is it not worry that brings on those white hairs in humans?" Cegan's voice was amused. He was smiling down at me. I couldn't help returning the grin.

And so Cegan and I traveled through our first storms safely. Through their passage, I think we learned much about our relationship and about each other. It would be lovely if I could say that it was our only battle, but Natharans do not lie.

Chapter Nine: Alien on the Farm

Cegan and I spent some time weeding the garden with Dad, then watering it and picking fresh vegetables for dinner. When we were done, I had early spinach, fresh corn, green beans, zucchini, and, of course, Dad's favorite, radishes. I made lasagna for dinner, leaving out the beef and using lots of cheese, fresh spinach, and mushrooms that Dad had bought at the store.

My father didn't mention the absence of beef in the lasagna, but he raised his eyebrows as if to tell me he'd noticed. "A recipe from your city friends?" he sneered.

I ignored him. Why was it that farmers always thought that a meal without meat was almost criminal?

"Thanks for putting Powder away," I said.

"No problem. Will you be black and blue tomorrow?" Dad asked.

Cegan was listening, but I don't think he understood what my father was implying. I shook my head and glared at Dad.

While I was cleaning up after dinner, Dad took Cegan into the living room to show him my trophies. He made Cegan sit there and watch old videos of me riding in barrel races at all the fairs. Poor Cegan!

Afterward, Cegan and I took a walk. Evenings and mornings were my favorite part of being on the farm. That evening was especially beautiful. After we watched the sun dance with a rainbow, as Cegan put it, my husband apologized again. "Your dad made it clear I was wrong, Kira."

"He mentioned it?" I asked, pausing to look up at my husband's face.

Cegan smiled down at me. His hands drew me up against his body. His fingers began to poke and pull at the elastic band I'd tied my hair back with. I thought he intended to remove it, but his fingers only studied it a moment and then moved on to tease my ears.

I pulled his hands down, backed away, and looked up into his face. "Did he?"

Cegan's smile broadened. "No, he just showed me a hundred videos of you doing exactly the same thing you did this afternoon."

I knew the evening light would fade before long, and there would be no moon that night. I needed to stretch my legs and feel the softness of the dirt beneath my feet. I took Cegan's hand and urged him forward. We walked all the way to Coon's Creek. There, we sat on a fallen tree and listened to the rushing water as it pushed pebbles and fought boulders.

"How long before we have to go back to the ship?" I asked Cegan.

"I'm giving us a week, Kira. We can get to know each other here on your father's farm. Then, you can decide if you still want to go with me," he said as he stared at the gurgling water.

I tried to ignore his lack of faith. Why did he keep telling me to trust when he didn't have the confidence to believe I'd love him no matter what? I didn't speak of it. I knew Cegan would have a rebuttal.

"Then after that, we'll lift off and head to Natharan?" I asked, tossing a stick into the water to watch it sail down the stream.

Cegan's eyes were also watching the stick. He was focused on it so intensely that I thought for a moment he wouldn't answer me. The stick rode the current down the miniature waterfall of stones. It bobbed about, whirling and dipping in front of us, then rushed off on its long, jagged course downwards and out of sight. Cegan's eyes came back to me.

"No, Kira. When we leave your father's farm, we will return to the ship and start trade negotiations with your government. Hopefully, those will be established quickly. Then, after that, we will leave your Earth."

I plunked a couple of rocks into the shallow pool beside a boulder. "Will we go to Natharan first or someplace else?"

"Natharan. I must report back, and my parents will want to meet you, Kira."

We discussed his parents only briefly. Cegan said it was better for me to draw my own conclusions instead of his answering my questions about what they were like. "But will they object to me?" I worried.

Cegan grinned. "They will be delighted with you, my wife. What other subjects do you wish to drill me on?"

I pushed in one of the small boulders at the side of the creek. It fell into the water and made a delightful "plunk." I looked around for another.

"Do you play, or is there a purpose to your efforts?" Cegan asked.

I turned to look at him. His brow was wrinkled with curiosity. I laughed. "I just like the sound of the splash, don't you?"

Cegan rose up from his perch. He walked closer and stepped beside me. His hands tilted my face, so I was staring up at him. "Of course, you like the sound of splashing, Kira. You are a Siren. Tell me it is not wrong to take you away. Will you still play as enchantingly when I take you far from here and enclose you in my metal ship?" He gave me no chance to respond. His lips stole away my words.

It was a while before we got back to my questions. I had so many, but it required little thought before one bubbled out. "What do you usually carry in your ship's hold?" I asked him.

"Tiraneum ore, musical instruments, garments, whatever sells," he answered idly as his fingers pulled off the elastic band from my hair. He studied it a moment and handed it to me. "I like your hair down, Kira. My fingers find pleasure stroking your curls."

I didn't want to discuss my hair. I wanted to know more about the planets Cegan visited. "Do you ever go to places where you don't know what to bring in trade?"

For a moment, his fingers were still. "No, Kira. I'm not an explorer. I'm a trader. I must know first what a planet needs so the trip will be profitable. Besides, new planets are often dangerous and unpredictable. I will not take you to any planets outside the established Trade Grid."

He reached down, picked me up, then carried me back to the boulder where he'd been sitting, shifting me into his lap. I trusted him not to drop me into the water, yet I was sure I would have resisted had anyone else brought me so near its edge.

I twisted about slightly so I could look up into his eyes. "Why did you come to Earth then if you're not an explorer? You told me that Earth isn't in the Trade Grid."

"We think you are ready to join, My Curious One. I volunteered to check it out."

"But you said you weren't an explorer."

"I think it's getting dark, Kira. We had best get back." Without removing me from his lap, Cegan suddenly stood up, and I found myself on my own two feet, with his arms still wrapped around me.

I knew from the finality of Cegan's voice that our discussion was over. I'd heard that same tone many times when we'd spoken on the transline. It was obvious there were still things that Cegan didn't want me to know and pieces of the story that didn't quite fit. I kept thinking about that as we walked. We were both quiet as we returned to the house.

Dad was reading when we entered through the backdoor. Cegan called out a "goodnight" to him and walked on towards our bedroom. I was tired, too. I followed my husband's lead. Inside our room, Cegan disrobed quickly, placing his clothes on the chair by the bed. Then he crawled beneath the blankets. I wished he'd say something, but he only closed his eyes and acted like he was falling asleep.

I undressed slowly and debated whether I should sleep nude like he did or put on my usual nightgown. I suddenly felt shy and nervous. I opened a drawer and pulled out one of my gowns. It was long-sleeved and high-necked, in a pale, yellow-checkered flannel. It wasn't glamorous, but it was warm, and I was shivering.

I slipped into the bed quietly, trying not to disturb him. Cegan didn't speak, but one arm reached out and pulled me over to him, gently placing my head on his chest. He kissed my forehead and then fell back to sleep. With the sound of his slightly quicker beating heart and the rhythm of his chest rising and falling under my head, I, too, drifted off.

I woke up the next morning to an empty bed. I dressed and found that my father and Cegan had already breakfasted. Their dishes were in the sink. There was half a cup of coffee still on the burner. I finished it off and started another pot.

Dad and Cegan came in while I was eating my toast. When Dad moved off to go use the bathroom, Cegan stood there watching me. He reached over and stole the piece of toast left on my plate. It had strawberry jam on it, which I already knew Cegan didn't like. His mouth twitched with amusement as he caught me watching him. Then he finished off my coffee, even though the rest of the fresh pot still sat on the burner.

I stood up, put two more slices of bread into the toaster, and refilled my mug. I offered Cegan a cup, but he smiled mischievously and said, "I don't really like it." I laughed, and Cegan's smile disappeared. He bent over me, acting like he was kissing my neck. "Do that again, Siren, and your coffee will get very cold."

I stood up, threw my arms around his neck, and kissed him fully on the mouth. He picked me up and was carrying me off to our bedroom when Dad walked into the kitchen. "Good morning, Dad," I called out as Cegan carried me away.

When we returned later to the kitchen, my coffee was gone, and so was Dad. I took a cola out of the refrigerator, popped its top, and drank. I tossed a bottle of water to my husband. He caught it with one hand. Did they have baseball on Natharan?

"Cegan," I said. "I'm going for a ride, OK?"

He didn't say anything, but his eyes glittered dangerously for a moment. I didn't stick around to watch Cegan battle his conscience. I went into my room and changed into my jeans. When I came out, Cegan was sitting in Dad's recliner, reading a book. I waved goodbye and ran out the door.

Dad was out working on the tractor. When he heard my yell, he crawled out from under the motor. Then he sat there looking at me, just waiting for me to say what was on my mind. "Dad, you do like

Cegan, don't you?" I asked, climbing up the arena fence so I could perch at the top. (It was a low fence.)

"Yeah, I like him, but I wouldn't marry him," Dad said.

I knew he was teasing me, but he was also making a point. I nodded that I understood his meaning. "He loves me, Dad."

"Yeah, that's a fact," he said, pretending to study the tractor frame.

"I love him, too, Dad."

"Do you?" He looked up again, measuring something he saw in my eyes.

"Yes," I told him.

I watched Dad's eyes shift up the mountain peak. My eyes followed his. There was a cloud up there that looked just like a horse with its tail stretched out in full gallop. As I watched, part of its tail separated and drifted off into the mountain winds.

"I thought you might love him when I saw you wear that dress over your jeans," he told me. "You have to be either crazy or in love to do that kind of thing."

I ignored Dad's teasing and leaped into the problem. "But, Dad, he's hiding something."

My father looked up then, studying me. He reached into his pocket and pulled out a pack of gum. I watched him stick two pieces into his mouth and start to chew. He balled up the wrappers and stuck them into his back pocket. He didn't offer me any. Dad knew I didn't like gum. I thought it turned people into cows, chewing away with lifeless, non-thinking eyes.

"Kind of thought he might be hiding a few things," Dad said. "What makes you think so, Kira?"

"I don't know," I said, climbing down off my post. I picked up a rock and tossed it out of the arena. "It's just bits and pieces that don't make sense. Like there's a big chunk missing in the puzzle. You know what I mean?"

"Like why he wanted to marry you before you saw each other?"

I moved up beside Dad and leaned against the John Deere. "Yes," I said, staring up at the seat where I'd sat so many times, pulling the small plow in the family garden.

"I wondered about that, too, Kira. There was something phony about the way he wooed you from outer space. But, sweetie," he said, and the pause lasted so long that my eyes moved away from the tractor to look back at Dad. "If you really love that big green alien enough to leave Earth with him, I'd let all those little puzzle pieces go. Whatever his reasons then, he's got different ones now."

Dad took a step closer and lifted up my chin. "You're not having second thoughts now, are you?"

I pushed his hand away. "No, Dad, it's not anything like that."

"You know, I thought at first that Cegan was too controlled for you, but when he got all steamed up over your barrel racing, he was real."

I felt my face turning red. I wasn't too comfortable discussing that scene with Dad. He didn't seem to notice.

"A man that reaches that point where he's so mad he can't think straight, he only goes in two directions. Either he loves you enough to work it out, or he leaves. Cegan didn't walk away and say, "Forget it." He stayed. That makes all the difference, girl.

"If he'd walked out on you, I'd have worried that one day on some planet where you couldn't do anything to get yourself untangled, you'd get him seeing red so bad he'd just take off and leave you.

"And you will get him mad, Kira. I saw that yesterday. I don't know what you two will tangle over next, but there's a fire in that man — and you lit it."

I started to back away. The direction of the conversation was making me uneasy.

"Hold on, Kira," my dad said, grabbing my arm. "I'm not prying into what's personal between you two. It's not the bedroom I'm talking about. What I'm trying to tell you is that Cegan won't run off on you. I saw that. He won't let you be the rooster, either. And that's worth a good deal. You wouldn't respect any man you could boss around."

"Dad, stop it," I said, starting to get angry at his macho attitude.

"All I'm saying, Kira, is that Cegan proved to me he's a good man."

I relaxed and smiled up at Dad. "I thought you said he wasn't a man."

"Well, Kira, I'm not sure what he is, but I do know one thing about him."

"What?"

"He's got the balls of a bull to stand up to you!"

Dad was chuckling when I backed away. I hated it when men talked like that. Usually, my father didn't, at least not to me.

Grabbing Powder's halter from the tack room, I headed out to the paddock. As my horse munched on his treat, I saddled him up.

Dad came around the bend just as I was heading out. His eyes scanned Powder. "So you're going out on the trail, huh?" I nodded. "Kira," he said, putting his hand on Powder's shoulder. "You've always pushed yourself to be the best. I've never seen anyone ride like you do or dance like you used to in those competitions, but you can ease up a little now. You didn't choose to pursue either of those sports, and I'm glad of it."

I sighed. This was one day for lectures. "What are you trying to say, Dad?"

"Well, Cegan and I were watching those old rodeo tapes of you riding barrels, and you got close to that fence at the end every time, but yesterday, you were a lot closer. Don't take risks, Kira."

"Now, both of you are against my barrel racing?" I asked.

"No, Kira, but Cegan sees things you don't," Dad said.

There were times I felt like adopting a favorite swear word. When I wanted to let it all out, all I could do was sound like a teakettle, letting off steam. I exhaled my aggravation, whirled Powder away from Dad, and galloped out of the yard. It wasn't good horsemanship. I should have walked Powder first, but I guess it was better than exploding.

The corn was busy forming ears. It wasn't frowzy topped yet. It had weeks of growing before it'd be ready to harvest. I rode down the path between rows, thinking how I wouldn't be there when the harvesters came. Already, I was missing the farm, even though living in the city, I hadn't been able to watch the changes either.

Farming ties you to the earth. It makes you aware of the passing of seasons in each crop rotation and stage of growth. Plants sprout and grow tall, then green and brown in their cycle. Farmers don't need the calendars they plaster everywhere. They feel the seasons in their bones, and they smell them in the soil around them: the disking time, when the birds are all diving for wiggling worms, the frozen smell when the ground is like coffee in the can that has no aroma until you open it, and in the summer when the soil lifts up into the wind and coats you as if trying to make you a part of it all.

How would you know a season when you couldn't feel the breath of the wind, see the soil beneath your feet, the color, and variety of crops, or even the feel of rain on your face, cold as sleet or hot as a furnace? There wouldn't be any seasons on Cegan's ship. Would there be any on Natharan, and would I know the feel of them or the smell of them?

I looked up at the sky in what I thought was the correct direction for Natharan. Cegan had pointed it out.

"Right now," he'd said, "it's at 32 East."

It was funny how you couldn't see stars in the daytime, yet you knew they were still up there. Just like you couldn't see Natharan, but Cegan knew where to look.

What would it be like in space up in the darkness, a constant night between the stars? I'd be alone with Cegan then, except for the crewmen I couldn't wear jeans in front of. Did the crew look like Cegan? Would I be able to tell them apart? Humans varied in skin color, hair color, eye color, and height. Did Natharans? Why wouldn't Cegan talk about his crew? Why did he avoid so many questions?

I let Powder stretch his legs. The wind streamed through my hair. It felt like Cegan's fingers, the way he liked to play with the strands of my hair. Thinking about Cegan's fingers sent a shiver of need through me. I wanted to urge Powder to go faster, but the sweat was collecting on his neck. I eased him back to a walk.

The ground beyond the corn was freshly disked. The soil was resting temporarily, churning the rotted stubble of its prior crop into fertilizer for the next. It was a rightness I had missed in the city where garbage served no purpose. Coffee grounds were tossed into the garbage can beside the eggshells and vegetable peelings. In the country, all of that was the strength of our garden soil.

A bobwhite quail questioned me. His stubby body strutted out to peer at Powder before he bobbed back into a patch of weeds. I heard his voice long after we were far from his home, "Bobwhite? Bobwhite?"

"No," I answered him. "I have no interest in your nest."

I urged Powder into a relaxed jog. We left the fields and meandered into the silent woods. I knew that if I stopped Powder long enough, the woods would eventually fill with animal babble, but the sound of my horse's hooves on the silky leaves of the trail still seemed loud in the stillness. The deer, raccoons, and squirrels preferred to hide while we invaded.

I stopped to inhale the scent of rotting leaves and maple trees. With my eyes closed, I always know my exact location on the farm. Under the canopy of towering trees, there was a delightful coolness. I had not realized how hot my body had become. Its city whiteness no longer held my farmer's tan.

I headed over to Coon Creek, where Cegan and I had sat and talked. The running water beckoned, babbling its secrets and stories.

Why had Cegan seemed so cautious in the things he'd said yesterday? Could it be that the language was still so new that words were hard for him to find? Cegan always seemed to know what he was doing. He copied us so well. Yet everything was new to him. Like the peaches he mashed before he learned to cut them and the coffee and food he didn't like. Maybe he was just doing his best to cope, and I was expecting too much.

I felt Powder's neck and shoulder. He was cool. I threw my leg over and dismounted, dropping the reins to the ground. A giant boulder was just the right size for me to perch. In years past, it had often been my thinking post. Like a friend, its warmth welcomed me. I picked up pebbles and tossed them into the water, one by one, just to hear their plunk.

Powder neighed an alarm. I stood up to see the cause. It was Cegan walking towards me. "Hi," I called out.

Cegan came up to me and kissed my lips. His arms stayed down at his side. "I know what you're thinking," he said, "and I will leave if you want, or I'll stay." There was a question in his phrasing and in his eyes.

"Stay," I said. I stood and let my hands rise up and reach around his waist. I leaned my head against his chest.

"Maybe I can answer some of those questions I see in your eyes, Kira," he offered.

His words reminded me of all my doubts. "It doesn't do any good for me to ask them if you hedge, Cegan."

"I will try not to evade, Kira, but there are things I still cannot tell you." Cegan's hand was once again petting my hair. I remembered how he'd stroked Muffin. I'd craved his touch then. The same current was running through my body, bringing goose bumps of desire. Yet, there was a stiffness in Cegan that hadn't been there that day. Was it his way when he was unsure?

I should have kept a distance between us. The creek and the woods were ripe for a lover's tryst. Was he aware? I wanted answers to my questions, yet my hands of their own volition rose to play with the shimmery green petals of Cegan's chest. In his eyes, there was no answering spark to my fingers or to the fact that I was wearing jeans.

I was irritated, but I asked my first question. "Why did you come to Earth?"

"To see if Earth is ready to join the Trade Grid."

I sighed, wanting him to notice my desire, wanting him not to so I could go on with my questions. "How will you know if Earth is ready? You just ask?"

Cegan reached up to hold my hands still. "Kira, you're my wife, and once you've been to Natharan, I will trust you with Natharan trade secrets, but I cannot answer that yet."

Another refusal to explain. Were Natharans always shrouded in secrets? I was watching Cegan's eyes. He was aware of my interest, but he deemed my questions more important. I sighed. I wanted both. "Why did you call me back on the transline?"

A flash of teeth told me Cegan's amusement. My hands had been stilled, but they still rested on his chest. I felt the stiffness leave his body. Apparently, he was on surer ground.

"I liked your voice. I still do. It's full of Earth magic."

A blue jay lit on one of the maple trees near us. It scolded us, complaining about our visit to its waterhole.

"Did you come to Earth intending to find a wife?"

"I hoped," he said.

I turned away to pick up stones. I was thinking about what he meant when he said, "he hoped." I threw the stones in, one by one. They were flat. I tried hard to skip them, but I'd never been any good at that. My dad could skip a stone four times across the water. Mine just plunked. "How did you plan to find a wife?" I asked.

Cegan sat down on my boulder. I could feel his eyes on my back. "Kira, did you have plans when you went to parties? Or did you just hope to meet someone you could love?"

He had not really answered my question, yet I realized there was some truth in his words. I turned to study his face. This was the most important question. "Cegan, did you marry me because you were told to?"

"How could you think that, Kira? I love you." He stood up and walked closer.

"You didn't answer the question," I said, backing away from him.

"I did answer it, Kira." There was a rebuke in his tone, but I persisted.

"Did you marry me because Natharan told you to?"

"Natharan did not order me to marry you, Kira."

"Did they order you to marry a Terran?"

"No."

Cegan's hands turned my head to look up at him. I could feel that he wanted to tell me something. It was in his posture and in the intensity of his eyes. For a moment, I didn't know if I wanted to hear it.

"You have an inquisitive mind, Kira. It is the evidence of a good brain."

I knew there was more. My dance instructor in high school had always tried to say at least one good thing about our dancing before she told us all the things that were wrong. This was the same feeling.

"Kira, two things I can freely promise you. I will not hurt you. And I will love you with all my soul as long as I live. But I think I was wrong about answering your questions. I'll have to ask you to trust a little longer."

"I do trust you, Cegan, but I still have an awful lot of questions. Please answer just one more so I can stop worrying. You say you won't hurt me, but does that include my father and the United States and Earth?"

There was relief in Cegan's eyes. He leaned towards me, kissing my brow. "Kira, I swear on my right to be a Natharan that I bring no harm to your planet, your country, or anyone living here."

"Thank you," I sighed.

It would have been a lovely place to make love, but I knew that Dad was probably already worrying. He always did when I rode out alone. I took Cegan's hand and led him over to Powder. "My horse only gets rowdy around barrels. Will you ride with me, Cegan? Please?"

I mounted Powder and looked down at my husband for his answer.

"I do not wish to be thrown off," he told me, but his eyes held no fear.

"Trust me," I said, grinning down at him. "Put your foot in the stirrup . . ."

Cegan was up behind me before I could finish the sentence. "I trust you, my Siren," he said, wrapping his arms about my waist and lifting me up so he could slide into the saddle. He placed me down in his lap. "Your horse is not that comfortable, Kira," he complained, "but I will concentrate on the pleasure of holding you."

Powder fidgeted a bit, but he settled down when I spoke to him, and we set off for home. I walked Powder the whole way back. I did not attempt a faster pace, knowing Cegan had never been on a horse before. When we reached the barn, we groomed Powder together. I often caught Cegan's eyes on my jeans, but he stayed on his side of the horse.

However, after we'd put my horse into the paddock, Cegan was not as well behaved, and his hands started roaming where I didn't want my dad to see.

I could smell the burgers cooking on the barbecue. I grabbed my husband's hands and pleaded for him to stop. He smiled down at me and whispered, "I understand the word 'torture' now, my Siren."

We were almost to the barbecue when I remembered what I'd only guessed at. "Do you eat meat?"

"It is not my preference."

"I didn't think so," I said. "Just tell that to Dad. It's not like he won't survive one more shock."

Cegan nodded, but I didn't know if he was agreeing or only acknowledging my opinion. "The ship will program for whatever you like, Kira," he told me. "The vegetable protein duplicates any taste you prefer."

I smiled. "Cegan, I'll miss jeans more than I'll miss meat."

"Be sure to bring the jeans then. You can always wear them for me." His arms swung around me, and he drew me close, his hands again traveling to places they shouldn't be.

"You help Dad," I told Cegan, pushing him away. "I'll go put on a dress."

Cegan said nothing, but I could feel his eyes. I looked back at him. I saw the fists at his side and the faint yellow of his green petals. For a moment, I wavered, but Dad was already calling out for me to come set the table. "Coming, Dad," I yelled.

When I returned, Cegan was busy slicing onions.

"You're not crying!" I said, standing there a moment to watch.

"Why would I cry?"

"Everyone does when they slice onions," I said as I tossed the blue-checkered tablecloth onto the picnic table.

"Onions irritate human tear ducts," Dad said. "You know what that means, Kira?"

"What?" I said, knowing Dad had a punchline. I was laying out the plates and silverware and tucking the napkins where they wouldn't blow away. I didn't turn to look at my dad, but it didn't stop him.

"It means Cegan's not . . . human!" My dad began to hum the Twilight Zone song.

"Cut it out, Dad." I groaned and picked up the tray for my next trip.

"Why? You getting cold feet?" Dad called out. His words followed me as I entered the kitchen through the backdoor.

The window was open, and I could hear Dad explaining the expression "cold feet" to Cegan. I placed condiments on the tray and listened to their conversation. Then, I grabbed the buns and carried everything out. As I walked towards them, I wondered how a person I loved so much could be so irritating. Would Dad never stop?

Chapter Ten: Horses, Cats & Dancing

That night, Cegan went to bed with Dad's book, and I stayed up to talk with my father. We sat on the porch on the old, padded swing. I forgot my irritation as I started thinking how few days we had left together. It was going to be hard to say goodbye, and I knew he'd be awfully lonely when I left. Even while I'd been living in the city, our phone chats had been an almost daily occurrence.

Dad didn't like to talk about Mom's death, but I figured that maybe this was my last chance to say what needed saying. But how did you go about telling your father it was time to start looking for someone to love when he was still grieving after all these years? I wasn't a diplomat like Cegan. I just blurted it out. "Dad, you need to get married again."

Dad chuckled. After about a minute, he said, "Kira, they call a person like me either a fool or a romantic. Depends on who's talking. Your mother and I, what we had together was perfect. I reckon it's not fair to ask someone else to measure up to that."

"But maybe there's someone who'd be perfect in a different way, Dad. Couldn't you try to find out? Go out on a few dates. Please. I don't want you to be lonely when I'm gone."

"Ah, Kira," he sighed. "I'd miss you, even if your mother was still here."

There was a long silence then between us, or at least we didn't talk. The crickets were chirping away, singing their own kind of song. A night owl screeched into the moonlight. Muffin came out and jumped up into my lap. Her purr was a steady hum, blending in with the other night sounds.

The stars were brilliant, even with the brightness of the moon, and Dad and I stared up at them. I pointed out where Cegan had told me Natharan was. I think I got it right.

Dad nodded, accepting the information. For a while, we sat there watching the spot, but there was really nothing to see. Even the Natharan sun, Koreo, wasn't very bright in our sky. Our eyes moved on into the sea of a hundred other stars. I wondered which ones had planets Cegan would take me to.

After a while, I kissed Dad good night and handed over Muffin. She curled up, just as happy to be in my father's lap as mine. When I left, my father was still gazing up at the stars. I watched him for a moment, trying to etch the memory into my brain.

When I went into the bedroom, I found that Cegan hadn't gone to sleep. His eyes were fastened on the book he'd been studying since the afternoon. He didn't even look up when I came in.

"What are you reading?" I asked him, sneaking a peek. "Horse Husbandry! What are you reading that for? You going to start a horse breeding farm on Natharan?"

Cegan's mouth curled up in the corner. He looked up, amused. "It's a possibility," he said. "Know anyone who likes to train colts?"

I sat down on the bed. "Cegan, you're kidding, aren't you?"

"Why?" he asked, pulling me closer.

I pulled the book out of his hands and laid it down on the nightstand. Then, I perched up on top of his chest, my legs sprawled on each side. Cegan's eyes were gratifyingly interested.

"You don't even want me to ride," I said, pulling gently and teasingly at his petals.

His hands made lazy circles on my legs. "I was wrong, Kira. If horses are important to you, then we'll have them. Just tell me 'yes' or 'no.'"

For a moment, I wasn't sure which question I was answering. Cegan's hands were sliding my dress up and off.

"Wait!" I said. It was too late for the dress. It was already lying on the floor. "Is this because of what Dad said? I'm scared, Cegan, but I don't have 'cold feet.'"

"Yes or no?"

His hands had stopped, and his eyes were no longer focusing on my body. I felt a stab of disappointment that he would give up so easily. "Yes! If you can bring horses to Natharan, I would love it!"

Cegan's eyes darkened. They weren't even seeing me then. He had already started planning the steps in his mind. "Tomorrow, we'll look for a source. The stallion sperm is no problem. It's the eggs. I'm not sure Earth is that advanced yet."

"You mean the eggs would be removed from the mare and 'hatched' in a lab?"

"Yes."

"Would you freeze it all or start off the process on the ship?"

"That depends on the level of technology you have here."

"Oh, thank you, Cegan. I think you're wonderful," I said, attacking his lips with kisses. He seemed only confused by it. His kisses were disinterested. I sat up to stare at him. His eyes watched me with an expression I couldn't read.

"Do you have grain on Natharan?" I asked, kissing his face and running my hands over his cheeks, feeling the hardness of the bones and muscles in his jaw line.

"Yes," he answered, but he was sliding my hands off his face, and then he was lifting me up and off his body. Was he already growing tired of me? Maybe I should put on my jeans? Yet, he was willing to bring horses to Natharan!

I moved away to brush my teeth and get ready for bed. Thinking about horses and taking them to Natharan turned into a beat that my feet just had to carry: *horses on Natharan, horses on Natharan.* In a moment, I was singing one of my dance songs, and my body found the old, familiar rhythm that carried me through the routine.

I stopped at the end of the dance, exhausted by muscles no longer used to the hard work of daily practice. Why had I stopped dancing when I went to the city? Music made me feel alive in the same way as riding barrels. I was still panting when Cegan called my name.

Something in his tone made me turn to look at him. He was moving towards me like a panther stalking his prey. His petals were paled into blotches that looked like someone had mixed mustard with canned spinach. Despite being winded, I had breath enough to back away from the look on his face. It didn't stop this, Cegan. He seemed oblivious to my fear. He backed me to the wall and stood there glowering down at me.

"Have you danced like that for others?" he demanded.

I was in unexplored territory. Cegan's eyes, with the diamonds, narrowed to a solid vertical line, held no hint of his normal disposition. I nodded to his question. When I saw the sudden flash of anger in his eyes that followed my response, I made a frantic attempt to dart under his arms.

Cegan allowed me no escape. His hands gripped my arms like two steel vises, not tightened into pain but secured and locked into place. His voice, when he spoke, was cold and hard. "In other places I have been, Kira, only certain females dance like that . . ."

Why had I accepted so believingly Cegan's assurance that he was a pacifist? There was no friendly light in the eyes that pierced me now. Cegan looked like a warrior prepared for battle.

"Yet . . ." he said, and he paused, examining me. The wildness in his eyes began to fade. The panther-look disappeared. The diamonds in the center of each eye widened. "Yet, you were untouched," he said, completing his thought.

With those words, I could feel the friction in the air die down, like a storm dissipating as it traveled through. Cegan's arms let go of their grip on me, and they dropped to enclose me in an embrace. As suddenly as it had flared, the maddened violence was gone.

"I have frightened you," Cegan said, and his eyes were once again the eyes of my husband, and the voice was the one I recognized, the one I'd grown to love.

I didn't bother to respond. I knew Cegan could feel the trembling in my limbs. I'd been scared enough that if I hadn't had an empty bladder, I would have wet my pants.

"I am sorry, my little Kira. I was angered, but I would not have hurt you." Cegan's lips kissed my hair. One hand began to slide deliciously over my skin. A familiar warmth took control of me, crowding out my terror. I lifted up my head to let Cegan reach my lips, but the kiss he gave me was far too brief for reassurance.

"Earth is strange to me, Kira. Although I am used to dealing with the dissimilarities of many cultures, I am not familiar with the emotions of love. And loving a Terran seems to carry with it a discord that plays havoc with my inner peace. Yet I crave this discord you bring. Will you forgive the insanity of my rage?"

"Yes," I said, reaching for his lips. Cegan granted only a token kiss, and then his lips were on my forehead and in my hair.

"But I don't understand what I did wrong, Cegan."

"Hush, my little one. It was not your fault. It seems there is more to learn about your culture than your books have told me. We will not discuss this now. I must once again soothe your fears away."

Cegan carried me to the bed and lay me down on it as if I were the most fragile of all possessions. Then he took me with the same gentleness he wooed me with on the ship. I craved his wildness and his passion, but I didn't tell him that. There was fear in me, not of the violence in Cegan's nature, but of the depths within him that I still didn't understand. Whatever I'd done or not done, I'd be a little more cautious in the future.

The next morning, it was as if nothing strange had occurred. Cegan appeared to have forgotten the incident. His mind was on horse breeding. He woke me up with his preparations. I could see that my husband wasn't a person who sat around and waited for things to happen. He was already pulling on his pants when I sat up to ask him how many stallions we should use.

"You will decide that, my lovely wife. Now, out of bed. We have work to do." He pulled back the covers and flung them down to the ground.

"I'm up," I protested.

"Then get dressed," he said, eyeing my nude body as if considering options.

I darted past him and into the shower. I half-expected him to follow me, but he didn't, and when I came out, wrapped securely in my towel, he was gone.

I entered the kitchen, suitably attired in a dress, to find Cegan and Dad with their heads together over a horse catalog. I poured a mug of coffee and started cooking breakfast. But as I mixed the pancake batter, I kept my ears open. The way the two of them were talking, money grew on corn stalks.

"Cegan," I said, setting down syrup, butter, and sliced peaches. "Horses are kind of expensive. Are you sure you can afford to do this?"

Cegan's arm reached out to circle my waist. "Kira, you have not married into poverty. My family can well afford a horse farm."

"But a ranch takes a lot of land."

"The entire population of Natharan is only about one hundredth that of Earth's, yet we have a planet that is almost twice as big. My family, your family now, owns about the equivalent of 7,500 of your acres. That's room for all the horses you could ever want."

When I got my breath back and picked up the margarine tub I'd dropped, I fell into the chair. "7,500 acres! Acres?"

"We can buy more if you'd like," Cegan said, laughing at my expression.

"Uh, no. That will do it. But is there water? Can it grow pasture?"

Cegan smiled up at me. I could tell by the sparkle in his eyes that he was amused. His hand moved up my back, and he pressed me gently down towards him. His lips caressed my brow. "I told you I lived in the grasslands. The land is fertile and has sufficient water, my wife."

When he released me, I walked over to the sink and poured each of us a glass of orange juice. Dad and Cegan were already bent back over their lists and were adding still more supplies. I carried the full glasses to the table and handed one to each of the men.

I paused to try to explain once more. "Cegan, all the supplies you and Dad are figuring on cost a lot of money. I have a little more than $2,000 in the bank. You can use it if you want, but your list is going to cost a lot more than that."

Cegan took the glasses I was holding out to him. He passed one to my father and then placed the other glass down on the table. I saw him flash his double row of teeth. It was the Natharan chuckle. Dad stared and started to choke on his coffee. Cegan ignored him, turning his eyes up to mine.

"There is a saying known throughout the Grid, Kira, that a Terran only fully commits his trust when he hands you over his money." Once more, Cegan flashed the double row of teeth. Then, he took my hand and brought it up to his lips. Briefly, he kissed the palm and then pulled me closer. His hands circled my waist. "I appreciate your trust in me, my wife, but I do not need your money."

I would have been offended by the Grid's statement if Cegan had given me the opportunity, but he continued speaking. His next sentence stunned me so completely I forgot about what others said about Terrans.

"You see, my lovely wife," Cegan said with a smile that only slightly curved his lips, "it is your government that is going to pay for our new horse ranch."

With his words, I backed away. "What? You said that you weren't going to harm my government. You said . . ."

"Kira." Cegan rose up. His massive hands seized my shoulders before I could retreat further. Almost roughly, he pulled me back towards him. "Kira, listen," he ordered.

"Let go of her," my father yelled, rising up from his chair.

Cegan didn't even turn to look at my father. His eyes were holding me to him as much as the strength in his clasp.

"Sit down, Hank," my husband ordered. It was a voice of command and was expected to be obeyed. Without a word, my father sat back down.

Still not freeing my eyes from his, Cegan said, "I will not hurt her, Hank. Never will I hurt her. But Kira is my wife now, and I will not allow your interference."

I couldn't believe this was happening. My dad never gave in to anyone. I tore my eyes away from Cegan's to glance over at my father.

"Kira, look at me," my husband demanded with the same fiercely commanding voice. I shifted my gaze back.

"A Natharan does not lie, Kira. Have you forgotten that I gave you my word?" Cegan's voice was stern, but his eyes were not panther eyes. They didn't frighten me. They softened even more as he studied me.

"But you said . . ."

"I said that your government is going to pay for the horse ranch. Perhaps I should have said they will trade."

"Trade what?"

"I am not yet free to tell you that, Kira. Can you not trust me a little longer?"

I didn't answer with words. I slid my arms around my husband's neck and kissed him. I was delighted when he pulled me down into his lap and kissed me back.

"All right. Can I get up now and get some more coffee?" Dad interrupted.

I'd forgotten my father's presence. I bolted up and turned away. My face felt hotter than an August day. I walked over and opened the door.

Outside, the birds were singing. The air felt fresh and smelled like morning dew. I breathed in deeply and tried not to listen as Cegan and Dad resumed their conversation.

After breakfast, when Cegan suggested it, I pored over the latest of our horse magazines. In the back, breeders listed the pedigrees of their stallions and described the strengths of each animal and the ribbons received. I chose three stallions to launch our ranch, an Egyptian Arab for spirit and refinement, a Thoroughbred for speed, and a Quarter Horse for endurance. I passed over the Morgan, which was also high on my list, deciding that it was necessary to breed for a larger horse. If Natharans were all like my husband, they were not small people.

While I was doing that, Dad and Cegan started making phone calls. Earth did have all the equipment and the Quarter Horse eggs we needed to get started with. "Project Breeding Farm" was a "Go."

By the time dinner rolled around, we'd accomplished everything except paying for it all. I examined the list that Dad and Cegan had made and tried to cross off some of the things that we could do without, but Cegan wouldn't hear of it. "Are you doubting me again, Kira?" he asked, holding the list above my reach.

"I'm not doubting you, but I'm kind of wondering if you clearly understand our system of money. What you and Dad put on this list probably costs more than a whole farm."

Cegan studied me. Then his eyes moved to the sudden doubt in my father's. "You both need to practice Trust."

"Right!" I said, and I turned to walk away. I didn't want to get into another discussion like we'd had over breakfast. Cegan's hand whipped out like a snake and wrapped around my wrist, pulling me back towards him. "Kira, I am a professional trader. Do you not think I have the knowledge to assess the value of a cargo?"

I was staring at Cegan's shirt, not even seeing what he was wearing, but remembering instead the vest I'd first seen him in, the one with the silver buttons I'd kept counting because I was too afraid to look up into his eyes.

Cegan dropped my wrists. His hand tilted up my chin so he could view my eyes. They were brimming with tears. He spoke words I didn't understand, but his tone was angry.

"Kira, I thought I knew everything about you by the sound of your voice. Yet the song of your words is not nearly as expressive as the message of your eyes."

He shot a glance over at my father. Dad hadn't tried to interfere this time when Cegan grabbed my wrists. He'd sat down in his old brown recliner and was pretending to glance through the daily paper.

Cegan's eyes moved back to mine. "Kira. Twice, I've needed to secure your wrists when words didn't grant me your attention."

"Yep, I had the same problem with her. She never listened to me either," said my father, turning a page of his paper.

Cegan ignored him. "I do not like forcing you, and it has made you cry."

I think that was all the apology I was going to get. I reached up and placed my hands on his shoulders. "Couldn't you just say, 'Kira, I need you to listen?'"

Cegan's eyes twinkled. "I have tried that, my love. You do not listen. Only one thing seems to work well." There was a quiver at the sides of his mouth. He was teasing me.

"What's that?" I asked.

He didn't answer. His lips slid down to mine. We temporarily forgot about my father until he shook his newspaper rather loudly and turned another page.

Then Cegan picked me up. I thought we were on our way to my bedroom, but he carted me over to the couch and set me down on it. Sitting beside me, he said, "Now that I have your full attention, I want you to understand that I have not underestimated the value of my cargo. What I have in the hull of my ship could buy you the whole island of Hawaii if you wanted it."

"Would it fit in the ship?" I teased.

Cegan squeezed my hand. "No. What else shall I buy you then, Kira? Would you like fancy clothes to wear on Natharan? Or perhaps Terran Jewels would be better? We could weave them into your hair. Name your desire, my Siren." Cegan tilted his head slightly to the side, waiting for my reply.

I looked down, giving the question a moment of thought. My eyes again fastened on the tee shirt Cegan was wearing. This time, I truly saw it. A huge, brown, ugly camel leered at me, one eye winking. Its nostrils were emitting a cloud of dirty, gray smoke. It was supposed to be an advertisement for a brand of cigarettes. Dad had bought it because it was the only shirt large enough for Cegan.

I placed my hand over the stupid camel and felt the soft, feathery feel of the petals on my husband's chest. I stroked the camel's mane, enjoying the feel of the steady beat of Cegan's heart. His eyes flickered with a slight widening of desire. His hand moved up and removed mine. He did not want me distracting him.

"Kira?" he questioned.

"There's only one thing I'd really like, Cegan, but I don't think it's possible. . ."

"Tell me."

I looked up and then into his face. "A cat?" I said. "Not for when we reach Natharan. I know that would be easy for you. You could bring cats to Natharan just like horses.

"What I mean, Cegan, is that I'd like a cat that I could have on the ship so it wouldn't seem so lonely up there. I know you'll be there with me, but sometimes you'll be busy, and I could hold her like Muffin, and home wouldn't seem so far away."

"A cat on the ship?" He said it with a voice that sounded as amazed as if I'd asked for a pet water moccasin.

"Cats can use a litter box, you know, a box filled with sand, and lots of people keep cats in the city, even in tiny apartments. And cats are never a problem. They don't tear up things or dig holes."

Dad stood up and folded his newspaper. He let out a loud yawn and said, "Time for some more coffee. Anybody want anything?"

Cegan and I shook our heads. I watched as Dad walked across the room. He must have felt my gaze. He smiled back at me. "A cat up in space, Kira. What will you ask for next — a swimming pool?"

He continued on. The kitchen door started swinging back and forth from his passage through it, but we could still hear his chuckling.

Cegan took advantage of my dad's exit to tease my hand with his pointy tongue. When I gasped, his teeth bared an amused amount of teeth. "How long until night?" he asked.

I was saved from answering. My father pushed his way through the swinging door and strolled back into the living room.

"The litter box is the problem, Kira," Cegan said calmly as if he hadn't changed the conversation while Dad had been gone.

How did he switch gears so quickly? I blinked my eyes and tried to focus. "But, I'll clean it," I managed to get out.

"And what would you do with the sand, Kira? If you sent it into space, then what would you have in the litter box?"

I sighed heavily. "Sorry. I guess I shouldn't have asked. Dad's right."

"I didn't say it couldn't be done, Kira. Just let me think about it. Maybe I can figure out something."

I nodded, but I didn't look up. I didn't want Cegan to know how important it was. It was a silly wish, yet his ship had seemed so cold and devoid of life. A fuzzy, purring cat would make all the difference.

I went off to use the restroom. When I came back in, Cegan and Dad were talking about my dancing. I wanted to stop their conversation before Cegan told my father what Natharans thought about dancers, but I took the coward's path and stayed out of it. I thought that maybe Cegan's talking with Dad about it might help.

I retreated and went off to take a relaxing bubble bath, figuring it might be the only opportunity I'd have for a long time. The smell of gardenias permeated the air from the bubbles' scent, and I closed my eyes and lay back in the fragrant, hot water. Would Dad show Cegan the videos he had? Dad had taped every competition so I could analyze my mistakes. And he'd kept them all.

I'd practiced so hard for those performances. It was almost ridiculous. So much work for trophies and ribbons that now had no value. But I remembered how much fun they'd been to earn, and Dad had been so proud. He used to brag that the rodeos and the dancing were what kept me out of trouble. I know I hadn't had the energy to do much else.

Lying there in the warm, sudsy water, I was almost half-asleep when my giant, green Natharan stormed into the bathroom. He took one look at the soap all around me and shook his head. "Another strange preference. You wash yourself exactly like you do the dishes," he said as he sat down on the toilet seat, treating my bubble bath as a public thoroughfare.

I slid further under the water and waited for Cegan to tell me what he'd come in to say. I hoped it wouldn't take too long. The water was starting to get cold.

"Kira, I have watched some of your dance tapes with your father. He regards them with great pride, so I assume that the competitions where you exhibited yourself so scandalously were only considered as a Terran recreation contest."

My brain was locked into the word "scandalous." That was enough to raise my blood pressure to new heights. "I'm getting out, Cegan," I warned him abruptly. I didn't care if that bothered him or not. Let him deal with it!

I was surprised when Cegan held the towel open for me and wrapped me up in it. But then, he tossed me over his shoulder and carried me back into my room — which all happened so quickly that I had little time to squawk.

"How dare you . . ." I choked out when he laid me down on the bed. He didn't wait to hear my complaints. He started right in, telling me his philosophy.

"By Natharan standards, your dancing is not acceptable, Kira. It would bring shame to the honor of my family. ."

"Get off of me, Cegan," I snapped, wiggling furiously as I tried to get unraveled from the towel. His lying on one end was keeping me trapped.

Cegan stopped. I could see the puzzlement in his eyes, but I was too angry to explain. I was tugging at the towel and pushing at Cegan, both at the same time.

Finally seeing the problem, he shifted slightly, freeing me. I rolled away and sat up to glare better.

"There is nothing wrong with my dancing," I yelled. "I'm sorry it upsets you, you, you Natharan prudes!"

Cegan started to interrupt, but I wasn't finished. "If I am not perfect enough for you, then leave Earth without me!"

Before I could move away, Cegan had reached over and yanked me back down onto the bed. His eyes narrowed. I recognized the panther-look. This time, I was too angry to be scared of it. "You will not say that," Cegan ordered. "You are my wife permanently by Natharan law. Only your choice can separate us."

His hands were doing their "vise around my wrists" trick again. I was about to complain about it when he continued, "Kira, I am merely trying to explain Natharan culture."

His eyes lost their anger. I could see he thought he was being patient with me. Perhaps he was rationalizing how this was necessary to hold my attention.

"Kira, I am not criticizing your Terran civilization. I am trying to explain the situation on Natharan and other planets. Do you understand?"

Finally, I got to speak! "Get off of me, Cegan," I spat out.

His lips curled into an amused smile. "I am pleased to see that you are not frightened this time, my wife. I realize you do not enjoy being held against your will, but again, you have not listened when I asked you to hear me out. I am not hurting your body, Kira. I will not free your hands until we have discussed this calmly. Now, answer me. Do you understand what I'm trying to say?"

"I understand that your list of do nots is growing longer!"

"I have not forbidden you to dance. I have simply warned you that such behavior is not acceptable."

His eyes were staring into mine, urging me to accept. I looked away. "Isn't that the same thing?" I asked bitterly.

Cegan moved swiftly. He lifted my arms and brought the wrists together, seized them with one hand, and then brought my chin up so he could look into my eyes.

"Stop it! Let me go, Cegan!"

"No, it's not the same, my wife. Mine is a proud family, but we will not be ruined by conduct that is distressing. It is your pride, my little one, that I fear for. Can you accept being snubbed by those who do not accept such outrageousness?"

I was so angry I was reduced to sputtering. "Outrageousness? How dare you say . . ."

Cegan interrupted as if my words were not important. "We do not have dance competitions, so you will have no opportunity to display your . . . *skills*."

The way he said "skills" was like waving a red flag at a bull. I struggled against his hold on my wrists, fighting, knowing there was no logic to the battle, but my anger needed an outlet. Only when I was out of breath did I stop to glare at him and snarl, "Maybe Natharan needs to see dancing. Maybe you Natharans are so puritanical and straight laced, it would be good for you."

Cegan sighed. Then he shut his eyes for a moment and drew in a long, deep breath. "Kira, you still do not understand. That is not your fault, although it would be easier if you were quieter in your listening."

"Cegan, that's . . ."

"Kira!" His lips followed the warning. He was right. Even in anger, the touch of his mouth on mine could make me quiet. All the fight left me in the breathlessness of that kiss. Cegan lifted up and stared into my eyes. He shook his head at me and then continued as if he'd never been interrupted. "Natharans are not puritanical, my dear, only caste snobbish."

I was lost. I had no idea what Cegan was talking about.

"Castes are like social stratum, Kira, except more so. You have nothing like it in your country, so it will be hard for you to understand. But Natharan dancers are not of our caste."

I shrugged, as much as it was possible, with arms anchored to the bed. "So I'm on a lower level," I told him carelessly.

Cegan's body recoiled, and then he stiffened away from me. His eyes had grown pointy with a sharpness that chilled. "Kira, I cannot talk about this further with you. Not now," he told me in the icy voice of a stranger.

He let go of my wrists and left me lying there. I closed my eyes, drained by the look I'd seen in his eyes. I listened as the door of my room closed softly. A few seconds later, the bolt was retracted in the back door of the house. I heard that door close, too. I remembered what Dad had said about Cegan's willingness to work through our problems. I wasn't sure that Dad was right anymore. Cegan had just walked out on me.

Sometime in the night, Cegan rejoined me. I'd cried off, and on ever since he'd left, and when he returned, I couldn't believe I had any more tears left to cry, but the petals on his chest grew damp before I could stop.

"I'm sorry," I told him over and over.

"I know, Kira. I'm sorry, too." He kissed my forehead and my eyes. "There isn't anything we cannot work out, my love," he promised me, planting kisses over the bridge of my nose.

"I don't know why I'm so stubborn. I don't listen when you try to explain things," I told him and met his lips with mine.

"Hush, my Siren. It's all right."

"I thought you'd left and gone back to your ship. I thought I'd never see you again." I cried. His fingers wiped at my tears.

"Kira, there is nothing you could do that would ever make me leave you," Cegan vowed. His hands cupped my face so that he could see my eyes. "I love you, Kira, always and forever."

"I love you, too, but I was so scared!" My lips melted into his. The taste of his kisses was of vanilla and sweetness. I knew I couldn't live without them.

We talked long into the night, and it was almost like the days when our voices had traveled on the transline. I don't remember falling asleep, but when I woke up, Cegan's arms were still clutching me tightly even while he was asleep.

We had two more days on my father's farm before we had to leave. We spent them lazily, happily, and, thankfully, with no more arguments. Yet, all too soon, I was saying goodbye to Powder and then to my father. I knew I'd see Dad before we left for Natharan, but I couldn't help crying.

The fact that we were flying back to Cegan's ship via his yellow smoke machine wasn't making me any more cheerful, either. I pleaded desperately with Cegan for us to take a train or a bus or even rent a car. My father laughed, and Cegan turned to him with a broad smile. The two of them shared one of those "looks" when men think women are saying something ridiculous.

It was my father who pointed out that Cegan would be a little difficult to disguise. "Big green aliens often frighten people, Kira," he said. "People with any sense, anyway."

My dad was smiling, and Cegan never took offense to anything my father said, so I let it slide, but it was obvious the 'Yellow Horror' was still our method of transport.

Dad handed back the control he'd taken when he'd driven off the farm. It had allowed him to leave and re-enter without a problem. Dad had already told us how it was in Roxanne that day — reporters everywhere. Apparently, all the locals had thought it funny that Dad slipped in and out without the media noticing, and the townsfolk had played along, calling Dad 'Mr. Grange.' I think Dad enjoyed it.

We kidded him about it again, and then I hugged and kissed him. It didn't matter that we'd already done all that at breakfast. Something told me, perhaps Cegan's foot position or the shift of his body weight, but I knew that Cegan was restless to leave. Without a word, my husband reached down, picked me up and carried me up the nonexistent stairs.

"I love you, Dad," I called as my feet touched down. Cegan's arms immediately turned me about, and his strong arms gripped my body tightly. I had no chance to speak before yellow smoke was billowing out all around us, and we were rising elevator-fashion into the sky. I was just as terrified as the first time and kept my eyes closed. I buried my face in Cegan's petals. The only bonus came in the fact that on the return, I didn't have to give directions.

Chapter Eleven: The Ambassador

It didn't seem like the flight was as long as before, and the landing was so gradual and gentle that I never realized we'd touched the ground. Cegan just started unlocking my arms from his waist, and I panicked. My screams must have drawn all the newspaper reporters at SpacePort, but I was oblivious.

"Kira. Kira! It's all right. We are on the ground." Cegan told me, but he held me tightly until I opened my eyes.

When I saw it was true, I kissed him with such gratitude that the "thank you" got out of hand. A sudden flash of a reporter's camera reminded us that we were not yet on the ship.

The ship was seemingly as empty as before. We went directly to Cegan's quarters, and there he stripped off his clothes. He'd been wearing that awful camel shirt. I hoped it would disappear forever. While he was changing, I took another look at our quarters. I hadn't noticed before, but there were camouflaged machines, like the clothes machine he was using at that moment, across an entire wall of the room. The other walls were bare and white, stark and unfriendly. Then, there was the charcoal gray bed platform and a dark gray ceiling, and that was it. It was hard to imagine being cooped up for months and months in such a room.

"Don't you ever get bored or claustrophobic in here?" I asked.

"I do not spend a lot of time in it," Cegan told me, slipping into clean trousers. He turned and looked at me. "Kira, you know you can change anything you want. Would you like a bed more like the one in your dad's house?" He sat down on the platform and started putting on clean jogging shoes. I sighed. The bed was the only part I did like about the room.

"No, it's fine," I told him, but I wondered if it was dangerous to hang pictures on the spaceship's walls.

I watched Cegan tying his shoes. He did the bow backward, but I didn't mention it. I figured that soon, he wouldn't be wearing Terran clothes.

"Could you introduce me to your crew today?" I asked.

I handed Cegan his clean vest, and he slipped his arms into the holes. "Why?" he wanted to know.

I couldn't keep my hands from slipping up the petals on his chest. When I reached the top, I started buttoning. "Please."

I think he was amused, but he captured my hands and held them still. "You play without meaning, my wife. Do you know that is confusing? If you want to be bedded, do not ask me questions. If you want to talk, do not initiate sex."

"Are you restricting my freedom?" I teased.

"Merely indicating an area of confusion, my wife," he said as he led me out of the room.

As we walked through the long, barren white corridors, I thought about asking if I could tack up posters. Pictures of horses or mountains with snow, anything would help liven the place up! I was just about to ask about it when we went through a door into a huge chamber filled with squatty washing machine-sized boxes. They looked wooden and had tree-swirled patterns on the sides and top.

I would have asked about them, but we were passing the front of one. I paused to look inside the horseshoe-shaped opening. It was empty, except for what looked like a flooring of soft gray carpet. Cegan tugged me forward, and we came to the next one. A huge egg yolk-yellow man was curled up inside it.

Cegan spoke to the person in what I assume was Natharan, and the yellow man erupted out of the box and began speaking in a weird, high-pitched wail. All at once, giant yellow-petaled nude Natharans started popping out of other boxes and running towards us. I backed up into Cegan and clung to his arm.

The people were as enormous as my husband. Their eyes were diamonded like Cegan's, but they didn't reflect the same keen intelligence. They stared at me like they thought I was from a horror movie and was there to attack them.

Cegan spoke to them. Whatever he said, their eyes dropped immediately, and they crossed their hands over their hair and bowed, saying, "Dram Kira, Dram Kira."

Again, Cegan spoke to them, and again they answered, "Dram Kira, Dram Kira." Cegan kept it up, over and over, until I wanted to scream.

"Please," I pleaded with him. "Please don't do that anymore."

Cegan swung me around to face him. Then he pressed his lips on mine and kissed me.

He loosened his grasp and raised his head, but his eyes continued to stare into mine. "Siren, your lips sing to me. We will not linger long here."

His eyes darted then to the crewmen who were huddled all together, still looking terror-stricken at the sight of me. Cegan looked irritated with them. I was afraid he was going to make all the yellow men start bowing and "Dramming" again. I tugged on his sleeve. "Cegan . . ."

He must have misunderstood my confusion. "Do not be angry, Kira. The kiss was necessary so the Yellows would understand your position on the ship."

I didn't understand why Cegan couldn't just have told the crew who I was. Why a demonstration? "But what were you saying to them? Why were they . . .?"

"The Yellows are very simple-minded. Keep your voice low."

I sighed. "How do I say 'hello' in Natharan?"

"Sedupt."

"Sedupt," I said, turning towards the Yellows. They moaned as if I'd offered to torture them. "Sedupt," I said again.

Their hands went to their hearts, and they fell to their knees.

"Cegan, didn't I say it correctly? Why aren't they responding?"

"They are, Kira," Cegan said with an expressionless voice. I looked up at him, trying to figure it all out, but Cegan was ignoring me. Suddenly, he hit his palms together with a low, dull thud, said more words in his language, and without a squeak or a squawk of their high-pitched vocality, the yellow people took off running.

It was the strangest thing I'd ever seen. I didn't understand any of it, and my husband didn't seem to be volunteering information.

"Talk to me, please," I said, but he was still staring after the Yellows, a frown on his face.

When they were all out of sight, Cegan turned back to me. "What do you want to know?" he asked. There was a note of despondency in his voice. Was he ashamed of his crewmen or bothered by the way he treated them?

"Why are they yellow instead of green like you?" I asked.

"They are a separate caste than I am."

"But they are completely different from you! They're almost like a distinct species. They don't even have your crest of gold hair."

"Yes. That is correct, Kira," he said, pulling me closer to him. "The castes do not look alike, nor do they act the same."

"But they're Natharan? Why do they look different?"

"They were born that way," Cegan said, suddenly smiling and teasing me into frustration.

I placed my hands on Cegan's chest. It almost always brought his eyes down to mine. "Are all the crew like them?"

"Yes," he said. His eyes watched my hands stroking his petals.

"How many of them are there?"

"When you do that with your hands, Kira, why do you continue asking me questions?" He didn't wait for my answer. "Fifteen," he said, and he swung me up into his arms and carried me back to his quarters.

Much later, although we were still lying down in Cegan's odd, high bed, the Ambassador from the Bureau of Alien Communications and Interrelations called. Cegan didn't pick up a phone or anything. He simply sat up in bed and said something in Natharan, and the ambassador's voice came out of the wall.

I started to sit up and move away. I didn't want to disturb Cegan, but his arm circled my waist and pulled me back next to him. He was kissing my forehead while the ambassador was inviting him to discuss trade negotiations.

"It is considerate of you to so quickly return my call," my husband told the man as his long green fingers parted a strand of my hair and gently tugged through a tangle. "Yes, my communication link was only initiated minutes ago. I had no use for it before that. Two o'clock? That will be convenient. Yes, a pilotcar will be fine. No, the media is no problem."

A word to the wall and the conversation was over. I removed the hand holding me still and sat up. "How did you call him? How did the ambassador call here? I don't understand how you could talk without . . ."

Cegan's eyes assumed the closed-off look he got when he wouldn't or couldn't answer my questions.

I sighed. "I understand. No questions about the ship. What should I do while you're gone? Do I have to stay in this room, or can I roam around?"

"Kira," my husband said in the way he has of telling me I've said or done something incorrectly. He sat up and stared at me. "You are my partner now. Of course, you will not stay here. You will always go with me on trade negotiations."

I was relieved. The thought of being on the ship all alone with the strange Yellows was rather frightening. Besides, I'd much rather see where negotiations were held. It sounded fascinating to think I'd get to listen in.

It was in the middle of sharing a Natharan shower, a process all too much like being in an automatic car wash, that Cegan began to explain how I must learn to be an acute observer during the Terran negotiations. That way, he said, I would master the process of negotiations more quickly and could participate in the family business when we went to other planets.

My skin felt pinpricked by the force of the water, but as I stepped out of the shower, I was feeling assaulted by more than water pellets. How could Cegan think that I could be an interglobal negotiator? That was too big a step from being a transystem programmer. My knees started shaking.

By the time Cegan followed me out, I was begging him to let me stay on the ship. "I can't do this, Cegan," I told him. "I don't have your training. Do you expect me to master negotiations on alien planets? I can't negotiate anything, not even on my own planet, except maybe the distance between barrels in a rodeo."

Cegan didn't smile at my quip. He folded me into his arms. I was amazed that his petals weren't even wet. "Kira," he scolded. "Do you think I would expect you to have knowledge without exposure? Relax. I will guide you."

"But you don't understand. I don't know what to say or how to act. And we're still on my planet, where I should know what to do. How can you expect me . . . ?"

"Why?" he asked. "Why do you believe in *shoulds*? I will guide you, Kira, if you need it, but I think you underestimate yourself. You have conquered fears and challenges that would have defeated most Terrans. Already you make an excellent partner, my dear. Stop worrying."

I won't say that Cegan's words cured my doubts, but I guess the Romans had the right idea when they coined the expression "the die is cast." Besides, I loved Cegan, and if I had to learn how to be a negotiator to be his wife, I guess I could do it — if only my knees would stop knocking together.

Cegan seemed to think if his words hadn't given me the courage, machinery would. He took me to the clothes machine and showed me how to select the style, color, cut, and fabric for every clothes item I could possibly desire. He'd programmed hundreds of Terran catalogs into the system. I could state any type of garment in Engspan, and the machine would duplicate it for me.

Using the visuals, I could display the variations of sleeve length and collar, determine the length of my dress, and choose different trims or buttons. I needed hours, but he gave me only minutes. Hurriedly, I scanned, and then I punched in my completed selection. Within minutes, the article was finished. I chose shoes, undergarments, and a short matching jacket, all using the same techniques.

When I was dressed in what I'd produced, Cegan's looked me over. Immediately, his eyes shot down to my legs. I could tell he thought I wore my dresses too short, but wisely, he said nothing. I figure that while I'm on Earth, dress lengths á la Terran fashion are one thing I do understand.

We nibbled on crackers and cheese, and each of us popped our capsule of the Neutralizer that Cegan had told my father about. Then, it was time to go.

The ambassador and a large number of reporters and cameramen were waiting for us when we stepped through the ship's door. When I saw the crowd, my heart started thumping. I kept remembering the reporter who'd been so crude. I wouldn't risk that again. I didn't want to talk to anyone connected with the news. That's why it surprised me when Cegan stopped and turned back to look at them.

"We will speak with you this afternoon," he told the media. The newsmen all groaned loudly about the concept of "later." I wanted to know what Cegan meant about the *we* in his promise, but we were already striding forward, and there was no time to ask.

I was glad to see that the ambassador had brought the pilotcar. I don't mind flying as long as I'm surrounded by metal. We walked up the ramp, past a couple of guys in suits who might be FBI or CIA, at least the kind of men who hide guns in their breast pockets.

Then I viewed the interior of the pilotcar! It was nothing like anything I'd ever flown in. The commercial ones were all wall-to-wall seats. This one had bucket seats that swiveled and displayed new red velvet upholstery. The carpet, in a rich dark blue, carried an artistic swirl of the same red as the chairs and looked like it had never felt feet on its surface. Unfortunately, it smelled of formaldehyde.

The moment Cegan and I sat down in the plush, cushioned seats, a man rushed up to ask us if we'd like coffee or something. I asked for a diet cola, but Cegan, in a voice that blasted out mine, declined for us. I think the man heard my order, but he looked at Cegan and scurried away, advising us to "let him know if we changed our mind." I shot my husband a dirty look. I knew he'd done it intentionally. Cegan shook his head and said, "Not here, Kira."

The ambassador had hardly said anything to us before we entered the pilotcar. When we sat down, he excused himself and bolted to the back to make a phone call. The door of the pilotcar shut, and we were up in the air before the ambassador rejoined us. He came over, apologizing, and Cegan stood up just as the man thrust out his hand. As the two were becoming officially acquainted, I stood there and waited for my turn. The ambassador gave me a nod, but he didn't stretch out his hand.

"Please," he said, instead pointing to the swivel chair where I'd been sitting. Obediently, I sat down, but the two males continued to stand.

"Congratulations on your marriage," the man told us both, but his voice was heavy with disapproval, and his eyes were polar icecaps. I thanked him politely, but I was thinking about how much his face looked like a weasel's, with his small, tapered mouth and narrow, long jaw line.

I continued watching him as Cegan, and he talked. His eyes kept flitting back and forth from my husband to me, yet it was not like he was trying to make eye contact. It was more like a moth, unsure where to land.

The pilot called out that there might be some turbulence ahead and asked that the ambassador and Cegan sit down. The ambassador went up to talk to the pilot. I squinched up my nose to show my husband that I didn't like the guy. Cegan wagged his finger at me in a scolding way, but his eyes smiled. I think he was agreeing.

The ambassador attempted to return to his seat about the same time we hit the turbulence. He was walking like a drunkard, lurching back and forth and stumbling. He would have fallen, but Cegan reached out and gripped his arm.

"The Natharan's attacking!" the ambassador called out to the agents. Three guns were drawn before everyone realized that Cegan had only offered assistance. Apologies followed quickly, but they were strained. After seeing the guns, I had such a bad case of nerves I was ready to argue with Cegan about that cola I wanted.

"Kira," Cegan whispered. "Move very slowly and come here."

The turbulence outside had settled a bit. I stood up and walked the few steps between Cegan's seat and mine. All eyes watched me. The tension in the room had not eased off, and my movement seemed to resurrect it. When I reached him, Cegan's arms slid around me with the same slow carefulness he'd urged on me. Just as cautiously and gradually, he pulled me down into his lap.

The ambassador's eyes glared at me, but neither he nor the others said anything, and we flew on in silence. I leaned my head back against Cegan's chest and sighed contentedly. I didn't even ask why Cegan had wanted me to come. For the first time since we'd left the ship, I began to relax.

The atmosphere, ten minutes ago, buzzing like an electric fence, began to calm. The ambassador ordered a shot of bourbon and asked us if we'd like to join him. Once more, Cegan declined for us. When the drink was delivered, and the ambassador had had a chance to sip it, Cegan asked where the negotiations were to be held.

The ambassador shifted in his seat, gulped at his drink, and then turned back to Cegan. His eyes avoided looking into Cegan's. He stared at a spot somewhere up on the wall. "The Pentagon," he answered, at last, speaking as if it were the greatest of honors to be taken there.

"That's not where trade negotiations are held," I said, sitting up as much as Cegan's arms allowed. "Why aren't we going to the White House?"

For the first time, the ambassador looked me directly in the eyes. His studied appraisal was no friendlier than his coldness. I felt like he suspected I might resemble a face on the "Most Wanted List" hanging up in the post office. "You're mistaken, young lady." The way he emphasized young made me cringe.

"Mistaken?" I countered, meeting his gaze. "I've seen the conferences on TV, Mr. Ambassador."

He sipped at his bourbon, peering at me over the glass. "When other worlds are involved, Mrs. . . . ."

"Dram Kira, Caste Five," Cegan supplied. I hadn't realized Cegan was even listening. His eyes had been watching the scenery through the pilotcar's window. I'd noticed because I never liked to look down and see the ground so far away.

The ambassador thanked Cegan and then turned back to me. "Dram Kira, Caste Five, when other worlds are involved, these meetings are held at the Pentagon."

"But Sporoff worked out agreements at the White House. That's what it said on the news," I persisted. I was confused. Something in his words and his tone of voice was slightly off-pitch, like a tune going flat.

Cegan's hand languidly rose to creep under my hair and up the back of my neck. Once there, his fingers began to massage my skin. Was he trying to tell me to relax?

"You watched the announcements of the agreements," the ambassador said. "Those announcements, Dram Kira, Caste Five, were held at the White House."

I ignored Cegan's fingers and sat up straighter. "But the Pentagon is for military purposes. . ."

"Kira," Cegan interrupted. His quiet voice had a firmness to it that pulled my eyes from the weasel's. "It's all right," Cegan whispered. His eyes were giving me the "trust me" bit again.

"But . . . "

"Kira." This time, it was a demand. I knew its meaning, and I knew the look he shot at me. I closed my mouth and sat silently, smoldering. I didn't resist it when Cegan's arms tightened and pulled me gently back against his chest, but I was wondering if being a negotiator-in-training would mean that Cegan was always telling me to shut up.

The flight was not long. Cegan spent the rest of the time talking small talk with Ambassador Decluson. I was surprised to hear that the man had twin sons. How had he found someone willing to marry him? Maybe his wife had used artificial insemination like the horse breeders.

The two males started discussing football. I was surprised that Cegan knew about Terran teams. Did he know about them because of my father or because he was a negotiator and tried to find commonalities? Maybe I shouldn't have argued with the ambassador. I didn't really know anything about trade negotiations except what I'd seen on TV, and now Weasel-face said I was wrong about what I'd thought I knew. I sighed heavily, worried that I would only be a hindrance to Cegan. Once more, I felt his fingers sliding under my hair, massaging the tension in my neck.

The pilotcar began to land. I could see out the window that it was headed for a little red circle of concrete. We set down almost exactly in the middle of its bull's eye. The door opened, and a couple of the men who'd aimed their guns at Cegan preceded us down the ramp. Cegan's arms gently pushed me up, but even when I stood, he didn't release me. One arm had a grip on my shoulder that almost hurt.

"Cegan," I complained, whispering so the ambassador could not hear.

My husband bent over me and spoke into my ear. "You must stay close at all times, Kira. Do not argue this. It is the only way I can protect you."

I nodded, remembering how quickly the guns had been drawn when Cegan helped the ambassador.

The ambassador was glaring again. I think he thought we were kissing. He waved his hand for us to go in front of him. As we headed for the exit, we had to pass two more of the agents with bulgy pockets, their hands on the guns inside them.

The sun was in our eyes as we walked down the ramp, but even squinting, I could see the squad of marines, all in their dress uniforms. Apparently, they were there to escort us into the building. They didn't bother me, but the bunches of Army men in their ugly pea-greens were a different matter. They had their rifles, not pointed at us exactly, but ready in case of need.

The center of my stomach was beginning to feel like ulcer heaven. The Pentagon looked like the kind of place where, if they decided you didn't fit, they used a firing squad to dispose of you.

When we reached the bottom of the ramp, Cegan stopped me, pulled me close, and whispered in my ear, "It is all merely a show that the generals and I will put on for each other, Kira. We call it the game of negotiations. Do not be frightened by whatever occurs, promise?"

The guns all around us were real. I'd guess that the bullets were real, too, but I nodded and swallowed hard.

Inside the Pentagon, it was surprisingly not as gloomy as one might suspect from the outside. Fluorescent lights gave it an ugly atmosphere, about like Cegan's spaceship, but I didn't think even the presence of a cat could soften the rigidity on the faces around us. If there were any smiles in the building, I suspected we'd have to be the ones bringing them in.

"You are expected," the ambassador said. "Come this way."

I wished he'd said it the other way, like Willem, the hair stylist, who always said, "Walk this way," and we Transline girls had always tried. We'd never been able to wiggle our bottoms quite in the same manner as Willem, and he'd joked with us about it. I smiled at the memory and wondered if I'd ever get to go out on an all-girls night again.

You could hear the feet of the guards all around us, slapping at the flooring with their heavy leather tread. Their feet were beating such an angry sound. It matched perfectly with the sterileness of the walls around us.

The man's stride was much longer than mine. As we continued walking, following the ambassador through the longest corridors I'd ever been in, I had to put in an extra hop. Cegan looked down at me, squeezed my shoulder fondly, and slowed down, making the others walk at his new pace. I smiled up at him, thinking again how wonderful he was.

But his eyes were no longer on me. They were flashing all about. He looked like he was studying the building's architecture and, probably, memorizing the route. Now that we were going more slowly, I found that I could look around, too. I stared up into the faces of the guards to our left. They were so serious, so set. Had these guards once played with GI Joe action figures and dreamed of marching through the Pentagon corridors? Was it special to them or just another duty?

We came to a guarded door, where two soldiers stood posed like mannequins with their eyes painted on. The ambassador stopped. He turned and spoke to Cegan as if I were too stupid to understand. "Dramsté Cegan, Caste Five, your wife will be far more comfortable in the waiting room. There are magazines and a TV there, and, of course, she will be perfectly safe, but I'll be happy to post a guard if you have any concerns."

Cegan did not bother to ask my preference. He responded curtly, "My wife stays at my side, Ambassador." The arm around me tightened slightly like it was necessary to secure his hold in case the ambassador decided to play tug-a-war.

Did either of them remember that I was of legal age and capable of speaking?

For the first time, I saw the ambassador fully meet Cegan's eyes. I think he'd planned to debate the issue, but my husband's eyes took a little getting used to. The ambassador took a step back and then kind of melted inwards with his fear. Cegan moved us forward.

As we passed through the door, which one of the mannequins graciously held open, I looked back at poor Weasel-face. The ambassador was staring after us with his mouth open like a landed fish trying to take in air.

Chapter Twelve: The Pentagon

A whole table of men, twelve or thirteen, I'd guess, all in officer's uniforms, stood up to greet us. Their military jackets were trimmed with badges just like my old Girl Scout uniform. Theirs had more stars than I'd ever earned.

The star for Girl Scouts means the number of years you've been a member. Theirs probably meant decades instead of years because they were all old guys. Each one of them had hair whiter than my dad's, except the one who was bald. Most of them had paunches hanging down over their belts, and they looked like they'd rather drink beer than play war games. I sure hoped so.

Their eyes were pinpointed on me, which I thought was pretty incomprehensible. I mean, I was standing next to someone who looked like a cross between the Jolly Green Giant and an angel. And I wasn't the one who'd come from hundreds of light years away to negotiate a trade agreement!

"Greetings, Cegan," said the one with the most stars on his uniform. He stepped closer with his arm outstretched and offered his pale white hand to be shaken. Cegan took the hand and pumped it politely.

"You may call me Dramsté Cegan, Caste Five, sir," said my husband, with the coldest voice I'd ever heard him use.

"Of course. Forgive me. I am General Kershberger, Chief of Staff of the US Army," said the man with the stars and the pale hand. "I see you brought your lovely wife, Kira Stevens."

Cegan's backbone arched, and he suddenly looked even taller than his usual enormous self. In an even colder voice, Cegan said, "My wife, General Kershberger, is to be addressed as Dram Kira, Caste Five. Anything less is an insult to her rank and position."

If words were bullets, General Kershberger would be moaning on the ground. For a pacifist, Cegan was an awfully good shot at disparagement.

My eyes rose to his face. He was like a different person in this room: domineering, superior, and cold as walking on snow barefoot.

The general's eyes moved to me grudgingly. I could tell he thought me an insignificant bother to his valuable time. "Congratulations on your marriage, Dram Kira, Caste Five," he said grudgingly.

Did he think I couldn't read his eyes? I wondered if he hated all women or just the ones who married aliens. He held out his hand to me. I took it and shook it quickly. It was slimy as an old dead fish — but maybe that was his eyes, and I just imagined the handshake being worse than it was.

Cegan's eyes were viewing the room. I think he'd memorized every man's position and was examining the number of ribbons and buttons on each uniform. When the general introduced each one of them, Cegan listened as if he were fascinated.

"Dram Kira, Caste Five," said the general formally, his attention once more on me. "I believe that you will be more comfortable in the room next door. We have prepared a nice, comfortable place for you so you are not unnecessarily bored by the tediousness of our business."

I swear Cegan's golden hair bristled like a cat meeting face to face with a dog. It was as if the general had delivered the worst possible insult to a Natharan woman, and Cegan was utterly enraged. My husband pushed me in front of him, draping his arms down to my waist. Then he spoke with a voice that, had it been water, would have scalded.

"The wife of a Natharan trader never finds business tedious. A Natharan wife is always a full partner." Cegan enunciated so slowly and precisely that it sounded as if he were talking to a very young child — or an idiot.

The general nervously stepped back, cleared his voice several times, and said, "Yes, of course, but we just thought she might prefer . . ."

Cegan turned his eyes fully on the general. He must have given him the panther-look. I heard the general gasp. Then, Cegan demanded, "My wife stays, or I do not."

The words were not addressed to me, but they still sent shivers of fear down my spine. I knew that if I'd been the one addressed like that, I wouldn't have argued.

The general let out a noise that sounded like a beer can opening, and then he called out to one of his men, "Bring Kira, I mean, Dram Kira, Caste Five, a chair."

But Cegan didn't wait for its arrival. He pulled out the chair intended for him and spoke to me loudly enough for all to hear, "My dear wife, please be seated. I shall stand behind you and admire your beauty."

Cegan never said "please." The shock of it almost made my mouth fly open. I sat down, and Cegan stood there with his hands on my shoulders, waiting for the promised chair while all eyes watched us.

When the chair was finally brought into the room, Cegan bent over and kissed me on the brow. Several generals winced and looked disgusted. I wanted to tell them that I bet Cegan's lips were sweeter to kiss than theirs had ever been, but I stayed silent.

Cegan made a big production over his chair. The aide had evenly spaced it between another general's and mine, but Cegan noisily scooted the chair closer to me. Then he sat down, turned my face towards his, and kissed me slowly and thoroughly on the mouth. Even with a room full of frowning old men, I had no complaints about that kiss!

Cegan's eyes were twinkling when he released me. I knew he was pleased with the way I was following his lead, but I didn't understand the game he was playing or any of the rules. "Trust me," said his eyes.

When we were finally all sitting around the negotiation table, and the generals were looking eager to plunge into the discussion, Cegan made it clear that he was still not ready to relinquish the floor. "Gentlemen," he said, "I see your coffee cups are half-empty. Perhaps fresh coffee could be brought in. My wife and I will be quite content with bottled water. You do have those small, sealed bottles we can open ourselves, don't you, General?"

I had never seen Cegan like this. What had come over him? He was being so pushy, he was lucky they hadn't ejected us out the door yet. Besides, he knew I'd rather have a cola than water. Cegan saw my look. He reached over, threw his arm around my shoulder, and bent over my neck as if to kiss me again, whispering, "Only water here, Kira. Trust me."

Of course, I trusted him. The strange part of it was that I trusted Cegan, a heck of a lot more than all the rest of these men. I met his eyes and nodded almost imperceptibly, but Cegan saw it and smiled.

The coffeepot made its rounds, and two bottles of ice-cold water were placed in front of us. Cegan opened one and drank from it, making a face as if testing it. Then he bowed his head courteously to me and placed the bottle into my hand. The second bottle was still sitting there on the table when Cegan turned back to the general and said, "Thank you. I think we can begin now."

It was as if he had set the stage and now sat back to watch. Cegan's feet pushed forward, and he backed his chair slightly, reclining as if he were in my dad's living room. Then he draped his arm possessively across the back of my chair, choosing a lock of my hair that his fingers could play with.

The general cleared his throat, leaned forward slightly, and began, "Gentlemen and Lady . . ."

Cegan swung his arm away from me and shifted forward, reaching out for his water bottle. His sudden movement drew everyone's eyes. The general's speech stopped as everyone watched Cegan's long green fingers sliding up and down the bottle. Cegan looked up as if it had just dawned on him that the general was waiting for his attention.

Once more, seats scooted. Several men coughed. The coffee cups were almost unanimously lifted and drunk from.

The head general again cleared his throat. "As I was saying, we welcome you, Dramsté Cegan, Caste Five, and Dram Kira, Caste Five, but we have matters that we would like to clear up first before we . . ."

The sudden twist of a water bottle being cracked open made everybody jump. Cegan smiled and nodded, raising the bottle up to the men as if saying "cheers." He tilted his head back and took a long swallow. Not an eye in the room was still on the general.

I was not scared anymore. Cegan was turning the meeting into a circus. I was trying not to laugh. My eyes circled the room, looking for a smile and a bit of warmth. There was none. Cegan was only making them all angrier. I hoped he knew what he was doing.

"If you are quite finished now, Dramsté Cegan, Caste Five . . ." the head general barked.

"Of course, General Kershberger. Please, go ahead," my husband urged him with a relaxed smile. He sat back once more, swinging his arm back around my shoulder.

"How did you evade our warning, and why?"

Cegan smiled at the general. "General Kershberger and Gentlemen," my husband said, as his eyes made contact with each man at the table, "If a missile were aimed at you, now I ask you, in all honesty, wouldn't you evade it?"

I gasped. A missile aimed at Cegan? I shot up out of my seat. "You tried to shoot my husband?"

"Kira," Cegan warned. I looked down at Cegan. His eyes were telling me the same thing his voice had. He shook his head and nodded for me to sit. With a loud sigh, I obeyed him, but I still glared at the head general.

Cegan took my hand and squeezed an "I love you," or maybe it was a "thank you" for my compliance.

General Kershberger did not look at me. It was as if he had not even heard me speak. His eyes were shooting daggers at Cegan. "You were ordered not to come closer to Earth," the general said.

"Ah, but I knew there was a mistake," Cegan responded amiably, sliding his chair back even more so his feet could stretch out. "Free traders have been welcomed by Earth for fifty years," he continued.

"Free traders without weapons," snapped one of the generals to our right.

"But, General Kershberger and General Stone, I carry no weapons of war," Cegan said, picking up his water bottle and taking a large gulp of water. The bald general started to argue with Cegan's statement, but my husband lifted up his hand briefly, indicating he had more to say. Placing his bottle down on the table, Cegan continued. "Natharans have been pacifists since your caveman days, gentlemen."

The way Cegan said caveman was almost a Terran slur. I sat up straighter, feeling insulted. Cegan's grip on my hand tightened.

"Our scanners saw weapons in the bow of your ship," said General Stone, the one with the bushy, white eyebrows that kept moving up and down on his brow each time Cegan spoke or did something that irritated him.

"That?" Cegan shook his head as if he could not believe the general's accusation.

Personally, I thought my husband was hamming it up a bit too much. I, who had lived with him, knew he was not appalled at all. He was enjoying every moment of this. Didn't the generals understand that? Couldn't they see that Cegan was playing with them?

"Those are blasters," Cegan told them. "Their sole purpose is turning asteroids into pebbles."

"Yeah, and why is it only you have need of them?" asked a rather rotund general. I think he was General Blade or General Farat. I got the two names mixed up during the introductions.

"But you are wrong, General Farat," said Cegan. "All free traders have them." Cegan smiled all around the table.

General Stone was turning red with anger. His eyebrows were at their topmost peak. "Now, you listen to me," he said. "Who do you think you are, coming in here, huffing and puffing like King Kong?"

I tried not to smile at General Stone's mixed metaphors, but the big bad wolf didn't look like a green King Kong!

The fat general spoke up again. "Don't you think we've given a reading to every ship that enters Earth's atmosphere? Why is it that only yours showed — what did you call them — meteor blasters?"

"Gentlemen," said Cegan in his most congenial voice. "Calm yourselves. I know you have done your research. You have discovered that Natharans do not lie. I have told you that all Free Traders have blasters. Therefore, the inconstancy troubles you." Cegan left the generals dangling there as he paused to empty his water bottle. "Terra, or Earth, if you prefer, has a reputation for being xenophobic. We free traders have known your fears for over fifty years.

"Perhaps, gentlemen, if you consider that I had just married this beautiful lady . . ." Cegan stopped to hold my hand up to his mouth and place a kiss on the back of it. Then he sighed dramatically. "You might have a theory about why, in my approach, I was a bit in a hurry and did not shield the blasters from your probe."

The bald man, General Farat, stood up, yelling. "That is preposterous." His fist was clenched, and he looked like he'd love to give Cegan a punch with it.

"No, what is preposterous, gentlemen," said Cegan, "is the fact that we have been here . . ." He held up my wrist and made a show of looking at my watch. "According to my lovely wife's time piece, we have been here forty minutes, gentlemen, and we have not once discussed possible trade agreements."

"Nor shall we," General Stone yelled out, "not until you and that traitor of a whore . . ."

Cegan jerked me up abruptly. His arm swung around me tightly, and he said through teeth tightly clenched and with a cold finality that was like the sound of ice cracking in the spring, "This meeting is now ended."

The yellow cloud that I'd grown to hate spread about us, and Cegan half-dragged me up the invisible steps. We lifted at once into the air. The yellow cloud grew thick until I could see nothing in front of us. Then it whisked us through the building, right through the walls of the Pentagon.

Outside, guns were exploding. I saw bullets whiz by us. One pinged against the force field. The yellow cloud absorbed the others. My arms circled Cegan's waist, and my head lay against his chest. With my eyes shut, I could almost believe we were still in bed, and none of it was happening.

We hung there for a moment, and Cegan whispered into my ear. "I am sorry, my wife. I did not mean for them to strike at you."

I didn't care about generals or whether the Army was shooting at us or not. I only cared that we were once again up in the sky, with nothing underneath us. The thought of it frightened me so badly that I buried my face in Cegan's chest and refused to look up. "Can we go home?" I asked.

"To your father's?"

"No, to the ship."

"You honor me, my wife," Cegan said, kissing my head.

I opened my eyes to stare up at him, wondering at his words, but his eyes were not looking down at me. He was looking at something in his hand.

"What is that?"

"It will return us to the ship, Kira. With this, I do not need to guide us."

I felt us going higher then and moving sideways. I quickly shut my eyes and tightened my grip. My nose was pressed against Cegan's chest. His petals never tickled. They were soft and luxuriously comfortable to press against. I breathed in deeply, enjoying his spicy scent. The wind against my cheek was chilly, but Cegan's body warmed me. The feel of his arms around me was security. If I didn't think about being sky high, I could be content.

My ears told me when we lowered. I firmed my grip, and Cegan again kissed the top of my head.

"We have reached the ship, my love," he said a moment later. "Open your eyes now." He did not loosen his hold on me. I had panicked the last time he did that.

I opened my eyes and relinquished my grip. Then I tried to move away, but my legs were still so wobbly I could barely stand.

"Are you all right, Kira?" asked Cegan, looking down into my eyes.

I nodded, but Cegan's arm was already sliding under my legs, and he was lifting me. "I know you do not like my holding you like this," he whispered, "but you can scold me later."

What could you say to a husband like that? I kissed his cheek and looked out at the reporters waiting for Cegan's promised words. They were standing there watching us, one or two of them taking pictures, and some of them were already scribbling in their notebooks.

"I have a story for you, men and ladies," my husband told them. His words froze their attention. They edged closer. "I came here to trade with you, Terrans," Cegan continued. "In doing so, I fell in love with and married my beautiful wife. You know all this, yet today, when we went off to the meeting with Ambassador Decluson today, instead of taking us to the White House where negotiations are normally handled, we were kidnapped and taken to the Pentagon, where generals gathered around like an inquisition team demanding answers about Natharan secrets.

"When I attempted to steer the matter back to negotiations, the generals turned on my wife and called her a foul name. Kira knows nothing of Natharan technology. She could not answer a single one of their questions if her life depended on it, yet it was she they attacked.

"I will not tell you falsehoods. Lying is so repugnant to Natharans that we would choose to die rather than endure the curse of an untruth. So, I do not lie when I tell you that the Pentagon shot at us with bullets from rifles. They attempted to murder my sweet, young wife.

"I am an alien: green, diamond-eyed, golden-haired, and different from you. I can understand your suspicion, perhaps even your hate. I have never done injury to you, and I have come here peacefully, but I am not Terran. I am not one of you. I could understand if bullets were aimed at me.

"But Kira. That your own military would attack her? Kira is only eighteen years old. She's lived on a small farm her whole life. She knows nothing about weapons and violence. How could you try to murder one of yours? One still child-like in her innocence, barely out of school, on her own for the first time? Why would you try to kill Kira unless it is because I love her?"

As if, suddenly, the emotion had overcome him, and he could say no more, Cegan turned and carried me into the ship. As the door slid shut with the solemn, heavy chords of a funeral dirge, I burst into laughter. I knew my husband was shocked. He probably thought I was becoming hysterical. His eyes darkened and widened in a way that informed me that he was concerned yet unsure how to proceed.

I tried to stop laughing. I tried to explain. "Cegan, you're such a ham!" I said and burst out laughing again, recalling Cegan's speech. Despite the eyes that were glowering down into mine, I could not stop. The tears cascaded down my face, and still, I laughed.

Cegan paused a moment, searching my eyes for understanding, and then he carried me the rest of the way to our quarters. Inside his room, he let my feet touch the floor, but his hands held me still while he looked down at me. "There's a healthy light in your eyes, Kira, so I would think you quite capable of explaining why you called me a pig. I do not believe that it refers to gluttonous behavior nor to a lack of neatness."

That started me off again. But when I looked up into his face, something in his eyes warned me that it would be unwise to continue. I breathed in deeply and fought for control.

"It's an acting term, Cegan. Being a ham means that you delivered all your lines with great skill and enjoyment. You were a bit overly melodramatic, I thought, at the end, but you sure played every moment!"

Cegan released me then, and I sat down on the bed. It was easier to talk with Cegan when I didn't have to stare straight up into the heights of him. And with his arms around me, he had a way of getting me off the subject.

He stood there, studying me. That was fine. I had lots to say. "I'm a child, am I, barely out of school?" Actually, now that I was no longer laughing, I was rather irritated by the way Cegan had milked the sympathy of the newsmen, using me as a baby needing protection. "What am I, nine years old?"

Cegan was still speechless. Then, his mouth started twitching, and his smile broke out. "I did not misrepresent the truth, Kira," he said, smiling and showing both rows of teeth. "You are an innocent in matters of trade and policy. And your youth," he said, dropping down on the bed beside me, "is obvious." His arms pulled me closer.

I wanted to lean back and rest my head on his chest, but I wiggled away and turned to face him. "Right," I said, "and you emphasized it to the hilt! And, earlier, you played games with the Pentagon that almost got us killed."

My husband's smile was wide with amusement. Once again, he was sliding me to him. His lips traveled across my forehead. "Kira," he said, "you were never in any danger. You should know better than that. I would not risk you for a hundred trade agreements."

I sighed. "I know. *Trust you.*" I said. Again, I pulled away to look into his eyes, where I hoped to read at least part of the truth. "You may not lie, Cegan, but you sure do connive."

The diamonds in his eyes were focused. What was he reading in mine? Did he know how confused I was about what he was doing? "Cegan, you intentionally lured those generals into anger, and then you let them fall into their own trap, knowing that Natharan technology would keep us safe."

Cegan's eyes twinkled. His teeth flashed his fullest smile. "My Kira," he said proudly, stroking my shoulders with his hands.

It shouldn't have distracted me, but already, a current of electricity was purring through my body. I knew the time remaining for coherent thought was running out.

"How is it that you can out-think Pentagon generals," he continued musingly, "people who've been in politics and diplomacy longer than you've been alive?"

I ignored my husband's praise. Gritting my teeth against the heat of desire, I brushed aside his hands. I'd seen how well Cegan could maneuver conversations. It wasn't the generals or me that I wanted to talk about. "Why did you do it, Cegan? What are you after?"

Cegan nodded his head slowly as if I'd confirmed something he'd already known. He was smiling, but his eyes were thoughtful as he stared into mine.

"Amazing, Kira. I've known from our first talks that you were highly intelligent, but I never realized until today how intuitive you are. Your instincts are excellent. If you can always overlook the extraneous and pursue the goal like you just did, you are going to make one hell of a Natharan trader!"

It was the first time I'd heard a swear word from Cegan. Obviously, he'd learned it from my father. And obviously, he was using it in an attempt to derail my thinking. I stood up and stared down at him. "Cegan, you still haven't answered me. Why did you do it, and what are you after?"

His smile broadened. He looked up at me as if I'd just done something wonderful. Again, he nodded, and his fingers formed the "OK" sign my dad used, except with Cegan's longer fingers, the gesture didn't look right. "Ah, Kira, you are persistent," my husband said fondly. "That is another necessary characteristic of a good trader."

He stood up so he could stand beside me. His hand reached down to clasp mine in his. "I am most impressed with your abilities, my wife. I wish I were able to reward you with answers. I can only repeat, Kira, what I have told you before. We Natharans bring no threat to your planet, nor do I propose to harm you or any other Terran. I can tell you no more, my honored wife, without betraying my purpose here."

I sighed. It irked me to have reached another dead end. Yet, I didn't protest when Cegan once more pulled me close.

"My Siren," he soothed, stroking my hair until I relaxed into him, "I am sorry that the quiet general hurt you with his words. That was not something I wished to happen. I meant their anger to go in another direction."

"Perhaps so, Cegan," I said, leaning my head back to stare up at him, "but you envisioned everything else. You manipulated that whole meeting."

He didn't argue. The diamonds watching me were unreadable.

"I don't understand why you did what you did," I continued, "but I see more of the pieces fitting together. What will you do when I have figured it all out?"

"I love you, Kira. No matter what else, remember that," he said, grasping my arms.

"Yes," I sighed. "I believe you. But I think that it's very convenient for you. Isn't it, Cegan?"

For a moment, his eyes were focused on the wall behind me. Then, once more, he looked into mine. "I cannot answer that yet, Kira, but will you forgive me if there is truth in it?"

What other answer can a wife have when her husband's eyes are looking into hers, and he is filled with adoration?

"I have never been in love before, Cegan," I said. "It is difficult to envision every possibility, but if Natharan is truly not trying to hurt my planet and really only wants to help us, I think then I will forgive you anything."

Chapter Thirteen: The Wonders of a Natharan Ship

For the rest of that day, Cegan escorted me leisurely through his ship. The computerized library with every subject imaginable was a joy. Whatever novel or text I wished could be formed into whatever size book I desired.

"I have downloaded the Library of Congress in Washington into the ship's data banks," Cegan told me, "and I have the computer taking a tour of Paris, London, and Moscow libraries for various subjects I am interested in. If there is anything you want in particular, please order it. Simply speak the name of the book, and the computer will find it. You can do that in our room if you prefer, of course. It is not necessary for you to come here. But you must order the books before we leave Earth's system."

I nodded, and we moved on to a rounded globe room. As we entered, Cegan spoke, the lights dimmed, and you could see stars across the ceiling. When he spoke again, constellations appeared in the sky, many from systems I'd never heard of, yet Cegan told me that Earth astronomers had labeled them. My neck began to ache from staring up at all the wonders he had to show me.

"Another day, I will tell you of other galaxies, other constellations," he said, lifting up my hair and massaging my stiffening neck. "Close your eyes and relax, my Siren." Then, I heard him speaking words I couldn't understand.

A bagpipe began to play in sliding atonal screeches. Like a wind rushing through deserted, lonely cliffs, it moaned and mourned until I put my hands over my ears and begged Cegan to stop it.

"You will need to become acclimated to it, Kira. The sliding pipe is favored by most Natharans, but you will have much time before we land there. We will stick with your western Earth music for now." Cegan smiled at me, seemingly not upset that I found his choice of music obnoxious. "Schubert," he ordered the ceiling, speaking in EngSpan.

The orchestrated melodies that came through the walls sounded like elevator music. I wrinkled up my nose and sighed.

"All right, Kira," Cegan told me, giving me his gentle, nonjudgmental look. "You choose. Composers are in the name of origin. You may ask for one you like."

For a moment, I thought about naming someone Cegan couldn't have heard of. I found Cegan's nonjudgmental look so irritating! It was superior and tolerant, but I knew it was important to Cegan that I liked his ship. "Mozart," I said, not knowing what else to choose.

I assume it worked. Whatever was playing sounded like a windup toy spinning in circles. I could almost picture people dressed in funny costumes twirling and curtseying to the music.

"You can do better than that," Cegan said, watching me in that amused manner he had at times. Was there a twinkle in his eye? Was he laughing at me, at least laughing in the Natharan way? I stilled myself not to react.

"You are not limited, my dear," he said, lifting up my chin so he could read my eyes. "Try something obscure. I think I have collected almost everything. Natharans are always intrigued with the multiphonics of different cultures."

"Grofé?" I said cautiously, still not looking into my husband's eyes. I remembered hearing about the guy in Music Appreciation.

With my words, the room filled with the "Grand Canyon Suite." Violins swelled sweetly, rising in their enthusiasm. I could hear the vibrations in their strings. More and more of them joined. A group of instruments jumped in and then copied the melody. It wasn't bad. I was surprised at how well donkey trails went with constellations.

"Grasshoppers!" I cried out suddenly, beginning to enjoy the game. "Yesterday, the grass always seemed so wet with dew . . ."

I hugged my husband's big body and laughed as the famous oldies from Dad's radio channel crooned their harmonies.

"But what if you don't want to hear that particular piece?" I asked, pulling back to look up at Cegan. "Maybe I wanted something else by them."

"Just say the name, Kira."

I could tell Cegan enjoyed sharing his "theatre" with me. His eyes were no longer superior, but warm, and with the particular glint that told me that at any moment, a double row of teeth would appear.

"Why did it have to dry up and brown like that . . ." the song continued. Cegan's head was tilted slightly. He was still waiting for me to change the music, but I could see he was becoming curious about the song. Before he could ask me any questions, I ordered "Visions of Blue Satin."

Cegan looked slightly puzzled when the song stopped, and nothing played. "Visions of Blue Satin? This is an insect song?" he asked.

"A Grasshoppers' song," I corrected him, trying not to laugh. "It's one of my Dad's favorites. I think he and his father used to sing it together."

Cegan spoke gibberish for a moment. I hoped he wasn't expecting me to respond. My mouth flew open when the ceiling answered him back. Did it listen? Did the computer inside the ceiling always hear everything? I started to ask about it, but Cegan had already informed me that my song was by The Grape Poodles, not The Grasshoppers.

"Oh, I knew that," I said. My face was heated from the mistake. How could I have been so stupid as to confuse the two groups, like I didn't even know my own Famous Historical Earth songs? I shot a glance up at my husband, expecting for a moment to see him mocking me, but he was only watching me with his usual patient half-smile.

"Does the computer . . ." I began.

"Try again, Kira."

"Grape Poodles, Visions in Blue Satin," I said, but I was far more interested in how the computer worked. I could hear oldie songs anytime I wanted.

The music began, and I forgot all about my questions. Dad had a great system, speakers everywhere, the latest in hypersound, but it was nothing like hearing the "Purple Poodles' *Visions in White Satin* in that globe room. I expected to turn around and see long ago musicians with scraggy hair and belted pants flopping around their bell-bottomed ankles. In that globe room, it was live sound, real and vibrant.

I listened to the whole song. Then, I left that kind of music and started on some of the stuff I liked. Cegan had it all. Tornado Twister, Sanded Scorpions, and even the new song by Thong Shang. The sound was riotous. The vibrations and tonal gyrations, even the color-coded jazz-toned replications, all accompanied the music. It was ecstasy.

I think Cegan merely endured my selections as I played through the computer banks. His head never bobbed with the beat, and he didn't move into the rhythms, but at least he never turned a funny color like he did sometimes when things got skewed. He just stood there watching me, his eyes all hazy in thought and his hands playing with my hair.

I was ready for Painted Shoeshine and had just asked for its newest number when Cegan said something to the ceiling and overrode my request. I started to protest, even though I knew I wasn't being fair about it since I hadn't listened to his music. Cegan said "Kira" like he did when he wanted me to be quiet, and that was that.

He spoke in Natharan, and a bed platform, like the one in our room, rose up. Cegan's arms propelled me to it. "Lie back now and watch the ceiling, Kira. We shall compromise on the music and listen to your Schubert."

The room produced a light show. Laser beams of violent colors danced and twirled, sunsets bloomed and faded, and rainbows arched in the sky. I heard the sound of leaves rustling, branches creaking in a slight breeze, and then water, gurgling and rushing over boulders and pebbles. A little later, birds began to sing, hoot, and caw. They were the wood birds I heard on my father's farm, and all the sounds were those of home. I relaxed into them.

My head was laid against Cegan's chest. My eyes were shut. I think I might have started to doze off, but I heard Cegan's voice issuing another order. One end of our bed slowly began to rise and become a lounging seat. I opened my eyes to find a platform in front of us, raised up into a stage. Hamlet appeared with a skull in his hands, discussing life and death in a Shakespearean tongue. Once again, Cegan spoke, and a scene from the musical Oklahoma appeared. The hero, I couldn't remember his name, was riding his horse through the cornfields, singing, "Oh, What a Beautiful Day."

I started to get up. I wanted to touch the horse. It seemed so real. I wanted to pet its coat and find out if it was warm with the feel of life. Cegan reached out with his huge hand and grabbed at mine. "What is it you want, Kira?"

"Let go," I demanded, pulling away.

He released me, and I backed up and walked towards the holographic horse. The smell of saddle leather, sweet and familiar, and the musky odor of sweating horse drew me closer as if I were spellbound. The horse pawed at the ground. Small bits of grass flew up from its movement. Its eyes watched my approach, but they were without fear. It nickered softly. The man on top continued his song, seemingly unaware of me.

"You may not touch it," Cegan's voice commanded.

"You're not my father, Cegan. Stop telling me what to do," I threw back at him. I stretched out my hand for the horse to sniff.

Immediately, the holograph disappeared, and there was only an empty stage in its place. I twirled around to glare at my husband. "Cegan! I just wanted to touch it." Cegan stared at me. I couldn't read his eyes. Was he angry because I'd disobeyed him? A part of me was analyzing, attempting to see his side, but I was feeling itchy with irritation and ready for a fight. My chin raised up, and I glowered at him.

Cegan's voice, when it came, was soft and irritatingly placating. "Kira, I do not know if touching the 'vida' would be safe for you. I will not allow you to be harmed."

Irrationally, his calmness angered me. Why wasn't he upset? Why did he never argue with me? I needed to argue, to fight, and to vent my frustration. I sighed, crossed my arms, and dropped my eyes, examining the mosaic pattern of the carpeting.

I could feel Cegan's eyes on me, searching my face. I looked up and met his gaze. There was no rebuke in his eyes, no impatience. I flushed and once more dropped my eyes. I studied the diagonal lines of the carpet. What color was it? Gray, black? Why couldn't I tell? Did it keep changing?

How ridiculous my anger must have seemed to Cegan. Did he understand? Did he know how irksome it was to be near someone who was always in control, always perfect? I dropped my arms to my sides and sighed.

Cegan was still sitting there, his eyes analyzing. He had not started up the music again or begun another play. Was he still waiting for me to calm down? What was he thinking? I wanted to ask him, but I didn't dare. What if he was having second doubts? What if he was wondering if all Terrans were as emotional as I was . . . or as immature?

I raised my eyes off the carpet's pattern and walked back towards Cegan. I sat down on the floor next to his raised bed platform. The silence continued. I stared up at the constellations, pretending to be fascinated by them, but I was extremely conscious of Cegan's eyes still watching me. I felt like a specimen under a magnifying glass. If I mentioned how irritating it was, I knew Cegan would look away, but his mind would still continue to observe me. The thought annoyed me more.

"Why do you show me Earth plays?" I threw at him. "Don't you have plays from other planets?"

"Of course," he said, "but you are not ready for them."

That was the last straw! I sprang up, recognizing a battle. "How do you know?" I defended myself.

Cegan didn't even attempt to answer. His eyes darkened, and I thought I saw a twitch in his lips. Before I could be sure, it was gone, and the stage was suddenly lit up with what he quietly informed me were Sanoran gholas.

I sat back down on the floor and prepared to watch.

The Sanoran gholas were nude, huge-chested males with bulging muscles that rippled on arms almost as thick as their thighs. A pelt of fur, thick as my cat's, covered their chests and shoulders. The fur was gray, glistening with drops of sweat, and gave off an odor pungent as overripe cheese.

The gholas were waving long, thin swords at each other, dallying as if in sport. Their heavy thighs supported them in a half-crouched position of readiness. Their maleness was uncovered and slightly upright.

I felt my face grow hot with embarrassment. I glanced up at my husband, wondering why he had chosen to show me this. His eyes met mine. I could not read his expression. Was he mocking me or daring me to admit that he was right?

I forced my eyes back to the stage. The gladiators were still prancing around, poking their swords at each other. Their gibberish was harsh, guttural grunts.

"Can you make them speak Engspan?" I asked. My voice had lost all its challenge. In the huge room, it sounded whiny.

Cegan spoke to the ceiling, and as easily as the music had changed upon command, I understood the speech of the warrior gholas. They were discussing the Boobalah and how they were ready to engage him in battle. Despite their frequent boasts about their competence, the prospect of meeting the Boobalah seemed to frighten them. I had no idea what a Boobalah was, but it seemed to me, as I watched the thrusts and evasions of the gholas, that they were well prepared for whatever it turned out to be. I was very wrong.

I heard a horrendous scream, and what I presumed must be the Boobalah was suddenly elongating itself down from the roof. If hell had a mascot, this creature was it. With mottled skin, lichen-green, and tree-trunk-brown, the Boobalah's body was growing larger each second. A mouth with dagger teeth screamed a challenge. Yellow saliva drooled forth from its mouth, dripping like liquid but burning huge rusty-green holes in the floor. Gaseous fumes that smelled like sulfur and ammonia mixed rose from the bubbly mess of the burning floor.

I covered my nose, trying to keep from gagging. I darted a glance up at Cegan. I knew this was all false, but my heart was throbbing, and my brain was sending messages to my body telling me to flee.

Cegan felt my gaze. His eyes moved to mine. They held no hint of fear. "Enough?" he questioned. I swallowed hard and looked away, giving him no response.

The gholas were attacking the Boobalah. They were attempting to ram their swords through its trunk like body, but the metal of their weapons was like a child's rubber toy. It bent and did no damage to the Boobalah's body. Still, the gholas darted about it, flinging themselves at his mighty neck.

The monster's tooth hit a sword. The metal tip of the sword broke off and flew across the room, hitting the wall and landing clear off the stage. I shot another glance at Cegan. His eyes met mine. They were twinkling with Natharan laughter. Again, I looked away, saying nothing.

One of the gholas darted out of the Boobalah's way, just missing a spray of the noxious yellow saliva. The fumes of it, billowing out into the room, made me cough. "It's not real. It's not real," I began to whisper over and over.

Arms had begun to sprout out of the sides of the Boobalah's trunk. They were growing, wiggling themselves long, like sea eels coming out of a small rock hole. All over the monster's trunk, these eel arms were shooting out faster and faster. Then, long claws with needle-like endings blossomed from the end of each arm.

I could see that the poor gholas were tiring. Their swords still battled, and their bodies shifted and evaded the raging teeth of the monster, but the gholas' eyes were darting about in a frantic appeal for escape.

"Run!" I screamed at them. "Get out of there!"

I think one of them heard me. He turned and looked at me. His eyes were sad. They stared into mine, and then he shook his head.

The Boobalah's trunk shifted its head to glare at me. Its one huge yellow eye glowered down at me. I couldn't move or look away. There was no air, no sound of my heart beating, only that eye filled with hate and cold, cold hunger.

Suddenly, the monster's mouth twisted sharply to the left, and one of its needled pinchers sliced across the neck of the nearest ghola. The ghola's head flew across the stage, and blood, gushing like a geyser, pumped itself out of the severed body.

My body was suddenly up and running. Without thought, I found myself buried in Cegan's arms. I no longer cared if I made a fool of myself. The feeling of my husband's arms around me helped to calm my shaking body. I wet his petals with my sobs, and my face breathed in the warm, spicy scent of Cegan. The smell of the Boobalah began to fade.

"Hush, my love. It is gone now," Cegan told me.

I heard him, but it was a while before I was willing to risk a look at the stage. When I finally did courageously peek, the Boobalah and the gholas had both disappeared, leaving no blood or severed heads. Even the rusted yellowish stains of sulfur on the flooring had vanished.

I dried my eyes and pushed angrily away from Cegan. "You did that on purpose! There were other things you could have shown me!"

"Yes," he said quietly.

I looked up, not understanding how he could have been so cruel. Cegan's eyes were not smiling down at me with the amused look I expected to see. His eyes were dark, with a strangely warning look and a harsh firmness that sent shivers down my spine. He met my eyes and held my gaze a moment before replying, "You ignored my warning, Kira. It appears that you must be taught to heed wisdom."

I wasn't about to hear a lecture. I thrust myself up out of his embrace and walked away, turning my back to him. My legs were still shaking, but I would not be cowed by Natharan tricks.

I did not look back at my husband, yet I was aware when he stood up and walked towards me. He came up behind me, almost close enough to touch, yet he didn't touch me, nor did he speak. I began to wonder then if I had made him angry, and remembering the time that I had done so before, my body trembled, but I didn't move away or look up at him. I was too stubborn to back down.

The silence between us became stiffer, and the tension in me was almost as bad as when the Boobalah first appeared. Then Cegan's arms were encircling me, and I was crying out, "Leave me alone!" and struggling against him. It did no good. My body was locked in as tightly as if I were a rodeo roped-and-tied calf.

"Kira," Cegan whispered into my ear.

I moved my head to the side, away from his mouth. His lips followed. Again, he spoke into my ear. "If I say 'no' to you, it is always with reason. Remember that, Kira."

His arms dropped then, and he moved back. I heard him speak in Natharan and saw that the bed-platform was sinking down into the floor. Again, he spoke, and almost instantly, I heard the sound of waves crashing against a sandy beach. A lone seagull screeched its sad, lonely cry. The smell of sand and salt and the fishy, wet odor of seawater made me turn.

Cegan was behind me still, but I ignored him, and looked past his huge green body. How could I believe what I saw? Not five feet away from me, there were ocean waves and a smooth-duned beach. I took a step forward, away from Cegan. Underneath my shoes, there was sand, soft and grainy, molding to my footprint.

I bent over and picked up a shell I saw half-buried in it. Where had the shell come from? In wonder, I examined it. It was real, rock hard and sharp-edged at the corners where it had been broken off from its other half. A dainty ribbing, like a miniature piecrust pattern, covered one edge. The other side was smooth but gravelly. The inside was a polished pearl. Tiny fragments of sand still clung to the damp outer surface.

"This isn't possible," I said, staring at the shell and then out into the tidal waters.

A seagull swept down to light on the sand hill in front of me. The gull's little arched toes paddled towards the water, then veered off to peck in the wet sand. I watched a moment, wondering what it could find in the sterile depths of a holographic ship. The gull, oblivious to my doubts, rooted out a small crab, then lifted up and flew away. The waves continued their drum roll.

It was easy to make the sound of waves, but how could the waves look so real? How could the distant water have that look of mirrors flashing in the sunlight? The ocean appeared to stretch endlessly into the horizon. How had it been made to look so believable?

Cegan stepped towards me, and I felt his closeness. When he placed his arms around me this time, I didn't fight him. I was too dazed. His hands began to lift up my dress. I grabbed at them.

"What are you doing?" I snapped.

"Cooling you down," he said, tossing my dress to the side. Before I could argue further, Cegan's hands were lifting me up, and he was carrying me into the surf. It was only then that I realized that my husband had stripped off all his own clothes. In the warm ocean water, I was soon as naked as he, and my anger floated away with the tide.

We swam and played. The ocean was so beautiful I thought it must have been modeled after Hawaii or somewhere equally perfect. Not only was it calmer than the Atlantic, but the water was just the right temperature. Without people about, the feel of it lapping at my naked skin was a sensuous delight.

We swam far out into the depths, racing, and diving under, pulling at each other's legs to slow the other's speed. I laughed so hard at times I got my mouth full of salty water, and Cegan had to hold me up until I coughed it out. Then, I'd push away and race him across the swells. We played for hours before Cegan pulled me down once too often, and I realized suddenly that I had barely the energy to get back to the surface. My arms and legs were refusing to propel me.

Cegan saw that I was exhausted. He pulled me up and pushed my body flat, stretching out my legs. I had never floated in the ocean, and the thought of being so far out began to panic me, but Cegan held my head back. I was far too tired to resist. I closed my eyes and felt the rhythm of the sea rocking me gently.

For a while, Cegan continued to hold me. The feel of his chest, its petaled softness, wet and warm against my side, made me sleepy. The sun lusciously toasted me while the ocean waves cooled me. I kept my eyes shut and listened to Cegan's voice as he spoke of other oceans. We lay like that for a long time, talking some, allowing the swells to bob us up and down.

"I'm too tired to swim anymore," I told him when he began once more to tickle my belly.

Cegan spoke in Natharan. I thought he was speaking to me, and I turned towards him, opening my eyes. The ocean was suddenly gone, and we were lying naked on the carpet of that strange, globed room. My limbs tingled from the fatigue of our long swim, but the water and the lovely beach were gone. There was only an empty chamber. How could a hologram have been so real?

"You said I couldn't touch a hologram," I whispered in awe.

"That was not a hologram," Cegan said. "Its rays are different and widely dispersed."

"How did you do it? I don't understand."

"I cannot tell you, Kira. You know that. I will answer all your questions when we leave for Natharan."

I sighed. "You keep saying that, but it doesn't make sense. If we're going to return to Earth in a year or two, what difference is there between trusting me now or later?" My words were more gesture than debate. I was really too tired to argue.

Cegan heard the difference in my voice. He smiled, then stood up. "I have shown you many secrets today: the library, this room, the nature of the ship," he said as he slipped on his pants. "These are mine to give you freely, my wife." He held out his hand for me, pulled me up, and then continued. "I trust that you will not let them slip out," he said, staring into my eyes. I shook my head, and his hands moved up to cup my face. "The technology of how they work, Kira, I am honor-bound not to give you until we leave Terra."

I smiled at him. "I wouldn't understand anyway, Cegan," I said, pushing away. It felt wrong to be naked when Cegan was clothed.

I scurried away to collect my clothing. I slipped on my dress first and then had to pull it off again when I came to my panties and bra. I was amazed that they were not wet or stiff with salt. I put everything on and then went to stand beside my husband. "I'm sorry about before, Cegan. I don't know why I was so angry.".

He drew me to him and raised up my chin. His lips met my forehead.

I waited, expecting him to say something, to criticize, to comment at least, but he did neither. His eyes were calm, his lips gently relaxed.

"I love you," I said, and his eyes and mouth answered.

Chapter Fourteen: Alien Food

I was too tired to explore any more of the ship that day. I could tell it amused Cegan when I admitted my fatigue, yet courteously, he only said, "Good. Then we shall go eat."

The dining hall was a special, enclosed, smoky-glassed inlet of a room. We apparently were the only ones using it, and Cegan said it was soundproofed from the rest of the ship. Yet, Cegan could ask for any room, and we were able to hear the sounds from within that room. I asked him the purpose of that, but as usual, he avoided my question.

We had only sat down in the comfortable black rubber-plastic seats when Cegan asked me to be quiet for a moment so he could speak with the crew. He spoke in Natharan, of course, and then I heard the voice of one of the crewmen respond in the Yellows' high-pitched, simplistic manner. I could not understand what the Yellow said, but I was sure he replied in short phrases and single word answers.

Cegan seemed satisfied with the response. He cut off the communication and then relaxed, reaching out his hand to mine. His long fingers swept underneath mine, completely enclosing my hand in green. His touch was firm yet gentle, but even the feel of his flesh gave me a flash of desire.

Cegan's eyes smiled into mine like he knew my thoughts. "Later, my Siren," he said. "I must feed you first."

I started to speak, but his middle finger rose to cover my lips. "Once more, I ask for your silence," he said.

I didn't answer. One finger still covered my mouth, and the others rode my chin and cheek. With the strength in Cegan's hand, I knew he could hurt me if he tightened his grip, yet I knew that he would not.

Cegan's eyes darkened. The diamond centers narrowed in desire. His fingers slid down to stroke my chin and throat. It was not a Terran gesture, yet I shivered. He held me like that, ensorcelled by his touch and his look. Then he smiled, caressed my cheek once, and removed his hand. Turning his eyes from mine, he spoke in gibberish. I heard words like "hamburger," "lasagna," "meatloaf," and "spaghetti." They were all foods he had eaten at my father's. Cegan's eyes smiled into mine for a moment, and then more words flowed: apples, bananas, bacon, eggs," toast, pancakes.

"What have I left off that we should add?" Cegan asked.

"Corn on the cob and peaches? I offered. "And pizza!"

We stumbled on, naming foods for several minutes, until Cegan raised his hand and called a halt.

I began to laugh. "How can a machine duplicate all those things if you haven't brought it food samples and fed them in?"

Cegan stared down at his hand holding mine. For the longest time, he didn't answer me. I assumed he'd gone into his deep-thinking mode and was examining my question, but then he looked up, and his eyes were twinkling, his teeth an open double row.

"Ah, Kira. There have been times on the ship when the days stretched out like the blackness of space. It was not boredom in me, for there are always matters to pursue, yet there was a restlessness that drove me to pace from hall to hall across the ship. I sought out the Yellows. From them, there was a temporary kind of relief, the presence of another beside one's self, but it was a hollowness that held no lasting content.

"Often, I read through the minds of the great men of each planet we have encountered, and for a while, the emptiness would not pain me. Feeling the presence of other minds, studying their thinking processes, their differences, and their similarities — it is a kind of food for the soul. But when I closed the books, the minds faded away, and in me, the hunger ate at my emptiness.

"Natharan knows this hunger. It is the need of the male to find his mate. Yet, the Caste Five females of my planet have not drawn me. I had never met, of course, the ones who would have been selected for me, but the Natharan females I came in contact with were too coldly aloof. Within them, there was no hunger for the essence that is within me.

"You have the same independence, Kira, but you have none of their Natharan coldness. Within you, there is also a need. That is why I believe we were able to reach out to each other. Do you understand, my Siren?"

I stroked Cegan's face with my free hand. I understood the need and that he was telling me he loved me. What I wasn't sure about was what it had to do with the computer and food replications.

Cegan smiled. "Your voice emotes, Kira. On this ship, I learned to listen to what you did not say in the silence between your words. I am learning that your eyes, likewise, hold the telling of your soul. They tell me now that I have confused you."

I would have answered him, but once more, he laid his finger on my lips and continued. "I have given you more than you are able to process at once, Kira. It is only that I wish to explain how you enchant me with everything you say and feel. Even when you are angry, my Siren, I savor the flash in your eyes. Is that wrong, Kira?"

Now, he was allowing me to speak, and I no longer knew what to say. "I'd rather not be angry," I told him.

Cegan's teeth flashed another double row. I had amused him extremely. It was as close to a laugh as a Natharan came.

"If I tell you I am amused by you," Cegan continued, "you will bristle up like Muffin when she first saw me, and then you will be angry, and I will need to let you swim again. I am hungry, so I will not say those words to you."

He was teasing me. Didn't he know that he was perfectly safe? I was much too tired to take offense. I sighed. "I will not bristle up predictably for you," I said. "And what does all this have to do with the food machine?"

Again, his teeth flashed, and I understood. What a diplomat Cegan was. He had only to say my question was so ridiculous he thought it was funny.

"All right," I said. "I understand you found me entertaining and think my question was laughable. I am not angry. But I don't understand how a computer can process and make food it hasn't analyzed."

"Kira, I do not laugh at you. I believe that you are too tired to think logically." Cegan's fingers stroked my hand. I attempted to withdraw it.

"Kira," he said warningly. I froze and stared at him. Cegan took advantage and continued, "Could a computer figure out the confirmation of an airplane, Siren, by stuffing bird feathers into its circuits?"

It was ridiculous when he said it that way. I sighed. "OK. It was an illogical question, but what I meant to say was that I thought you'd need a metal probe or something to analyze the food."

"It has been analyzed chemically, Kira. By our voices, we have only placed the foods in readiness for our orders."

"So I wasn't all wet." I shook my head and started over again. "I still don't understand why you told me about being lonely and needing a mate. I'm glad you did, but why did you tell me here and now?"

"What do you wish to eat, Kira? Tell the server."

His eyes had grown hard. He was staring at the wall across from me as if lost in thought. Why was he shutting me out? I wasn't ready to drop the subject. There were already too many puzzle pieces flying around in my head. I captured Cegan's chin with my hand and brought his eyes back down to me.

He did not refuse me, but his eyes, as they stared into mine, were unreadable. Cegan could do that at will, while I was as open to him as a news broadcast. It didn't seem fair. "Why do we have to drop it, Cegan? Why did you tell me now?"

Once more, his eyes flashed with amusement. He removed my hands and kissed them lightly. "I have two hungers at this moment, my Siren. Which do you prefer we appease first?"

I dropped my eyes and tried to hide my blush. I studied the shiny black of the tabletop. It looked polished and spotless. Who did all the cleaning on the ship? Would that be my job once we took off? "I want to try something, Natharan," I blurted out, braver than normal.

"You will not like it."

When I would have argued, Cegan stood up, and then, watching me, his eyes twinkling, he spoke into the room in his Natharan babble. The wall lit up and unwrinkled a patch with a window-like cupboard. Cegan opened it, pulled out a plate with my meal, and carried it over to me. The plate was of the same shiny blackness as the table, and in its middle lay four squares that looked exactly like the alfalfa cubes I fed my horse. Cegan placed the plate down on the table in front of me and stood there watching.

"Where is yours?" I asked.

"I will watch you eat yours first."

I picked up one of the cubes and examined it. Small strands of stiffened strings in a dull green were packed hard with bits of oat-shaped beige circles. It had no smell. I attempted to bite at the corner, but it was harder than I'd expected. I could not bite through. I gnawed at it a moment. Nothing noticeably broke away from the cube but the taste. It was of seaweed and sawdust. I drank from the bottle of water that Cegan had given me and put the cube back down on the plate.

One layer of teeth was grinning away at me. I met his eyes. "May I still order that hamburger?"

The twitch in the corner of his mouth was back, but he said nothing, only pulled the shiny black plate to his side of the table and spoke into the air. Once more, I saw the wall quiver and produce the window, and then he was placing a second plate in front of me.

The hamburger, peach, and diet cola I ended up eating weren't bad. I offered my husband a bite of the peach, but he shook his head and let me know his preference. He finished the horrible alfalfa cubes, drank my water, and admittedly seemed much happier than he'd been with the food at my father's.

We went back to his quarters then, and Cegan read the printout of calls. Apparently, there was nothing important. He tossed all the messages into the recycler. I figured he must have forgotten his romantic offer before dinner because, just like a bored husband, he turned on the translinevision.

I couldn't see a TV or projector machine. Cegan had turned on the wall with a couple of Natharan words. Lying on the bed, we were able to watch Cegan giving his speech on five news channels. It seemed that the commentary that came at the end was what interested Cegan most. Each one of them was different, but the consensus was that the Pentagon had erred grossly. The station promised more updates, but Cegan spoke in Natharan, and the screen went back to being just a wall.

Watching the news reminded me that my father might be worried. I asked if I could speak to Dad. Cegan agreed but warned me that the line would be tapped. What in the world could I say that the Pentagon would find interesting?

Again, Cegan spoke to the wall, and Dad's voice answered. I assured my father that I wasn't hurt. Dad hardly spoke with me before, demanding that I put Cegan on the phone. I wasn't holding a receiver, but I pretended that I was and told Dad that I'd go get Cegan.

"I'm here, Hank," Cegan said after counting out about twenty seconds.

"Listen, Cegan," my dad said. "If there's any danger to Kira, take her away from here. I'd rather you flew her to Natharan and never returned to Earth than have them try to hurt her again."

I wanted to reassure my father, but Cegan's finger was back on my lips. I remembered then what Cegan had said about the phone being tapped.

Cegan nodded at me and replied to my father. "I understand, Hank, but as long as she's with me, Kira is safe."

"How safe is the ship?"

"Impenetrable."

"I'm trusting you with her, Cegan. Don't let me down."

"Thank you, Hank. You have my word. I will always take care of Kira," Cegan said, smiling at me.

I rolled my eyes and sighed. Men! Like I couldn't take care of myself! What did they think I'd been doing these past months?

"Could I speak to Kira again?" my father asked.

Cegan said, "Here she is." His fingers lifted, then he counted 1,2,3 and nodded for me to speak.

"Stop worrying," I said. I was about to explain to him just exactly what I'd been thinking about. Dad needed to know I could take care of myself just fine, but he cut me off.

"You listen to Cegan, Child, and you do everything he tells you. You hear me?"

I stuck out my tongue, aiming it at my husband. He probably didn't know its meaning, but he knew me well enough to understand I was disputing my father's words.

"Dad, you'll still come before we leave, won't you?"

"If I can, baby, but I told Cegan to take off if there's any trouble. And don't you try to argue with him if he does."

"Dad!" I protested.

"I love you, girl. Call me tomorrow."

"I will." I wasn't crying then, but my eyes were leaking just a little.

"Kira, no cold feet, right?" he asked.

"No, Dad. No cold feet."

That night, all the swimming and the excitement of the day robbed me of my usual energy. I lay down on the bed after talking with Dad and fell right to sleep. I never felt Cegan pulling me towards him and cradling me in his arms as he did every night. I woke once in the night and found myself being held firmly. I closed my eyes and slept peacefully.

In the morning, I rose with a stretch that discovered sore muscles. I groaned. The swim hadn't affected Cegan. He kissed me good morning and pounced off the bed to check messages. After dressing, we went off to a breakfast where I was definitely not daring. My coffee, eggs, and toast looked much better than Cegan's hard cake of soybeans or whatever Natharan vegetable proteins are.

At 9:30, about the time I was receiving my third cup of coffee from the food machine, a crewman's voice interrupted us. I couldn't understand the Yellow's words but I heard the words *President* and *United States.*

We returned to Cegan's quarters, and he took the call there. It was really strange to hear a voice I'd heard so often on the news saying my name. I kept thinking every time that I was mentioned that the president had to be talking about somebody else named Kira. He couldn't really be referring to me, the girl whose only fame was in county fair rodeos and high school dance routines!

Cegan was the one who did all the talking, luckily. I couldn't have. I wouldn't have been able to manage "hello" without creaking like a meadow toad. Imagine hearing personally from the President of the United States of America!

Cegan told the president that he was willing to meet at 4:00 that afternoon. I started wondering if Cegan would expect me to go with him. I wanted to go, kind of. I mean, if Cegan asked me to go with him, I couldn't say "no," yet I knew my whole body would tremble like a Bobble-head in earthquake country. I'd probably make a fool of myself, too. And I didn't have the slightest idea what I'd wear.

I guess it was funny that the day before, I'd thought the White House was where we were headed, but I figured that we'd never see the president. Now, with the man himself on the phone, I couldn't help thinking how nice that small white frame house of Dad's was. Life hadn't been as complicated there. Why had I ever left it?

Cegan was laying down the law to the president. How could he be so calm? He was talking as if the president were doing us a favor! "One more thing," Cegan said. "You know that Natharan has the technology of force fields, as you call them. Your men won't be able to search us. The machine creates a three-foot radius around us, which nobody can enter. After yesterday, you understand its necessity. Do you agree to this?"

The president hesitated. I could hear someone in the background urging him to say "no." Cegan remained silent, not giving in until the president agreed. Then, the man offered to send his pilotcar to us. Cegan told him that we had our own transportation. I groaned, but other than giving Cegan pleading eyes, I let him handle it.

"Wait," Cegan said abruptly, just before the president was about to hang up. My husband was staring at me with his faraway look, which meant he wasn't really noticing me. "Yes," he said after a moment. "Send the pilotcar, but I want either your wife or the vice-president in it. And you need to know that if someone planned to blow up the pilotcar, the force field would not allow us to be harmed. Understand?"

The president paused. "I understand your lack of confidence in us. My wife says she will be delighted to meet you. She and the pilotcar will arrive at 3:30."

When the connection ended, I was still staring at Cegan. "You do understand that the man you were talking to is our president? I mean, the one and only President of the United States. Didn't that make you nervous? Even a little bit?"

I sat down on the bed behind Cegan and wrapped my arms around him. Maybe he didn't understand how important the president was! I kissed my husband on the neck, still waiting for an answer. His shrug almost flung me off, but his hands effortlessly grabbed me and slid me down into his lap. How could someone so strong be so gentle?

He pulled me closer, nestling me with his arms, kissed my forehead, and said, "The kind of traders we are, Kira, presidents will be fairly common. There will be kings, emperors, and dictators at each of our stops. The title changes, my sweet wife, but the position is more or less the same." His hand caressed my cheek and moved on to play with my hair. "Will you tremble each time I speak with one?"

"What makes you think . . .?"

"You vibrate," he said, cutting me off. "Like Muffin when she purrs." He smiled broadly. "I can hear it."

"You cannot!" I argued, but his lips had found the surest way to stop any debate.

Chapter Fifteen: The White House

Cegan had told my father that there was no danger for us in the twistings of the government's bureaucracy, yet Cegan made love to me that day with the same wildness as after our fight over the barrel racing. I suppose that, in some way, the speed and the power of my ride, and maybe the risk, although I never thought of it as such, were like the wooing of power. And power was what I thought, at the time, that Cegan was after. But for whatever reason, whether it was from a rush like I got from barrel racing or from the thrill of danger, what followed was wilder than either of us intended.

I had known Cegan was alien from the first, and anyone who viewed his big green petaled body could have no doubts about it. Yet, everything between us had been so normal that I think I had stopped believing aliens could also mean unworldly, strange, and beyond anything I could possibly have imagined.

The passion that burst between us that day was like falling into an old wooden well. I spiraled downward so far that I wondered if there would ever be any bottom. Then I plunged into the shock of it, and I was almost drowning in the icy chill of what I believed to be water. Yet still, I kept falling further and further down.

There was a kind of release then, an agony and an eruption of pleasure, all mixed up with the coldness, yet I wasn't cold. I was hot, burning with restlessness, but held suspended in time. Cegan was there, beside me, yet we were entwined inside each other, mingled and interwoven. It was almost as if we were two buckets of water that were poured into a basin and merged drip-by-drip. There was suddenly no separation, no feeling of individuality or self-identity, just molecules playfully blending, uniting, and joining.

Then, all at once, I had a body again, and I was swimming back up into awareness. Even at that first moment when I broke through to the surface of the water or whatever substance it was, even as I breathed in those great gasps of sweet, lovely air until my poor, empty lungs were filled, even then, I was sharply aware that I was not myself, not the person I had been before. There was a strangeness in me, some residue left behind from what had just occurred. I probed at this strangeness, attempting to push it out. I felt altered, changed, different. The feeling panicked me.

My arms were starting to grow weary of dog paddling. I looked upward and saw only blackness above me. If this were truly a well, and I was at the bottom, shouldn't I see a hint of light? I made an effort to relax and not paddle so hard with my arms, but I was struck then by a thought that almost sent me plunging back downwards and under the surface. I had been so busy fighting against the changes inside me that I had not recognized that there was also a loss. Some part of me had been left behind, and I suddenly felt its absence. Like a tidal wave of horror, the thought rammed against my stability. For minutes, I could scarcely breathe.

My arms and legs were waging war against the liquid I was in, fighting to hold me up on its surface. I knew I could not continue the effort much longer. I calmed my limbs, attempting to slow their agitation. I knew my body was buoyant and that my struggles were more against my loss and the differences I felt than in my need to keep my head above the surface.

I had wasted a great deal of energy, giving into my panic. My arms were already so heavy they could barely support me, and my legs were numb with the cold, but what choice did I have but to continue?

Again, I looked up, hoping to see some sign of rescue or at least a light that would tell me there was a way out. Why was I here? What was happening to me? Where was Cegan?

Cegan! Cegan had brought me here. He would get me out. "Trust me," he kept telling me. "I trust you, Cegan," I said, but there was no answering voice.

My arms were so tired. I lay back and rested, floating as I had done in the ocean. I knew I couldn't swim anymore, so I closed my eyes and accepted the strangeness, feeling it settle in and become a part of me.

I woke to feel Cegan's hand caressing my cheek. I opened my eyes to stare up at him. He looked the same, yet I could see subtle differences in the way he looked at me. His eyes held more tenderness, more understanding, more love. Yet I'd never once known him to show me any lack of them. His eyes were drinking me. It was as if I'd suddenly given him some gift totally unexpected, and his eyes were all lit up with contentment.

"You have taken all of me inside you, Kira," he said. "I did not know you were able. Our souls have merged in this union. A small part of you is now completely Natharan, and I am Terran. We are one now. The commitment is complete."

I opened my mouth to question him, to argue, I suppose, maybe to be indignant, but I couldn't speak. I barely had enough breath to keep my lungs from complaining.

"Your eyes hold fear. Do not be afraid, my little one," he cooed. "This change will not hurt you. I will never hurt you, my little Siren. Remember?"

He picked up my hand and turned my palm upwards. His lips gently kissed the inner surface. I could barely feel his touch, yet my blood raced, and deep inside me, there was an answering summons. "Feel it, Kira?" my husband asked. "The merge has brought us closer."

My body's response to his touch only frightened me more. It was too strange. All of this was beyond anything I'd ever heard or seen. I could adapt to Cegan's advanced technology, but this . . .?"

"Kira!" he shouted. It was one of the few times I'd heard Cegan raise his voice.

I gasped from the shock of it. My lungs filled with air. I breathed in deeply. Breathing is the most pleasurable sensation.

"Much better, my little one. Breathe deeply. You will be fine."

My eyes opened again to watch Cegan. He understood what had happened. Had he caused it? What had he done to me? Had I really almost drowned in a well? If I'd only dreamed it, he wouldn't be talking about it.

"Kira, easy, my love. The fear in your eyes still grows, yet you do not speak. Is it the alienness that alarms you?"

His fingers stroked my face. They were gentle fingers, long and thin, yet strong, stronger than human fingers. They were capable of bringing so much pleasure when Cegan wished it. But they were an alien's fingers. What had Cegan done to me? Why?

"Do not be frightened. Trust me. You know I would give my life for you. You do know that, do you not?"

I wanted to answer Cegan. I wanted to ask him a whole lot of questions, but it was like that frozen moment when the air is knocked from your lungs, and you can only focus on your needs. It was like that. I could not breathe, yet I was breathing, and each breath hurt with its strangeness and my fear.

Cegan continued to talk to me, petting my face, soothing me, calming me. "I am sorry for your fear," he said. "I should have prepared you, but I did not know or mean to . . ." Again, his hand stroked my cheek. "Easy, my little Siren, relax into it. You will be fine in a minute. Breathe, my little Terran, breathe."

I wanted so to talk. I wanted to tell him I was all right. He seemed so worried. And it was not that I was in pain, not anymore. Actually, my body was beginning to feel wonderful, clear, and clean. I was becoming drunk with the feel of it. My head was starting to reel. I was sure at any moment, I would rise into the air and float upwards towards the ceiling.

"Kira, I should not have allowed myself to take you so deeply. Forgive me. It was too great a shock for you. You are still fighting it. I should have known you would resist."

I opened my mouth to tell him I was OK, but nothing came out. Would he never let me talk? For a moment, a twitch of his lips, almost a smile, covered the worry in his face. "Was that argument I saw in your eyes, my darling Kira?"

I gave him the briefest nod, but even that made my head spin.

His smile broadened. "The worst is over then. Close your eyes, little one. You are tired now. When you awaken, you will feel the difference less. Sleep now. Sleep."

His lips touched mine, and I closed my eyes. I would have argued, even then, but my eyes refused to open, and the bed platform seemed so soft and comfortable.

When I woke, Cegan was sitting there beside me, gazing down at me. I wondered if he'd sat there and watched me the whole time. He bent over and kissed my lips, then picked up a small tumbler, like a jigger that served whiskey. He lifted me up and forced me to drink the liquid. I still didn't have the energy to argue.

I thought, at first, that the drink he'd given me was tasteless, and I'd smelled no odor, but as the seconds traveled, floating in the air like bubbles passing by me, I knew the taste. The taste of it was chocolate and ice water from a mountain stream, the first raspberry of the season, and Cegan's kisses.

"Do you trust me?" my husband asked.

"Yes, yes!" I laughed, throwing my arms around him.

Whatever he had given me, I felt alive. I felt like I did that instant when I looked down the arena and saw three metal barrels. I knew the promise of that moment and the absolute joy that was coming when I said, "Go."

I tried to explain to Cegan. His eyes darkened when I spoke of barrel racing, but there was an alertness to his look when he searched my eyes. Then he smiled. His arms enfolded me with his warmth, and as I leaned my head back against his chest, he spoke. "I tried to think of words while you slept so you would understand what happened. When Natharans merge, I think it is like finding a channel on your radio and then fine-tuning it. Does that make sense, my love? Do you mind the difference? Are you angry?"

"No, Cegan. How could I be angry? Why didn't you merge us sooner?" I laughed. The strangeness of it all seemed like only a bad dream. I didn't understand how I'd ever felt fear of Cegan's love or of anything Cegan did. Cegan was a part of me, my twin soul, my love!

He kissed me gently, tenderly. "I told you, Kira. I did not mean to merge you yet. A merging isn't always possible, not with races that are not Natharan. And even if I had dared to believe that we could attain it, I should have waited. Emotionally, you have had too much to contend with already. Your body did not need another shock."

I laughed. "I'm fine, Cegan. We Terrans are sturdier than you think. But do you mean your perfect control slipped?" I teased him.

He stared at me, and then the double row of teeth appeared. "I can see you are sassy as ever. Get dressed, woman," he growled at me, but his eyes glowed, and his teeth flashed fully.

I laughed as I rose. I felt strong and surer than I'd ever felt before. There was a link between us that hadn't been. I felt it in me, and my fear of it was gone.

Cegan's eyes continued to watch me as I went to the computer terminal. I saw that he was still worried. I flashed him a reassuring smile, and then I turned and began my search for the style and color of a dress appropriate for meeting a president.

Chapter Sixteen: The President's Wife

After searching through the computer banks in a study that should have taken hours but required a selection, according to Cegan, within fifteen minutes, I chose a navy blue, slender A-line long-length dress. It was conservative enough to ease Cegan's discomfort over short dresses, dressy enough to be proper for the White House, and elegant. A jacket made of the same material and color completed it. With only a minute more of Cegan's patience, the shoes I chose were simple Italian pumps but with rather daring three-inch heels. I figured if I leaned on Cegan, no one would be aware that I wobbled a bit.

When I modeled the ensemble, Cegan was suitably impressed. His eyes flared lustfully when I stood before him. He ran his hands down the side of the dress and threatened to wrinkle it delightfully. I laughed and pulled away.

Cegan looked pretty good himself in his three-piece lawyer's suit. There was just a hint of green in the gray of the suit that went nicely with the color of Cegan's skin.

I started to put up my hair to equal the formality of my dress, but Cegan had his own opinion. "Kira, I'd rather you let your hair down," he said. "You look about sixteen with it the way it is right now. It would be perfect for pictures."

If any other male had tried to suggest how I should wear my hair, I would have blown sky high. But I knew what Cegan wanted, and I thought I knew why. I left my hair down, long and simple.

At 3:30, we stepped out of the ship. The yellow powder surrounded us immediately with its barely visible coating. Cegan pushed me gently into the front. His arms held me firmly against his soft, petaled chest. I was glad for the support.

The next instant, the news reporters surrounded us. For a moment, there were so many questions thrown at us that it was like being a duck at the shooting gallery. Cegan raised up his hand to quiet them. "Yes, we are on our way to meet with President Clayton now. It will be my last attempt at bargaining. If anyone threatens my wife, we will return to the ship and take off, and Earth will not have the option of our valuable cargo."

Cegan ignored the questions about his cargo. It was as if he did not hear them, but when one of the reporters asked, "Is your wife OK after yesterday?" Cegan turned to him and smiled. "After tears and a call home to her father, Kira's doing much better."

"Kira, there's a rumor," said a TV woman broadcaster, "that your husband somehow caused the violence yesterday. What is your comment on that?"

I flared at the reporter. "That's a lie! I was there, and Cegan never threatened or initiated any violence, nor did he call the wives of the generals . . ." I couldn't say the words. I felt my face grow hot.

"Kira, please finish. What did your husband do when they called you those names?"

I don't know why the tears started. I hated it when I cried, but though my eyes dripped, I swallowed and finished telling my story. "Cegan put on this force field to protect us from them because they all started yelling and threatening us. Then we left, and they started shooting." I couldn't go on anymore. It was more frightening in the remembering than it had been the day before when it was happening.

Cegan turned me to face him so I could cry with his arms around me. "That's enough," he ordered the media. "Leave her alone now."

Four presidential guards marched up to us. One stepped forward and identified himself. I immediately forgot his name. I was probably still crying. He cleared his throat, obviously tired of waiting for me. I drew in a shaky breath and tried to think about Powder and running the barrels. I knew if I thought about the crowd surrounding us and taking a hundred pictures of me with red eyes, I'd probably cry some more.

The guard coughed again, even more loudly, and repeated, "We are here to escort you to the White House. If you will, please follow us?"

Cegan had us surrounded in force field yellow, and we were perched a couple of feet off the ground. I looked down at the guard. The guard met my eyes and winked at me. I guess he wasn't really too impatient with my tears.

"Be careful," one of the reporters said to us as we passed.

Cegan gave the man a quick smile and a nod, but my husband's eyes were focused on the pilotcar up ahead.

It was an enormous vehicle, twice as big as the one we'd been in the day before. Mrs. Clayborn was waiting for us at the door. As we reached her, she waved at the crowd and then backed away to let us enter.

Her posture and manner were elegant. Despite the crowd of reporters and Cegan towering in green petals above her, she was calm and politely casual. I was impressed. She urged us to sit where we liked. How had she learned to take everything in stride so graciously?

The seats were done in a dark, rich, blue velvet. They were soft, cushioned, and comfortable. They had been bolted into the pilotcar in a circle, so you couldn't move them from place to place, but you could swivel around to face whomever you wished. Cegan and I sat. Mrs. Clayborn took a chair next to Cegan. As the pilotcar took off, I exchanged a smile with her. Hers was warm and friendly, but I was so nervous I would probably have bolted out the door given the opportunity.

The guards filtered in after us. It seemed like they'd multiplied. They filled in the vacant chairs of the circle and overflowed towards the back of the vehicle. It made me nervous that some of them were behind us and out of sight. The officer who'd winked at me sat on the other side of Mrs. Clayborn.

The president's wife started a conversation with Cegan. I tried to listen, but my knees began to shake. I wondered if anyone besides Cegan could feel the vibration of my trembling.Cegan reached over and patted my arm. "Relax," he ordered, but my body was on alert. It wasn't listening to him or me.

Mrs. Clayborn ignored Cegan's interchange with me. She kept right on talking. She either didn't realize that I was so nervous I could hardly swallow, or else she was used to people being stage-struck. "Tell me how you two met," she said.

How could she not know how we'd met? Even *People Magazine* had done a spread on the strange story of our wedding, thanks to my friend Frances. Yet, Mrs. Clayborn was pretending she'd never heard. She was treating us like any other couple.

Cegan told her the story, but the way he gave it was dry. He might as well have been talking about someone's tax return. He left out most of the highlights that Frances had stressed, the parts that made me fall in love with him. Nevertheless, Mrs. Clayborn went on and on about how romantic it all was.

It was strange how Cegan didn't seem the least bit nervous about the pilotcar full of guards ready to shoot him if he flinched. He just kept answering Mrs. Clayborn's questions calmly. I wished I could relax enough to give the conversation my full attention. I really was curious about how Cegan viewed "our courtship," as Mrs. Clayborn put it.

A couple of times, a guard moved, shifting in his seat; one man got up to use the john. I realized then that Cegan was very aware of the motions behind him. I could see the tightening of his thigh with each one of the men's movements as if Cegan were ready to spring up should the need arise. Yet, each time, he glanced at me, patted my arm, and then continued the story he was telling.

The yellow powder all around us maintained its hazy quality. I couldn't feel it or smell it, and it never bothered my eyes. I could slip my hand through it and touch anything I chose. But I knew from the Pentagon fiasco that no one could touch us. So why did Cegan's thigh stiffen each time the guards moved? Why did I think sometimes that I saw a sudden alertness in his eyes? Why did I feel that beneath his calm, he was a motor with the throttle at full?

The flight seemed unending. My fear was causing my legs to tremble again. My hands cupped them and held them still.

"Excuse me, Mrs. Clayborn, but I think that Kira should give you her side of the wedding. I wasn't there to see, and I should like to hear her words."

Cegan expected me to speak? I couldn't talk to the wife of the president! Again, my husband's hand was reaching out to touch my arm. I wished the seats were closer. I wished I could crawl into his lap. I wished . . . I bit my lip to try to still my body. Cegan's eyes were on me, encouraging me. Everyone's eyes were on me.

"What a wonderful idea," gushed Mrs. Clayborn. "I realize you are shy, dear. I was dreadfully shy, too, when my husband first became governor. You'll get over it. How about a cup of coffee or a drink?" she offered.

"Bottled water?" asked Cegan.

Two unopened bottles of ice water were brought over by one of the guards. At Cegan's suggestion, the man set them down on the table in the middle of the circle. My husband stood up and opened one of them. He took a sip and then another and carried the bottle to me.

I reached out for it, but Cegan paused and stared down at me a moment. "Stand up," he said.

It was embarrassing to be ordered about like that in front of everyone. My face turned hot. I knew I was blushing, but I stood up.

"Take my seat, Kira. That way, you and Mrs. Clayborn can become better acquainted. I will sit in yours," he told me.

Cegan had moved me before I was coherent enough to argue. With my bottle in hand and Mrs. Clayborn's expectant eyes urging me to tell her about our wedding, I knew I was trapped. I concentrated on Mrs. Clayborn's kind eyes and tried to ignore everyone else. It was rather like being on stage before a dance competition. I felt that same surge of adrenalin pumping me up. My heart raced as I started. I was surprised when my words flowed, and my voice sounded normal.

Mrs. Clayborn had a lot of questions, but they were all of a friendly nature. At one point, I even laughed at a joke she made. I turned to include Cegan, and I saw that he was smiling. He nodded at me. I saw he was pleased. His eyes were full of pride.

Mrs. Clayborn questioned me for the rest of the trip. She was very upset about our wedding when she heard the actual details. She came close to lecturing Cegan, saying that I'd been cheated out of something that should have been very special.

"You know, Cegan," she scolded. "I don't know how it is on your Natharan, but here, most young women dream of their wedding. There's a long, full gown, all in white, with a train of material behind the bride that drags on the floor. A religious leader says special words. The groom, the man getting married, puts a ring on the woman's finger, and then he kisses the bride. It is a very beautiful ceremony.

"You two don't even have any pictures of your wedding," she continued, wiping at her eyes. "Your poor father, Kira. He never got to give you away."

I lowered my eyes in guilt. I didn't mean to make Cegan feel bad about the way we'd been married, but Mrs. Clayborn was right. I had hurt my father.

"My daughter's wedding dress is in one of the closets," Mrs. Clayborn went on. "I don't suppose you would want to pose for some pictures? Your father could come, Kira, and if you wanted, you could even have a little ceremony in our chapel. What do you think?" she asked.

I looked up at Cegan. His eyes were studying me. "We shall see how the meeting with President Clayborn goes before making any plans," he said a little gruffly.

I sighed. "It was a lovely idea," I told the first lady. "Thank you for offering."

"Now I feel like a boot," Cegan shot at me.

"A heel," I corrected him.

The landing of our pilotcar took place on the White House lawn. A score of plain-clothed policemen scrambled to the vehicle's side. Several men led huge German Shepherds that barked at us as we got out. I wondered if they barked because of the yellow cloud around us or because of Cegan's different appearance.

Mrs. Clayborn exited after us. She stood among our group with perfect tranquility. I guess she must be used to having an army of soldiers surrounding her.

One of the guard dogs was fighting its leash. Its hair stood up, its dog lips were pulled down at the sides, and its mouth displayed shark-like teeth. To be the one a dog like that wanted to attack was frightening, even if you were pretty sure it couldn't get to you.

We started across the lawn. It was spongy from the recent rain. My heels sank down to its surface. I wished everybody would walk a little slower.

We had almost reached the cement walkway when one of the dogs pulled free from its owner's hand. It rushed at us, jumping up into the air and aiming its teeth at Cegan's body. I screamed, but the yellow powder of the force field halted the dog's charge. With a dull thud and a loud whimper, the dog fell to the ground. The force of its collision must have knocked all the breath out of it. It lay there beside us, looking dead.

The suddenness of the incident stunned me. Like a flashback in an old movie, all I could see was Corky, my little golden-brown cocker spaniel, lying on the side of the road where some speeding motorist had tossed him.

The officer came running over, apologizing profusely. "I don't understand it," he kept saying. "It was against all his training."

The man bent over and lifted up his dog. As we continued walking, I looked back. The dog lay limp in the man's arms, but its tail was starting to wag.

Turning around almost unbalanced me. One of my heels wobbled slightly. Cegan took a firmer grip on my arm. "If the shoes are difficult, I can carry you," he offered.

"Don't you dare," I whispered, horrified at the thought.

Cegan flashed his double row of teeth. "You are like Earth weather," he said, grinning widely. "The variations of your temperament will always prevent boredom in our long space flights."

We entered via the side door of the White House and traveled through long passages of maple flooring. Pictures were on every wall: florals, nature scenes, portraits, animals, and scenes of relaxation. We walked by cabinets filled with medals and trophies, statues of the Greeks and Romans, and assorted figurines.

I paused a second in front of a rearing stallion. Its coat gleamed in ebony black. Its face demonstrated the breed's concave, dished head, small muzzle, and large and intelligent eyes. The statue, barely ten inches high, showed the horse's arched neck and a thick mane scattered from the movement of its position. It was an exquisite piece of art, at least to a horse fan like me.

Cegan hadn't said a word as I stopped, but I could feel the eyes of everyone urging me to move forward. I shot a final glance at the Arabian horse, then continued on, my eyes noting Chinese vases with pink lotus flowers, British tea cups in white porcelain with blue willow designs, and silver coffee pots with matching cream pots and sugar dishes.

And everywhere, there were guards in formal uniforms, saluting and opening heavy wooden doors. I wished we could have a tour, but no one spoke. Even Mrs. Clayborn seemed subdued by the majesty of the White House.

After the many turns and doorways we passed through, I was thoroughly lost. I wondered if even Cegan could find his way out of the maze. We finally stopped before a set of double doors. The handles were thick bars of golden metal, so shiny they looked new. The guards that stood in front of the doors made no attempt to open them. Instead, they stood in front of them, barring our entrance.

Mrs. Clayborn stopped and smiled at us. "It has been a pleasure talking with you two. I do hope that we are able to follow through on that matter we discussed earlier." Her eyes moved to look up at Cegan. She didn't seem in the least frightened by Cegan's great size or appearance, and the steel in her eyes made me think that she would keep urging Cegan about it.

The door opened, and Mrs. Clayborn stepped back. A white-gloved guard waved us forward.

My eyes searched for the president, and I saw him striding toward us. He looked so "usual," just like a man you'd pass on the street and not even notice. I'd expected him to be taller.

He was only a step or two away from the yellow haze when it occurred to me that I didn't know what I should do. I couldn't remember if I was supposed to bow or curtsey, and I couldn't shake his hand. I was the Terran. I should have been telling Cegan the proper protocol, yet my mind was a complete blank.

The president didn't act like we were supposed to do anything. He came closer and said, "I would like to shake your hand in welcome to the White House, but I think that will have to wait for another time . . . unless you are willing to . . . ?"

"We cannot do that," Cegan told him.

If I'd had control of the force field, I would have turned it off. It was horrible to be acting like I didn't trust my own president.

"I understand," the president said. "Perhaps next time. Still, I welcome you, Dram Kira, Caste Five of Earth, and Dramsté Cegan, Caste Five of Natharan."

"Thank you, Mr. President," Cegan replied.

I was about to follow suit when my eyes glanced across the room. I suddenly forgot about the president. I turned my back to him and glared up at Cegan. "I will not stay here with them. I don't care what you say. I won't do it!"

Cegan's hands took hold of my upper arms. His eyes stared into mine. "Kira, listen to me."

I shook my head determinedly. I was not about to hear excuses for the generals' presence. I'd had enough of their name-calling. I raised my chin defiantly.

"You are wrong, Kira. You will listen."

I don't know whether it was the tone of Cegan's voice or his words spoken with that emphasis on "will," but I froze for an instant. He didn't wait for me to recover. His eyes held mine firmly. "The generals are here because I demanded it. They are here to apologize."

The words were like a slap. I dropped my eyes and stared at the ground. I felt like such a fool. Why hadn't I thought of that? Why hadn't Cegan warned me? When had he talked about it with the president? My face heated. I suppose I turned into a catsup head, as my roommate used to say, teasing me about my constant blushes.

"I'm so sorry, Mr. President," I apologized, but I couldn't look at him. I couldn't bear to think how rude I'd been.

Cegan asked about our seats and then led me to my chair. I sat down, assuming that the eyes of everyone were scowling at me for my impertinence. I gazed down at my hands and wished I were anyplace but in the White House. My nose had begun to run. I sniffled a couple of times and shot a quick glance around the room. I couldn't see tissues anywhere.

President Clayborn was a kind man. He walked over and placed his fancy engraved linen hankie on the table next to me. Cegan reached out for it, opened it up as if inspecting it, and then handed it to me. I mumbled my thanks, used the cloth on my stupid nose, and continued to stare down at my lap. That didn't help my runny nose at all.

I could hear the president positioning himself at the head of the table. Cegan scooted his chair next to mine. A second later, his fingers were lifting up my chin, and he was smiling down into my eyes. That made my eyes water even more. How could Cegan not be angry with me? I must have embarrassed him dreadfully.

"I'm sorry, Cegan," I whispered.

His fingers released my chin, and he caressed my cheek. "Be easy, Kira. You've done no harm."

Once more, I dropped my eyes, feeling like an impudent child, one that deserved a lecture from my incredibly forgiving husband.

"Mr. President," Cegan said, his eyes still fastened on my bowed head. "My wife has had great reserves of strength and courage to endure what she has been through since we were married. Her ability to meet every challenge with bravery and acuity has been a source of great pride to me."

Again, I sniffled and held the handkerchief to my nose. This was torture. I'd rather ride the yellow monster mist than sit here with a runny nose at the White House, feeling like a fool.

Cegan pushed his chair back and stood up. "However, the events of yesterday have pushed her body's tolerance beyond acceptable limits. I am sure in your position, Mr. President, you can relate to and understand the considerable stress that my wife has been under."

Cegan's apology for my behavior made me feel even worse. I cried out. "Please forgive my rudeness, Mr. President," I said, fighting back the tears. "I did not mean to . . ."

"Kira," Cegan spoke my name so gently I stopped. I knew he was asking me to be quiet.

He moved to stand behind my chair. Placing his hands on my shoulders, his long fingers squeezed gently. It was a loving touch, not one of reproach.

"However, Mr. President," Cegan continued, "My wife's stress will be relieved considerably . . . when the abusive generals are no longer present."

Having concluded his speech, Cegan once more sat down beside me and reached for my hand. Then, he bent over and whispered, "Remember, trust me, Kira."

The president shifted in his chair. He reached for his coffee, took a sip, and then put the cup back down. He steepled his fingers and rested his chin on them. I could see that he was thinking about what Cegan had said. Perhaps he felt my eyes on him. He looked up and smiled at me.

"Please help yourself," he said. "The ice water is for you. I have been told it is your preference, but if you would rather, we have coffee, sodas, or even mixed drinks — although I'm afraid we can't serve them to you, Dram Kira, Caste Five for a few more years," the President teased, trying to ease the tension in the room.

"I'd love a diet cola," I said, surprised when my voice sounded almost normal.

"No, the water is fine for us," Cegan said, reaching for a bottle. He opened it, took a sip, and then handed it to me. "Only water," he repeated in a voice similar to the times when *Kira* became an admonishment.

I knew Cegan was afraid of someone slipping something into our drinks, but an unopened can of Coke didn't seem like a threat to me. I sighed, but I didn't argue.

Cegan flashed his teeth at me and then turned to observe the other end of the table. The president was bent over in conversation with the generals. They were not happy with what he was saying and were arguing with him.

My husband took advantage of the moment and leaned closer to me, whispering in my ear, "There is fire in your eyes when you are defiant, my wife."

I started to pull away, feeling a rebuke, but Cegan's hand was suddenly holding me still.

"I enjoy your rebellion," he continued, still whispering into my ear, "and I will not often curb it, my dear, but you must remember that it is I who is the seasoned trader and you the novice. Allow me my expertise, my wife." He kissed my cheek and then let me go, but his eyes continued to watch me.

It was the most gentle of censures. I thought back to the mess I'd made earlier when I'd been rude to the president. How could I do anything but nod?

Cegan kissed my hand. Then, as if the matter had been dealt with, he was once again all business. He turned to watch the president and the generals.

A moment later, President Clayborn looked up. "Each of the generals will give an apology now and then depart," he told us. "Before they start, are you sure I cannot offer you a sandwich or that coke you wanted, Dram Kira, Caste Five?"

I shot a glance at Cegan. His eyes held no expression. He was doing his "poker face." I shook my head. "No, thank you. I'm fine," I said.

Cegan's squeeze of my hand was his only response. He was an excellent manipulator. I'll say that for him. I picked up my water bottle and took a small sip.

General Stone stood up first. His bald head gleamed in the lights of the room. His eyes glowered at us. Two white eyebrows lowered almost to his eyes. They made his small, rather piggish eyes seem empty.

"I offer an apology for what I called your wife. It may not be true," he said gruffly.

Cegan shot up. "I take affront to your words, sir."

I stared up at Cegan. What did a pacifist do when he took affront?

"General," said the president, "I agree with Dramsté Cegan, Caste Five. To insult the wife of a man demonstrates no honor. You will courteously apologize now."

The general's eyes narrowed until he looked like he had slits for eyes.

"Mr. President . . ." he began.

President Clayborn bolted up, towering over the general. "Try again, General Penor, and get it right this time."

The general didn't fool around then. His face turned red. I thought he was going to have a stroke. "I apologize for my words," he croaked out. "I was in error, definitely in error."

The president nodded at him, and the general walked out of the room like a rooster who'd lost his battle. His round, bald head displayed tiny drops of sweat. For a moment, I'd even felt pity for him.

Cegan sat back down. His legs pushed forward, and he opened up his water, acting as if he were in my Dad's kitchen sitting around chatting. How could he be so relaxed?

My eyes roved around the table, attempting to take it all in: the president looking so normal, the advisors, each in their lawyer's three-piece suits; the one token woman in a sharp gray business suit, her hair neatly coifed — her makeup, an ad for Liz Claiborne. She saw me watching her. She smiled and winked. I returned the smile, and my eyes moved on.

One by one, all the generals stood up, apologized, and left. I wished they'd all counted to three and said it at the same time. I was thoroughly bored by the time they were finished. I couldn't help the yawn that escaped.

"Drink your water," Cegan whispered, but his eyes were smiling.

"Dram Kira, Caste Five, you are satisfied? And you Dramsté Cegan, Caste Five?" President Clayborn asked when the generals had all departed.

I nodded. I'd been satisfied when old Baldy left.

"Thank you, Mr. President. I believe the situation has been corrected," Cegan said. "Hopefully, we may proceed to discuss trade negotiations now. It would seem that trust on Earth takes a vast amount of effort. But I believe it is . . . How do you say it? A two-way highway?"

"Street," I said quietly.

"Thank you, Kira. A two-way street. We free traders do not wish to destroy our source of market. Nor should you have the wish to destroy the supplier of your needs."

The president leaned forward. His steepled fingers supported his chin a moment as he pondered. "It would be far easier to trust if we were as impregnable as you are." He took a sip of what must have been very cold coffee and continued, "You have shown us that our weapons are useless before your technology, Dramsté Cegan, Caste Five, yet you ask us to trust you.

"Don't fear me, you say, with shields on your ship far beyond anything we've ever dreamed of. 'Don't fear me,' you say as you lift yourself up with an antigravity machine that passes through buildings. 'Don't fear me,' you say, behind a force field that no bullets can pass through. What option do you give us?

"Is it any wonder that those generals — whose life-long passion has been the preparation for such an event — dissolve into bumbling name callers against a foe who says, Don't fear me — a foe whose technology is hundreds of years more advanced than ours?"

"I am not your foe," Cegan said, meeting the eyes of the president. "I am only a trader who wishes to engage in free enterprise without the illusions other traders have perpetuated."

That started a buzzing between the advisors. President Clayborn had to raise his hand for silence. "So, leaving off the shield that you claim the others use was intentional?"

I felt a moment's hesitation in Cegan. His eyes met mine. I could almost read his message. "Trust me," they urged. I nodded.

"Yes," Cegan said. "It is time for Earth to grow up. It has been fifty years now since trade was established with you. During that time, we on Natharan have observed. You have grown in your maturity and your acceptance, but you are still untrusting. You are still afraid, even perhaps more so. How long will you need to accept that the Universe is not your enemy?"

The president sat up straighter. "You are confusing me, Dramsté Cegan. You are the first of your species, to my knowledge, to land on our planet. Yet you speak as though your race has been here throughout the past fifty years."

"We have watched you. Let us leave it at that."

"What is it you really want, Dramsté Cegan?"

Cegan paused a moment. His eyes viewed the table full of men and one woman. "Acceptance, trust, and the freedom to bring my wife home to Earth without being afraid for her safety."

The president shifted in his chair, then gathered himself up as if readying for an attack. His eyes turned hard as the bullets that had shot through the air the day before. Although he didn't look at me, I felt a wrenching in my stomach, as if knowing that the weapon he was about to use was the one thing that could pierce our force field.

He leaned forward into the attack and said, "Perhaps to you, Dramsté Cegan, Caste Five, Earth is primitive in technology and immature in interspecies relations, but our distrust and fear have taught us to be cautious. When things happen, we Terrans *worry* them like a dog worries the meat off a bone. It is a rather a successful maneuver for us Terrans. When one gnaws at something like that, edges start to fray, and eventually the pieces come apart. Then one sees what is truly there.

"When an alien from a world almost unknown to us invades our space for whatever reason and then steals one of ours, however legally, and I suppose we could say in a morally correct manner, we want to know why.

"Sixty-three calls you put out to Transtel Systems across the planet. Were you so confused about where you wished to land, Dramsté Cegan, Caste Five?"

What was the president trying to say? I shot a glance at Cegan. His green had faded. Had the president found the answers to some of Cegan's mysterious secrets?

"You were only interested in the women, it seems, especially the nineteen of those operators who were unmarried," President Clayborn continued, watching Cegan. "Those were the only ones who received callbacks that were more than routine. Why did you concentrate your focus on only one woman on the second day? Was that not cutting your odds too fine?"

The president's eyes glanced at me. He paused and examined my face. I raised my chin. I was through with crying. His words were interesting, but they wouldn't change how I felt about Cegan. Nothing could do that.

My husband was always supporting me. It was time for me to show how completely I trusted him. I reached over and took his hand. His fingers squeezed gently, but his color didn't improve.

But President Clayborn had not yet run out of bullets. He pressed on. "How did you know that the one you chose would agree to marry you? Did you choose a neophyte? None of the other ladies were as young as the former Kira Stevens, although several were only a year or two older. Did that make a difference to you? Was youth a prerequisite?

"Or did you choose a girl who was a romantic? The Transtel application screenings certainly profiled your wife as such. Her roommate called her . . . where is that sheet? Yes, here it is, 'a dreamer who preferred old-fashioned novels to the reality of the party scene' and a business partner, Miss Frances . . ."

"Enough," I said. "This is pointless."

"Is it?" the president probed. "I find the analysis quite interesting. What was it that would make a young, beautiful girl like yourself choose a huge, green alien over a man of her own kind? Why would you do that, Dram Kira, Caste Five?"

I was itching to tell him it was none of his business. Could you say that to the president of the United States? I opened my mouth to begin, but Cegan interrupted me.

"Kira, let the president continue. I will stop him if he insults you, but his ramblings are hopefully only a prelude to our negotiations."

Cegan spoke so confidently. It was as if the words left him untouched, but if that were so, why was his skin the color of a squashed avocado?

"We will forget the other statements of your character, Kira . . . excuse me, I mean Dram Kira, Caste Five. However, please permit me to persist. If we can gather a firmer understanding of the circumstances behind his choice of you as his bride, it may indeed be the prelude to negotiations."

I sighed, and Cegan squeezed my hand. I drank from the water bottle and heaved another embarrassingly loud exhale. I let my eyes drift about the room, studying the wall across from us. It had a copy of the Declaration of Independence. It was artfully done. The paper had been aged to the color of dried pee. It was a copy, wasn't it? Surely, the original would be in a museum.

The president continued his musings. He was talking about how I'd been lonely and had recently left my home to live in the city.

"Is that what you were looking for, a lonely, young girl, one who was gullible and naive in every sense of the word?"

There were no tears in my eyes on hearing this. As my father had said, was it important what Cegan's reason was in the beginning if he loved me in the end?

I breathed out my exasperation in all this, wanting to interrupt the president's flow of words, but I restrained myself in honor of my husband's wishes. Once more, I lifted up the water bottle and drank from it. When I put it down, it occurred to me that the room was still. The president was apparently without more bullets. I looked up to see Cegan studying me.

I thought he was about to whisper to me about trust, but he didn't. Instead, his eyes left mine and roamed the room before returning to view the president again.

"I think your words have implied accusations," Cegan told the president. "Yet, you have forgotten that I'd only had occasional contacts with Terrans, and I'd never once met a female of your species. How could you suppose I would have personnel files or statements from Dram Kira's roommates? The coldness of your theories rejects the basic premise of love.

"Try to understand. It was far simpler than any of your conjectures. You see, the truth is, she laughed. She was trained not to laugh; she told me so, but the sound of her laughter tore my heart in two and carried part of me back to her. What was left inside of me grew like a graft around that laugh. Can you not understand that, Mr. President?"

"I understand how you won Dram Kira, Caste Five on words alone," the president said.

Cegan glanced down at me and then looked away. His eyes circled the group again, making eye contact here and there. "You Terrans fear what is different, even when the difference is inside you. You tear at it and attempt to fling it from you. But you are on the brink of learning that the souls of Baskan, Qweldon, Tegor, Cedtarant, Sleeb, Sefnor, and a thousand other worlds are populated with souls just like yours. The bodies of these worlds come in diverse packages, but the souls are all of one kind.

"I reached out for a Terran soul who could see beyond that fear. It was not a gullible or a young soul that I searched for, only one that had the openness to see that the differences between us did not bar us from the sharing of our minds and hearts."

Cegan shifted in his seat. He looked down at his hands and then back up at the president, searching his mind for the right words. "When love, with its power of understanding and respect for another individual, can bring two souls together to make a total commitment for the future's perpetuation of that love, and when that commitment happens between two people from different worlds and cultures and bodies, then that species is ready for a bridging to a higher level of co-existence."

Everyone realized at the same moment that Cegan had given us the key to all our questions. Around the table, various conversations sprang up. Everyone needed to talk it out and explore the possibilities. Cegan's words had opened up a whole new outlook, a new way of thinking.

The president once more steepled his fingers, deep in thought. His brow wrinkled, and his cup of cold coffee looked empty. What was he thinking?

I could feel Cegan's eyes on me, but I wasn't ready to meet them, not yet. I, too, needed to process his words. I didn't get the opportunity.

A large-boned man with reddish sideburns broke into all our thoughts. "Wait a minute," he said. "Do I understand you to mean that your wife was a guinea pig, a test subject, to see if Earth was ready for — how did you call it — a higher level of co-existence?"

I looked up then and met Cegan's eyes. They were sick with worry. His body was pale to the almost blue tinge of when I'd barrel raced. I had no more time to savor my thoughts.

"No, sir," I said, looking at the man who had spoken and then at all the others. "Your analogy is wrong. A guinea pig allow a scientist to be an uninvolved observer."

Glances were passing between the eyes all around me. Their faces were filled with looks of pity. Those smug-suited bureaucrats felt sorry for me, believing I'd been duped. They didn't understand how wonderful Cegan was and how I was the luckiest woman on Earth.

"Don't you see?" I cried out in exasperation. "Cegan didn't trick or deceive me. He didn't use me as a guinea pig. What Cegan did was to love me, and love requires the full participation of *both* individuals."

I met the eyes of my husband then. They were full of wonder, pride, and love. He stood up and pulled me against him, surrounding me with his huge, gentle arms. "Kira, you do understand," he said as if a great miracle had occurred.

"Yes," I said, staring up at him. "You trusted absolutely, Cegan. It is your faith that was the guinea pig. You had no way of knowing whether a Terran could accept you. Yet, you gave your love freely. Thank you for *your* perfect trust."

Despite the men watching, Cegan and I celebrated with a kiss, a kiss of commitment and faith. When we ended our embrace, Cegan pushed me tenderly back down into my chair. Without taking his seat, standing behind me, his arms resting possessively on top of my shoulders, he attempted once more to move us forward into negotiations.

"As you said, Mr. President, you Terrans worry over the frayed edges, but I think I have given you ample time to worry about the edges for now. Your attempts to place a wedge between my wife and myself have underestimated her astuteness. You can see that your plans have backfired. And, despite your obvious manipulations, I have been honest and open with you. Let us move forward, ignoring these false starts. I have come to you, as I have already said, to engage in trade. Have you no curiosity as to its nature?"

President Clayborn pretended that he hadn't been accused of underhanded dealings. "It appears that you've been truthful in what you've told us. I won't question your relationship further. However, I'm completely mystified as to what we on Earth would be able to trade *you*. What could we possibly have that you would value? Undoubtedly, it is not our technology. And, let us be sure of one more point first: isn't it in your power to simply take whatever you wish from us?"

Cegan almost smiled. "You are *worrying* it again. Trust cannot be stolen. It must be earned. Trade with us this time, and next time, your fear will not be as great."

"You avoid the question," interrupted one of the advisors, a fair-haired movie star clone.

"Which question?" Cegan asked, puzzling.

The president waved the advisor to silence. "Is it true that you have the ability to seize whatever you want?"

Cegan looked at me. "Kira, my dear wife, I am having language difficulties. I think your president is asking if I plan to wage war, yet he knows Natharans are pacifists."

He looked so sad. I knew that this time, he wasn't acting. I think he was beginning to believe the current meeting would also end in failure. I gathered my courage to leap into the discussion once again. Ignoring the table full of men and the woman who had remained silent throughout the afternoon, I said, "Cegan, forget the war and whether or not you do or don't have the capability of waging one. Please, just tell us what you offer in trade."

My husband gazed down at me for a moment. His eyes softened, and he bent over to kiss my forehead. "You, my little Siren, you are the future of Earth: the brightness, the promise, and the willingness to offer your trust. Do you hear me, gentleman and lady? If it is your youth who hold the faith that Kira has, do not let your fears bury them in age. I cannot believe that I have found the only one with such attributes on your entire planet. You must search for those like Kira, and you must nourish them."

I was still waiting for Cegan's reply. Impatiently, I sighed once again. Several people shifted forward in their seats. They also wanted to know the answer. Was it gold, diamonds, silver, platinum . . . What would be the valuable cargo that would make a trader fly across light years of space? And what would a Natharan want in exchange?

Again, Cegan smiled at me. "President Clayborn, Earth has already given me the treasure I most wanted, but I have a list as well because Kira is already mine, and she was never an object of trade."

"Cegan," I said, in irritation at his stalling.

All I got was an amused smile, and then he was flourishing a paper he'd pulled from his pocket. He placed it down on the table, and an aide came forward to run it to the president. Not a breath was inhaled while we waited to hear. Everyone watched as the president bent over and studied it.

"What does it say, Cegan?" I whispered, tugging at his sleeve. My sweet husband only bent down and kissed my forehead again.

The President looked up. "The first five items are paintings, museum pieces:

Asher Wertheimer by John Singer Sargent (Tate Gallery, London)

Mlle Charlotte du Val d'Ognes by Jacques Louis David (Met Museum of Art, NY)

Nude Maja by Francisco Jose' de Goya y Lucientes (Prado, Madrid)

The Cook by Jan Vermeer (Rijks Museum, Amsterdam)

Wedding Dance by Pieter Brueghel (Institute of Arts, Detroit)

Before that, there was a long list of equipment and horse breeding supplies, followed by 1000 bags of cat sand, 1 litter tray, and a kitten."

I stood up and flung my arms around Cegan's neck. "Thank you. Thank you. You *are* going to let me have a cat on the ship. I love you!"

Everyone at the table laughed.

"I think your wife asked a very good question, Dramsté Cegan, Caste Five. What will you trade for our old paintings, horse supplies, and a considerable amount of cat sand?" asked President Clayborn, wiping the tears of laughter from his eyes.

Cegan disconnected my arms and firmly placed me back in the chair. "As the wife of a trader, Kira, you will have to learn not to show what you value most in the bargaining," Cegan warned me with a fond smile.

Again, there was laughter. Cegan waited a moment and then grew serious. "What I have to offer you is useless without your trust. You will not be able to prove or disprove its efficiency with your technology. Nor will you be able to duplicate it for scores of years. What I offer is a drug."

Everyone began to talk. Cegan waited for their silence. Cegan continued. "This drug, when injected into a cancerous section of the body, will eradicate all cancer cells from the patient. It is not a preventative. It cannot be used as a serum, but it has no dangerous side effects on the cancer patient, and recovery is 100%."

The female advisor to the president gasped. "I have been diagnosed with a type of cancer. When will we be allowed to test the drug?"

"That is up to your president, Mrs. Chlow. I will provide your country a quantity sufficient for 100 people as a testing mechanism, and I will include, additionally, enough for a medical research team to attempt to analyze the drug. They won't have any success, but as you so aptly put it, Mr. President, you Terrans can *worry* it. When you agree that you wish the trade, I will empty my hold. It contains a quantity estimated to fulfill your planet's requirements for the next two years."

"How do we know this drug is safe?" asked the President.

"Gentlemen, Mrs. Chlow, President Clayborn — my wife and I are tired," Cegan said, pulling me up from my chair. "Discuss your fears and doubts without us. It is time that we leave." Cegan drew me closer to him. For a moment, he paused, staring down into my eyes. I was in shock. For once, I couldn't think of a single thing to say.

"Mr. President," Cegan continued, "if you will be so kind as to send our agreed-upon escort? I will be happy to allow your research team to pick up the drug samples at their convenience."

The president stood and gave the briefest of bows. Immediately, everyone in the room rose and bobbed their heads to Cegan. My husband was so wonderful I wanted to bow, too, but I was suddenly realizing, just as Cegan had said, that I was exhausted.

It was the vice president who escorted us back to the ship. He and Cegan kept up a conversation as we walked to the pilotcar, but I was too tired to come up with any more polite banter. I didn't even argue when Cegan picked me up and carried me through the still-soggy area of the lawn, and later, in the warmth of the comfortable pilotcar, I am ashamed to say, I fell asleep.

Upon our return, there were the usual crowds of reporters to pass through. Cegan was brief. "Our discussion with the president was friendly. No agreement has been reached yet, but I feel confident that there will be one."

I went to bed without dinner that evening. I think it worried Cegan, but I was too tired to try to reassure him.

Chapter Seventeen: My Father on an Alien Ship

I woke up the next morning with such a burst of energy I felt like I could fly to Natharan without using a ship. I struggled to contain my dancing feet, but Cegan only smiled. He was relieved to see me recuperated. It wasn't until later that he admitted rather sheepishly that he'd called my father and urged Dad to come for a visit because he was worried about me.

I was excited to hear that Dad was coming, but I teased Cegan about his lack of trust. "I told you I was fine. You didn't *trust* me." I teased him.

Cegan smiled and messed up my hair, a gesture he'd copied from Dad. It was one I wasn't fond of.

A couple of hours later, the Yellows informed Cegan that a man was knocking at the entry gate. Cegan and I were in the library at the time.

"It's my father," I cried out when the Yellow's words were translated.

"Probably," Cegan said, but his nose had the slightly contracted, squeezed-in look that it developed when he was suspicious.

"Who else could it be?" I demanded as we walked toward a monitor.

The ship's equivalent of a video camera had lenses that patrolled all segments of the exterior ship. It was computerized so that an alarm sounded when any surface was touched. However, Natharans believed in many layers of defense. Not only was the monitor visually patrolled by Yellows at all times, but the force field surrounding the ship was set within a second region, and anyone knocking at the outer border would not be able to go further than that area without Cegan permitting it.

The man was, indeed, my father. I told Cegan I wanted to go greet Dad by myself. I'd been in and out of the ship enough to know how to get through the force field borders, and I'd even learned the Natharan word that opened the entry/exit door. I knew it would relieve my father's anxieties if I were the one leading him inside the huge monster of a ship. But my sweet, gentle husband had other ideas.

"I will attend to him, Kira. You will stay inside," he commanded like some feudal lord.

At first, I laughed. I thought he was joking. I walked with him to the exit, and standing directly in front of the door, I gave the word in Natharan for the door to open. I couldn't believe that after all Cegan's promises about my freedom, the door wouldn't release for me.

I said "Chebufa" three more times before I looked back at Cegan and found him staring at me with a threatening look. Those eyes narrowed and almost glowing with a blackness so dark it was shiny obsidian sent a shiver down my spine.

"I told you, Kira," Cegan repeated. "You will stay inside."

"Why — because I'm only a Terran and can't handle news reporters as well as you more advanced Natharans?" I said, warming up to my anger.

Cegan pulled me toward him in what came pretty close to looking like anger. "Kira, there are going to be times that you must listen and just do as I tell you."

I gasped from the shock of it. Cegan took advantage of my moment of astonishment and threw me over his shoulder, carrying me away from the doorway. I struggled (and I admit I yelled a bit,) but, of course, there was no one to hear. The Yellows would never interfere with Cegan. Still, I was gathering up air for another protest when Cegan said, "Do you know what your father said to me after I carried you away from Powder that time?"

"What?" I screamed, not stopping my struggle.

"He said he didn't think a pacifist could handle you. He said I'd probably have to bend you over my knee and paddle you."

That stopped me. "He'd never say that," I scoffed.

"Do Natharans lie?"

"They don't beat their wives. You told me that."

"True, but no Natharan has ever had a Terran wife before."

Cegan had carried me into a room that I'd never visited. It had a single chair. He tossed me into it, said a word in Natharan, and stood there a moment watching. I wasn't able to move or speak. I couldn't do anything but blink.

"I will never hit you, Kira, but I have found that I cannot always give you your freedom as I once promised. You *will* wait inside the ship, not because it pleasures me to restrict your independence, but because I will not risk you."

I couldn't throw any words at him as he left. That angered me more than the confinement. The only movement I was permitted, besides blinking, was breathing, and the chair didn't seem to compensate for the fact that I'd been struggling and was out of breath. It was several minutes before I stopped feeling faint. At last, my body acclimated to the chair's cycle of breathing. Only then was I able to relax enough to notice that I'd gained an audience of three Yellows, who seemed fascinated by my subjugation.

They came closer than they normally did and began to discuss the situation in their high, squeaky voices. They stood like that for maybe five minutes, keeping their distance not coming closer. Their eyes looked worried, and their voices sounded even more high-pitched than usual in what I hoped was concern. One of them heard something. He turned, faced the door, babbled several squeaks, and without even bidding me goodbye, they all ran off.

It was a moment before I heard the noise that had frightened them. I recognized it as the sound of footsteps coming closer. Cegan entered, with my father right behind. Why had he brought my father with him to see my disgrace? I was mortified.

"I am sorry for the necessity of this, Kira. I ask your forgiveness," Cegan said formally. Then he spoke in Natharan, and the chair released me. I would have rushed to my father and cried on his shoulder, but my husband's hands were on each side of the chair, trapping me.

"How could you do that?" I cried out, wanting his arms around me, yet too angry and frightened to ask for it.

Cegan's hands slid down to my waist, and he lifted me up to a standing position. As if he knew what I needed, his arms wrapped around me. "Because I love you, my wife," he said, kissing my brow and then gently releasing me. "Your father is here, Kira."

I ran to my father and threw my arms around him. He said nothing about what he'd just seen. Had he really told Cegan that I'd need an occasional paddling? Surely not. My father had never laid a hand on me.

"The Yellows were here with me," I told Cegan as we left the room.

"I know. They watched over you, Kira. Had I been longer than fifteen of your minutes, they would have freed you."

Cegan had flung his arm about my waist as we walked, and, with his words, he kissed my head. Then he was telling Dad something about the ship. For Cegan, it seemed as if nothing had happened, but I hadn't forgiven him. We would have this out when Dad left!

I was glad for my father's visit. I'd missed him. Knowing that I'd be gone for so long and so far away made me treasure our time together. And it was fun showing Dad the ship, even if we couldn't show him the technology Cegan had shared with me. Dad couldn't see the globe room, the computer library, or any of the other marvels of Natharan superiority.

We ate lunch in the small, enclosed dining room. Cegan served my father and me with no offers of choice. Nor did he discuss the food machine or demonstrate its abilities. Instead, the talk was of the day before. Dad was impressed enough. He wanted to know all about what the president had said and done. (Cegan didn't mention anything about how rude I'd been to our US leader. I squeezed his hand to let him know I appreciated it.) When Dad heard about the drug Cegan had stored in the cargo bin, Dad stared at him as if Cegan were a movie star or a key basketball player. I knew the feeling.

While we were eating, the medical technicians knocked at the ship's border. A Yellow came in and, in his squeaky voice, rattled off about it. I figured that the technicians had come for the samples that Cegan had promised. I started to explain to Dad, but he was staring at the Yellow, and his mouth dropped open like a surprised cartoon character.

The Yellow ran off, and Dad's mouth closed just about the time Cegan turned back towards us and said, "I've given the crew instructions that they are to take the cases of drugs to the exit chamber. They will not carry it off the ship, so I must do that. Will you help me, Hank?"

"I'll help, too," I blurted out.

Both men turned to me and said, "No."

"Don't do this again," I glared at Cegan.

"You will stay inside, Kira. Will you listen — or do I need to take you to that room again?"

I glanced at my father. He was silent, fiddling with a leftover piece of bread. I glanced back at my husband. Once again, his eyes were rocks of coal.

"I'll stay here this time," I said with as much grace as possible through gritted teeth. "But we need to talk about this, Cegan."

He inclined his head cordially to show me his readiness to do so, and then he and Dad were gone. The three Yellows from before, or maybe different ones — I couldn't tell one from the other — entered the room when Dad and Cegan left.

"Hi," I greeted them. "Sedupt."

"Dram Kira, Dram Kira," they said, going into their bobbing and bowing routine. I waited for them to end it, but they kept on and on. "Stop it!" I cried out finally and then wished I'd kept silent. Their eyes were darting left and right as if searching for protection. I took a step towards them, wanting to reassure them. Their yellow petals grew pale, and their mouths began to wail. I put my hands over my ears and stepped back.

The door slid open eventually, and my dad came in with Cegan behind him. "What on earth is that?" Dad cried out.

A sharp word from Cegan and the Yellows ran off. "I told you to stay away from them, Kira," he said. I looked up to see his blazing eyes.

"Too many orders get all confusing, don't they," I snapped back.

"If you two could just show me where you want me to bed down, I'd be real content to watch a little TV and rest up for dinner," my dad interrupted.

Cegan's anger was instantly gone. "Of course, Hank. We should have shown you before."

Cegan put my dad on the other side of the ship. "Does he have to be so far from us?" I asked angrily.

"The room has been specially readied for your father, Kira. I am sorry if its location offends you."

"It's just fine," my dad said quickly.

By then, his door had slid open, and I was ashamed. Cegan had copied Dad's house, taking bits and pieces from each room. There was the same TV with Earth-type knobs on it, a refrigerator humming away, and a double bed. A heavy comforter, the kind Dad liked, lay across the top of it. There was even a bookshelf with a variety of books and magazines on it.

"There's a stereo over there with some CDs I think you might enjoy," Cegan told him.

Dad tried out the bed. It squeaked and groaned, just like his at home. The mattress gave to his weight. Dad plumped at a couple of pillows. "Turn on the telly, would ya, Kira?"

I turned it on and then handed the control disk to Dad. He reached out for it, but his eyes were already sagging, and I could tell he'd be asleep in no time.

Cegan and I withdrew quietly. We strode down the corridor without talking. I felt like I should apologize, yet I was still all mixed up about what he'd done. I stopped in the middle of the hall. "Thank you, Cegan. You never told me you were fixing up a room for my dad. I'm sorry I . . ."

"Hush," he said, and his arms pulled me towards him. "It is not easy, this co-mingling. I have made you angry. I have not explained it well. Be patient with me, my Siren."

How could I still be angry? His lips were melding with mine. His hands were playing music on my body. His petaled chest was emitting its sweet, spicy odor. When he lifted me and carried me back to our room, I made no protest.

It was only later, after we'd joined and danced in the Natharan well of oneness, that I remembered we had things to discuss, but by then, it was time to meet with my father, and there was no chance.

We had meatloaf for dinner, mashed potatoes with a dark, rich gravy, green beans, carrots, and strawberry shortcake for dessert. Dad eyed Cegan's horse-food cubes and shook his head, but he was suitably impressed with our dinner. Even the ink black coffee met with his approval.

"I don't know how you made that meal, Cegan, and I don't want to know, but I guess that Kira isn't going to starve on this ship."

We all laughed for some strange reason, and then we went to Dad's room and watched TV and talked. There were cokes, beer, and bottled water in the refrigerator, and it was almost like being out on the farm, except that we couldn't see the night sky. (I knew that Cegan probably could have produced that if he'd wanted to.)

When Dad got sleepy, we left and went back to our room. I thought we'd have it out then, but Cegan started telling me a story about Okriton, and I fell asleep in the middle of it. Then, the next morning, we slept late (even Dad) and had breakfast together, which took a long time because Dad and Cegan kept swapping tall tales. (Cegan explained that since tall tales are not meant to be taken seriously, it is acceptable for a Natharan to tell them. He said that such stories are used to teach Natharan children to discern lies from truth. Do you know how that made me feel since I couldn't tell which parts were true and which were false?)

Then we played checkers, with Dad cheating like crazy, watched an old movie on TV as we ate fish and chips, and while Dad napped, Cegan and I hiked up an old mountain trail in the globed room. It was a great day. I loved having Dad there, and I guess he thought the ship was OK, too, because he agreed to stay another night.

The next morning, over a breakfast of scrambled eggs and bacon, the president called. Cegan left Dad and me to talk in another room, and then he returned shortly.

"Hank, Kira," Cegan said as he walked into the smoky-glassed dining room. "The trade has been accepted. The drug's usefulness has been confirmed, and your president is ready to sign the agreement."

Cegan's eyes showed no contentment. They looked worried, and the hue of his green was faded. What was wrong with him?

"Why are you so somber?" I asked. "Shouldn't you be happy about it?"

Cegan came closer, and his steps deliberately slowed. "I am pleased, Kira, that your government has proved receptive to trade relations. I am well content with that, but I was hoping that their decision would not come for another day or so. I must leave for Natharan as soon as the trade is completed. It would be unwise to linger during this transitional time. Because of that, I'm afraid, my Kira, that your time to decide is too short."

"Decide? Decide what?" I shot a glance at Dad to see if he understood. He was sipping at his coffee, studying the wall.

Cegan stopped walking. He stood several feet away from me. The distance was uncomfortable. What was wrong?

"It will not take much time for the goods to be loaded. You will only have another day or two. You will need to choose then, Kira. It will be your last chance."

"Choose? Choose what?" I stared at him, not understanding his coldness, this feeling of separation. I took a step and then another. I couldn't stand the distance he'd placed between us. I put my hands on his chest, breathing in the smell of him, the sweetness of vanilla.

"Of course, I'm going with you, Cegan. Is that the choice? I'm your wife. I love you. I shall always stay with you . . . if you want me to."

Cegan lifted up my hand and kissed the back of it. "I shall always want you, Kira, my lovely Siren. It would tear me inside out if you did not choose to come with me, but the choice must be given to you. On the day that the ship lifts to return to Natharan, I am required to ask you one last time, and then you must make your final decision."

"Why do you doubt me?"

I threw my arms around his neck and lay my head on his chest. Didn't he understand that I would die without his arms around me, his lips on mine?

I attempted to kiss him, but he gently pried my arms off his neck and held me away from him. Keeping me still, his eyes searched mine. "I can feel that you are still angry with me for confining you. I was afraid that my actions might have changed your mind."

"I love you, but we do need to talk about that, Cegan. You have to promise me not to ever do it again."

"I cannot make that promise, my wife." His eyes traveled to my father. Perhaps he thought my dad would interrupt, but my father kept silent. Cegan's glance reminded me that we were not alone. It was not the right time to have this conversation, yet how could I back down or put it off when the issue was so important?

"What happened to equality?" I asked.

Cegan's face grew more serious, but he scarcely paused. "Equality occurs only between two individuals who possess the same years of experience concerning a given situation."

"Years of experience? You're saying that I'll never be your equal?"

"What time did you say this appointment you two have with the president is?" my father barged in.

Cegan didn't flinch. Once more, he responded without pausing, his eyes never leaving mine. "You are included in the invitation, Hank. We must leave in forty of your minutes."

"Forty minutes!" I cried. "Cegan, I can't be ready to see the president in forty minutes. I haven't even selected a dress . . ."

"Kira," Cegan warned me, and I realized how close I'd come to almost giving away one of his secrets.

"Hank, if you will stay here a minute, I'll return Kira to her room so she may spend a ridiculous amount of time dressing."

I had no chance to debate that before Cegan was hustling me off. "If you argue, you'll have less time," he told me as I struggled to keep up with his long legs.

I arrived out of breath, but I sat down at once to design my dress. I was just reviewing the colors when Cegan overrode my request and ordered a suit for Dad. In a minute, he was holding a handsome bluish-gray suit, shoes, socks, tie, and underwear.

"Sorry, my love, I have robbed you of three minutes, but I wanted your approval of your father's attire. Is it all right?"

"It's perfect, but where is my sketch?"

Cegan reached over and flipped it back up. He delivered the clothes to Dad and returned far too quickly. He was fully clad in minutes.

When I was dressed, Cegan asked me to leave my hair down again. Since he didn't put it like it was an order, I didn't mind the request. I'd also modified the heels on my pumps and made the cream-colored dress longer than usual, just to please him. Darn him! He never even noticed.

Cegan and I picked up Dad on our way to the exit chamber. While we were walking, Cegan attempted to convince my father that he should be inside the force field with us, but Dad kept saying, "No. You keep my daughter safe, Cegan. I'll be fine. Don't worry about me."

I tried to convince Dad, too, but he just pulled me close and said, "Hush, Kira. This is between your husband and me."

"Cegan," he continued, "I've watched you with my daughter. I feel real confident that you'll take care of her up there in space but be extra careful with her these next few days. You know she's the one they'll be after."

"Dad, stop it. That's silly! The government has already agreed to the trade. There's no danger to anyone now."

Dad rolled his eyes, shook his head, and pretended to pull out his hair. "For a smart girl, you sure talk stupid sometimes, Kira! Try using that pretty head of yours to think!"

I was glaring at him and just about to express my outrage when Cegan made the strangest-sounding noise. It was either Natharan or the call of the Seth. It forced both my Dad and me to turn towards him and gawk.

"Hold it, that's my wife you're talking to, sir," Cegan kidded, his mouth gaping open with a full-toothed smile. It was only for a second, and then his smile was gone, and his eyes lost their twinkle. Cegan took a step towards me, reached out, and brought my hand up to his lips. "I will always shield your daughter, Hank, even from her own naive recklessness . . ."

Cegan calmly assessed my irritation. His eyes flickered with a hint of amusement. "I adore you, my Siren," he said.

"Hank, do not lay the blame for Kira's ignorance on her lack of sense or thought. Neither is the case. It is because Kira is so trusting. That is a good thing, but she doesn't yet perceive the accompanying danger. That is her 'light of honesty'."

My sigh was almost loud enough for the reporters outside the ship to hear. "Are you two finished discussing me enough to explain what it is you're talking about?"

They were both silent then. My father studied Cegan for a moment. Then, he turned to me. "Kira, I don't much understand this 'light of honesty' your husband praises so much, but you should have enough good old common sense to see that there are crazies out there. They're more dangerous now than ever. With them half over their fear of Cegan, the scheming part comes next. If they could get you away from him, you'd be helpless as a babe. Now don't go arguing about that!" he said as I opened my mouth to defend myself.

"Anyone kidnapped by murderers would be helpless, except maybe this alien of yours . . . anyway, if they got you away from Cegan, he'd be forced to trade something he didn't want to trade to get you back."

I leaned against the wall, looking from my dad to Cegan and then back again. "But I don't understand. They're getting the drug. What else is there?"

My dad shook his head at me. "The ship, the force field . . . Don't you see, Kira? The Natharans are centuries ahead of us. Everything they know holds value, and that's easily worth taking a hostage or killing someone. To those kind of people, an easy billion is all that's important."

My eyes shifted to Cegan. He was watching me with an expression I couldn't read. It didn't matter. I was suddenly happy enough to do cartwheels. "That's why you clipped my wings! I thought you were starting to let your size turn you into a macho Terran."

Cegan didn't have a clue what that was. He turned to Dad for an explanation.

"She means you restricted her freedom," my father said, laughing. He wiped at his eyes and continued to laugh. "She gets pretty prickly about that. You're lucky she didn't explode at you!"

Cegan grinned and shook his head. "I think she has done that a couple of times."

"Ah, yes, the chair," my dad said, laughing.

I met my husband's eyes and raised my chin defiantly. "I don't blow up if you explain things clearly, Cegan."

My husband smiled both rows of teeth. He watched as my dad moved over towards the ship's door and pretended an interest I doubt he had. Cegan used the moment to secure me against him. "I'll try to remember. I'm supposed to stand there explaining things clearly when a Sanoran Boobalah decides your sweet little body looks tasty," he whispered into my ear.

I couldn't help my shudder. I still dreamed about that monster and the severed head. Cegan smoothed back a lock of my hair. "Ah, Kira, I shall always protect you from even the Boobalah. I only ask that you let me."

Chapter Eighteen: The Agreement

We stepped out through the ship's door and down the steps. The instant our feet touched the pavement, Cegan and I were enclosed in the yellow force field. I looked back at my dad and saw him walking off. He was almost lost in the crush of reporters. I think he thought he could just fade out and disappear into the crowd, but one alert reporter recognized him.

"It's Hank Stevens, Hank Stevens, the girl's father!"

From the moment he was identified, the reporters began pestering him. "You were in the ship. What was it like?"

"How many aliens did you see inside?"

"What do you think now about your son-in-law?"

Cegan looked worried. His eyes scanned the crowd for trouble. If I still had any uncertainty about how real the danger was, the look in Cegan's eyes took all my doubts away. "Cegan, what can we do?" I whispered, alarmed at the sudden crowd around my dad.

He didn't let me down. He caught sight of the approaching White House guards. "Surround Kira's father. He needs protection," Cegan ordered them, directing them to where my dad was. They obeyed without question, and Dad, slightly humbled by the experience, was escorted back toward us. Together we walked to the White House pilotcar, where the first lady was, once again, our assurance of safety.

I think it was the same vehicle as before. Mrs. Clayborn gestured a seat for each of us to sit in, and then I introduced my father. The two of them struck up a conversation right away. Unfortunately, their talk was mostly about me. After they had run through how intelligent, how sweet, and how pretty I was, much to my distress, the president's wife began to gush on and on about how she wanted to give us a second marriage ceremony. Within minutes, Dad was agreeing with her.

"I'd be grateful for even the pictures, Cegan, if you're against tying the knot a second time," my father told him.

Mrs. Clayborn had to explain the knot part. It was kind of interesting because I'd never heard the story she and Dad started weaving. But then Cegan tried to tease me about how it would be a lot easier to control me if I had ropes with knots around my limbs. I didn't find his kidding very funny. It reminded me far too much of the chair he'd placed me in and our unfinished conversation on "equality." He got up from his chair, scooped me up, and set me down in his lap.

That embarrassed me dreadfully, but Mrs. Clayborn and my father just laughed and went on talking. My eyes dropped to Cegan's hands, although I wasn't really seeing them. For some reason, I was close to tears again.

"I am sorry that I have hurt you, my Siren. It is a tender area for you, but do not *worry* it, as your president says. I will never clip your wings. You are my wife, and I will teach you to be my equal in knowledge and experience," Cegan whispered into my ear.

I stretched out my hand to caress his face. The soft-pearled feel of him, the hard bone beneath his cheek, and his gentle lips all felt normal to me now. He was my husband, and I loved him. I bent closer and touched my lips to his.

"Hey!" my dad interrupted. "We're trying to talk about a wedding here. Yes or no, Cegan?"

Cegan smiled down at me. His eyes were soft and slightly hungry for the sweetness of our unions.

"Wouldn't it be better if I sat in my own chair?" I asked, feeling his desire.

"I prefer you here," he said, but his arms loosened to show me that I was free to choose.

"If Kira wants a second wedding, of course, she may have one if it can be done safely," Cegan answered my father, not taking his eyes off mine.

I kissed his lips once more, just a token thank you for his willingness to please my dad and me, and his arms tightened, "A good rope with knots is always a fine thing to have . . ." he joked.

I demonstrated the strength of my elbow in his ribs. "That's still not funny," I said.

"Neither is a Sonoran Boobalah," Cegan reminded me, grinning with both sets of teeth. "I might need the ropes so I can tie it up while I'm explaining to you."

The President and his advisors were ready to sign the agreement when we arrived. Four of the pictures Cegan had asked for were being sent to the White House, but the fifth, "Wedding Dance" by Pieter Brueghel, had just been sold and was not available.

Cegan was prepared. He pulled out a paper from his pocket, scanned it, and said, "Call Detroit's Institute of Arts. I'll accept "Man and Machinery" by Diego Riviera, but you'll have to add wedding pictures to my list of wants."

"And a ring," said my dad. "You never gave her a ring, Cegan. It's no wonder that the general assumed . . ."

Everyone got quiet, and the president began to write down *wedding ring*."

But my dad wasn't through. "Make that a diamond engagement ring, a full carat, and a matching band."

"Dad!" I protested, but the president wrote a note on the list.

"Anything else?" he asked, looking pointedly at my father.

"Well, a wedding cake would be nice," my dad said.

"I'll pay for that and for the chaplain," the president said, and he passed the paper to the aide to bring to us.

The young man, looking rather timid about the cloud of yellow surrounding us, put the paper down on the table and backed away quickly. Cegan didn't pick up the paper. He waved for my dad to read it first. I think that pleased him. He looked the paper over, gave it a thumbs up, and placed it down where Cegan could reach it.

My husband didn't even glance at it before handing it to me. "You'll be signing it first, Kira, if you agree with the terms."

I didn't take the paper from him. I just shrugged and asked, "Why would I sign it? It's an agreement to you."

"You are one wise partner, Kira," Cegan said, kissing my forehead. Turning to the president, he said, "There is a mistake, I'm afraid. You have left off my wife's name."

"It doesn't matter, Cegan. Just sign it," I said.

With my words, Cegan's eyes stopped smiling. "It is Natharan law that both partners must sign a document for the agreement to be valid, my wife."

"But I'm a Terran, so it doesn't matter," I said, trying to tease him out of this sudden situation.

Cegan stretched out his legs and took a sip from the water bottle placed there for our use. "Mr. President, how convenient that you are here to settle one of our numerous arguments." I could see that the twinkle was back in his eyes. Was I being foolish again?

"Cegan, OK, I'll sign it," I said, reaching up for the paper.

"Not so quickly," he told me, holding it up in the air. "By Natharan law, Kira is both Natharan by marriage and Terran by birth. Is that not true of Terran law?"

The president consulted with his advisors. One of them stood up. "I am an attorney for the United States Government. I will speak to that: An American, born on Earth, who moves to Mars, may continue to be American and Terran if he chooses, and, likewise, by Martian law, may be American, Terran, and Martian until that time when he revokes his citizenship of the United States. There has been no test precedent concerning this particular situation, but a logical assumption can follow."

"Meaning," said the president, "that Dram Kira, Caste Five can be American, Terran, and Natharan?"

"Um, it would seem so," said the man.

"That is as much a 'yes' as you will ever get from an attorney," President Clayborn said, laughing at his own quip. The others followed. Only Cegan and I remained serious as the room filled with chuckles. Then the president cleared his throat, and the noise stopped almost as quickly. "Therefore," he continued, "I, as President of the US of A, proclaim you, Dram Kira Caste Five, formerly Kira Stevens, American, Terran, and Natharan."

"Does that mean that Cegan is also a Terran?" I asked, not sure how it all worked.

The president checked with his advisor, who was shaking his head "no."

"I'm afraid, Dram Kira, Caste Five, that Cegan, just like any other immigrant, would have to become a citizen first of the United States or whatever country he chose, and then he could be labeled a Terran."

"So I'm bound by his laws and mine, but he's only bound by his own?" I asked.

"Kira!" growled my father.

I sighed and took the pen from Cegan, aware that his teeth were flashing. After signing my name on the line, I handed the document to Cegan, who diligently read it over and then added his signature. Then, the document was officially witnessed and copied, and we were finished.

In minutes, we were all piling out like children from a classroom when the school day was over. There wasn't any pushing, of course. There was never any crowding with a three-foot radius of force field around you, but the feeling of great relief was the same.

The first lady rushed up to us the moment the doors of the chamber opened. She begged us to wait while she spoke to her husband. So we lingered there, standing in the doorway. There were guards ahead of us and some behind. None were close. Cegan silently eyed them and probably scanned for escape routes. My father was taking out a stick of gum. I contemplated the force field, wondering, again, how it worked. At that moment, it was almost translucent, its powdered yellow substance surrounded Cegan and me, but not with the thick fog-like texture it had when we were flying. I could look all about us and see through its faint dappling. The thing had no odor or taste, and it didn't bother my eyes or coat my clothes with dust. How could a gaseous substance stop bullets and dogs?

The door's archway was causing the mist to bunch up. It looked rather like a lady's hooped skirt billowing out in front and behind us. Did that mean that it wasn't gaseous? Could it be a solid stretched super thin? I wished I could talk with Cegan about it. Would I understand if he explained it? I'd never done well in chemistry. I'd never taken physics. I wouldn't be able to take them now. Did they have college classes on Natharan?

A guard stepped back to avoid an elbow when his partner sneezed. His foot knocked against the force field's surface. Like a ball thrown against a wall, his foot bounced off. The guard almost fell, but he recovered his balance and stepped back. The incident reminded me of the dog that had attacked earlier. I hoped it was OK.

"I am sorry, sir. No harm intended," the guard apologized nervously and backed away from us a good five feet.

I felt my husband's body swell up as it did when he took affront to something. I think he was going to remind the man of my presence. I tugged at Cegan's jacket. "Please, don't say anything. He didn't mean to . . . " I whispered. My husband's eyes softened as he looked down at me. His roving hand found a curl and began to stroke it.

Behind us, the conversation between Mrs. Clayborn and her husband was growing louder. They were discussing a marriage ceremony, and it seemed that they were in agreement about most of it, but you could hear Mr. Clayborn trying to modify the huge production that Mrs. Clayborn was imagining. It was hard to know if we were supposed to be hearing the discussion. Both Cegan and my father turned to face the room. They were making no effort to hide their eavesdropping.

"Dad," I called out softly.

"She!" he hissed at me.

Cegan glanced down at me. He pulled me close, then gently pushed me in front so that he could drape his arms over my shoulders. "You are sure you want this ceremony that will tie you in a knot?" he asked.

I couldn't tell if he was kidding or not. I knew he wasn't smiling, and his voice was rough with his concern.

"There aren't any knots, Cegan. But, yes, I'd like my father to see us get married."

"We are already married, Kira. This would be only for the pictures, correct?"

"The pictures and the memories. You weren't there the first time, Cegan. I'd like you to . . ."

"Kira, Cegan, the president's calling. He wants us to go back in there," my father interrupted.

"In a minute, Hank. I need to hear Kira."

"You can't keep the president waiting," Dad said.

Cegan ignored him. "Kira, you would like me to what?"

I turned around to face him. "Oh, Cegan, it would just be so nice if Dad could see us getting married and if you could be at my side this time, not up on a ship, far away from me. We could see each other the whole time, and when the minister says that part about kissing the bride, you could really do it instead of having Mr. Dee peck at my forehead. And, like Mrs. Clayborn said, we could have pictures made, and we could look at them and remember the day, and we could even show them to your parents if they wanted to see them and . . ."

"All right, Kira. I understand. It is important to you. We will try to find a way for this repeat wedding to happen if I can be assured of your safety."

We followed Dad back into the chamber we'd just left. Cegan and I started to sit in the same seats as before, but Mrs. Clayborn suggested that we all sit close, so Cegan pulled out the chair next to the president. I sat between Cegan and Dad, and then Mrs. Clayborn took the opposite side, next to her husband.

Mrs. Clayborn gave me another of her friendly smiles. While I was returning it, I decided that the first lady's teeth were her best feature. They were very white and straight. And the way she smiled, with her lips fully opened, made you feel that she was a person you could confide in and be friends with. Perhaps it was also the kindness I could see in her eyes when she smiled. You could relax in that warmth.

The president, on the other hand, didn't have a smile like hers, but he was very handsome. The wisps of white that trimmed the sides of his hair made him look distinguished. I liked the way his eyes crinkled when he looked at his wife. I think the two of them were still very much in love.

"Everybody else, clear out," the president ordered, and Cegan, Dad, and I watched as the guards retreated and closed the door. Only one agent remained. He held his walky-talky in his hand and was speaking into it. "Sir?" he questioned, in a tone that was more a reminder of protocol than a request. The president nodded that the man could stay there in front of the door.

We focused on the president, allowing him to begin, but Mrs. Clayborn jumped in before he could speak. "You're a size five, aren't you?" she asked me. I nodded, and she started telling me about the design of the wedding dress her daughter had left hanging in one of the closets upstairs.

"Clara," her husband interrupted. "I think we have some details to be worked out before we can spend a lot of time describing the number of pearls on the top of the gown."

The way he said it was just like when Cegan attempted to correct me about something — that same gently teasing tone. The love was so obviously curled around each word that Mrs. Clayborn took no offense. She merely smiled up at her husband, dimpling like a schoolgirl.

"Carry on, dear," she said to him and then winked at me.

"This ceremony can take place right here in the White House. It has its own chapel and chaplain. Is that acceptable?" the president asked after flashing a quick smile at his wife.

Cegan, Dad, and I all nodded. The president continued.

"I suppose, then, that the first step is to set a date."

"We will be leaving immediately after the items have been loaded and your medicine picked up. I estimate that those things should be completed by about 3:00 p.m. tomorrow. Therefore, today would be the only day possible for this repeat wedding," Cegan stated.

"Tomorrow? We're leaving tomorrow?" I asked.

Cegan didn't answer. His eyes studied mine.

"How in blazes can you expect a wedding to be staged in half a day?" Dad blurted out. "You can't send out invitations in a day!"

"It will be safer for Kira if there are no guests," Cegan told us.

"What kind of wedding is that, no guests?" Dad said, starting to get worked up.

"Dad." I waited for him to look at me before continuing. "We have a chapel, a chaplain, the president and Mrs. Clayborn, and wedding pictures. Please, Dad. It's so much more than we had before. And I *am* already married. Cegan doesn't have to agree to any of this."

Cegan took my hand and lifted it to his mouth. His lips lightly touched. His eyes spoke of his love. Once more, I felt the strength of our link and my desire for him.

"All right," my dad said. "No guests and it has to be today, but let's keep our attention on the discussion, OK?"

My face grew hot. Dad could make me feel guilty for even thinking about kissing Cegan.

The president called over to the agent. "Ted, have the chaplain available for this afternoon, and make sure the chapel is prepared."

"No media," Cegan added.

"Except a photographer," I piped in before Dad could.

"Right, call Ed Nodor to do the pictures," the president told Ted.

"The cake needs to be started, too," Mrs. Clayborn said.

The agent nodded that he would order that as well.

"OK, then here's the plan. At 3:00, Dram Kira . . ."

"Just Kira, please," I said.

The president glanced over at Cegan. When he said nothing, the president continued. "At 3:00, Kira will go upstairs with Clara and Dramsté Cegan . . ."

"Cegan?" I said. "We don't have to use those titles when we're with friends, do we?"

"If they are your friends, Kira, they are mine. You may call me Cegan, Mrs. Clayborn and President Clayborn."

"Now, isn't this silly!" she tutted, "Of course, you must call us Clara and Ben."

"If I may continue?" the president — Ben — said, and he looked around the table at each of us. "So Kira goes upstairs, and Cegan and Hank change into . . . Darn, we're going to need some suits for them. Ted, send for Jim Hawkins. He's a good man. He'll be able to figure out what to do about suits for Cegan and Hank."

"Ben," Cegan said, making it sound like it was a new food he was trying out. "Perhaps I do not understand this clearly. You are not saying that Kira will be separated from me during this time. I will not permit that. I cannot protect her if she is not at my side."

"You two have to be separated before the ceremony. It's bad luck for the groom to see his bride in the wedding dress until she walks down the aisle," Clara cried out.

Ben started in about how he would personally guarantee all the guards who would surround me, and he added that I would always be with Clara or my father.

"No," Cegan said, pulling his feet underneath him in preparation to rise. "There is no wisdom in this ceremony. It is merely for show. I wished to please Kira, but not at that price." So saying, he rocketed up to his full height, raising me up beside him.

"Cegan, please," I said, putting my hand on the widest part of his upper arm. Natharans have a protective bone cartilage there. Instead of making them insensitive to touch, the cartilage makes them supersensitive, and only the mate of a Natharan may touch one there.

I knew all that. I knew that my touch would either make Cegan angry because I had done so in the presence of others, or he would be amused that I had dared. I knew also that it would make him freeze for a second and give me all of his attention.

"Sometimes you have to trust. You taught me that, Cegan. These are our friends, and this wedding is an Earth tradition that is important to all Terrans. I trust Clara and Ben. They have given their word that we'll be safe, and so you must trust them, too. Please, my husband."

Cegan had not flinched from my touch. His eyes only studied mine. I watched as they changed: desire, amusement, love, and the smallest hint of warning. Slowly, his hand slid up to reach mine. It cupped my hand, then enfolded it, and tightened. His fingers, long and wide, stronger than a human's, lifted my hand and removed it from his arm. Still holding my hand, as if he feared it would fly away, he turned it over, examined it, and then lifted it to his lips.

"She is very brave," Cegan told my father without taking his eyes from mine. "Has she never listened to your 'NO's?"

My father laughed, as did the others around the table. I did not. Cegan had wounded me. I dropped my eyes in defeat.

Once more, the grip on my hand grew tight. I looked up, but Cegan was no longer looking at me. He began to speak. "President Clayborn – Ben. You said once that it was easy to trust when one wore a force field. You are correct. It is far easier. Yet Kira, my wife, my partner, has asked me to trust you without that protection."

Cegan glanced over at my father. "It is not easy curbing her youth. Kira is impetuous. She is untouched by treachery. Yet, she has a wise soul, a soul with the *Light of Honesty*. She is correct that sometimes you do have to trust."

Cegan's eyes returned to the president. "I will yield to Kira in this. I hope you will not mislay her trust."

I attempted to hug Cegan, but he had not let go of my hand, so it was a one-armed hug. I threw a kiss in for good measure. His free hand rose to my back, and he held me to him. "I have agreed to this ceremony only to please you and your father," he whispered into my ear. "You will sit quietly now so I can assemble some safeguards. Agreed?"

I nodded, and he released me. We sat back down, and the details continued for at least thirty more minutes. At one point, another round of bottled water was brought in for Cegan and me. I observed that my husband didn't say a word when Dad drank coffee.

Finally, it was all decided. A squad of men would be on patrol, the chapel where the wedding was to take place would be off limits to anyone not approved by the president, no press would be invited, there would be only one photographer — a personal friend of the president, and the cake would be prepared by the White House's own chef and would never leave his sight. A few other minor points were debated, and then, finally, all was approved, and the time for our second wedding was affirmed.

Chapter Nineteen: A Second Wedding

It was lunchtime when the details were finished. The advisors who had participated in the earlier meeting were invited to the wedding, but they were not free to leave the White House before it was over. They dined in an area set aside for them.

We were to have lunch with Clara and Ben. We walked to a patio area attached to the side of the building, filled with flowers, a small space of grass, and a massive block-wall fence on the three outer sides. There were cushioned lounge chairs in pretty flowered patterns for us to sit in, and several gigantic umbrellas in matching designs sheltered us from the sun.

An oversized picnic table was loaded down with a huge platter of fresh vegetables. Another equally large platter of fresh exotic-looking fruits surrounded a large watermelon boat with balls of cantaloupe, honeydew, and watermelon, along with fresh raspberries, blackberries, and blueberries.

Dad was pleased to see the huge tub of potato salad but not so pleased by the vegetarian burgers that were the main course. I noticed he ate two of them anyway. We were even offered a variety of desserts: chocolate cake with dark chocolate icing and chocolate curls on top, apple pie with fresh homemade vanilla ice cream, and a plate filled with the prettiest cookies and marzipan candies. If I hadn't eaten so much already, I would have eaten some of them.

Throughout the lunch, my fussy husband never said a word about what I ate, but the moment we were out there on that patio with the spread of food, and they asked me what I wanted to drink, I said, "diet cola." I guess Cegan decided it was a lost cause.

He seemed to relax after a while. Ben started telling some jokes, and then my dad jumped in, and we were all laughing pretty hard. Cegan only stiffened up when a waiter would come round to ask us if we'd like anything else. I almost had a second cola, but at the last moment, I ordered a bottled water. Cegan looked pleased.

The force field was so light by that time that I could hardly see it, and, at one point, my dad completely forgot about it, and he tried to hug me. We didn't make contact, but he didn't get repelled violently, either. Then, to my surprise, Cegan turned it off completely so my father could kiss me. My dad's cheek was rough against mine. I urged him to shave again before the ceremony.

All too quickly, it was time to get dressed. Cegan turned the field back on. I felt it before I realized what my husband was doing. "Cegan, what is that for? How am I supposed to get dressed if I'm . . . ?"

"It is only while I walk you to the chamber where you will clothe yourself in this extra-special white gown."

"Then?"

"Then we shall enter the period of trust."

By that time, we'd already reached the chamber where I was to change. Cegan took me in his arms and kissed me deeply. When I was sagging against him, uncertain that I could bear to be separated, he said. "You are my suns, my moons, my rainbows. You are my every breath. Do not fail me, Siren."

"Fail you? I don't understand."

"Be cautious. Without you, I could not tolerate existence."

He turned then, and I realized that the force field was off. Neither of us was protected.

"Cegan," I called out. "You be careful, too, please. I love you."

He'd stopped when I called out his name. He listened to my words and then continued on without a backward glance.

Clara stood waiting. She led me into the room, and I saw the dress that had belonged to her daughter. It was truly as beautiful as she'd said, with a bodice of seed pearls sewn individually across the front. It was high-necked, but above the bodice up to the neck was a see-through material with tiny flowers of the same seed pearls. The sleeves were long and slightly full. They, too, were of the lighter fabric and played at being modest. At the cuffs, the satin was back again, with beaded pearls worked all around. The train behind was long and flowing, and there was a pearl attachment for my hair. It held the veil that fell down over my face and around the dress, like a glaze of snow surrounding a frosted tree.

I told Clara how appreciative I was for allowing me to wear her daughter's dress. She hugged me and said, "There, now. I've been wanting to do that since we first met, and that husband of yours had that silly, yellow thing on, so I couldn't."

I laughed, feeling warmed by her friendship and pleased at the way this special day was going. As Clara removed the dress from its hanger, she told me that her daughter was pregnant. "How wonderful!" I said, and I meant it, but a part of me was also trying not to think about what I would do if the dress didn't fit.

My worries were unnecessary. The dress fit perfectly, and it was every bit as gorgeous as Clara had said. I twirled before the mirror. I couldn't wait for Cegan to see me. Would he think me beautiful? What did a Natharan female wear on her wedding day?

While Clara fixed my hair, she continued telling me about her daughter's wedding. I suppose all this was bringing back those memories. She was describing the bridesmaids' dresses when she stopped suddenly and cried out about there being no bridesmaids at my wedding. She seemed horrified, and I reminded her that all the people who really mattered to me were at the ceremony. I let her know, too, what a great honor it was to be married in the White House Chapel.

We almost started to cry, but sensibly, Clara stopped us, fixed my veil, and went to get my shoes. Unfortunately, her daughter's shoes were too big. Even with padding, I couldn't hold them on. My own shoes were bone, not white, and the heels were so low that the dress dragged at the front. Clara sent a guard to her own room, and he brought back the pair of shoes I ended up wearing. So, I had more to thank her for. I couldn't believe I'd be wearing the First Lady's own shoes.

"Why, that's perfect!" Clara said. "Now you have something borrowed!"

Everything was borrowed, but I didn't mention that!

Clara insisted that I wear a penny in my shoe for luck, and she pinned a blue silk flower to the inner hem of my dress. Then, after readjusting my veil once more, we walked down the stairs.

Five guards accompanied us to the chapel door. Even Cegan would have found that sufficient. As we entered the vestibule, a florist handed me a bouquet of red roses and baby's breath.

White-gloved guards held the door open for us, and we passed into another waiting area. There, we found my father, looking tall and handsome in tails. His eyes glowed with tears. "You're so beautiful," he whispered. "Just like your mother." He held a handkerchief in his hand and wiped at his eyes. "It's drafty in here," he said. "I think I got something in one of my eyes."

He waved me away when I offered to check. "Do you know how proud your mother would be of you?" he asked. I kept looking down at the elegant white leather sandals I'd borrowed from Clara. I was afraid if I met my father's eyes, I'd be crying, too.

"You two are so much alike, plucky as a couple of mountain goats," Dad said.

Mountain goats? My head flew up. I no longer felt like crying. I think I was about to laugh.

"But, are you sure, Kira, that this is a mountain you still want to climb?"

"Oh, Dad," I groaned. I didn't even bother to answer him. I looked around for Clara, but she was gone. I supposed she was sitting in the chapel next to her husband, waiting for the ceremony to begin.

The music started. Unbelievably, it was the same version of "Visions of Blue Satin" that I'd heard in the globe room of Cegan's ship. I smiled, wondering if Cegan had chosen the piece. I didn't have to speculate long. My father squeezed my arm and whispered in my ear. "Cegan picked that tune for you. He said you liked it."

The piece ended, and the familiar Wedding March began. A man with a red carnation on his lapel told us that it was time. The doors swung open, and we walked into the chapel. It was just like I'd always imagined it. The aisle was long, decked out with bouquets of red roses and baby's breath, and the scent of the roses lingered in the air as my father and I passed them.

Faces turned to look at me. I saw the diplomat who'd told us she had cancer. I hoped that she was well now. She smiled at me as we walked near her. Most of the other faces I didn't know, but that made no difference because Dad was at my side, and at the altar was the one I loved, standing there in shiny-black tails, a white shirt, and his usual lime-green sneakers.

Cegan turned to stare at me. I don't know if the dress was special to him or if he even understood the magic of weddings, but the look in his eyes, mainly relief that I was OK and love and fascination because he never knew what to expect from me — that look told me that I wanted more than anything to be walking down the aisle to him.

Dad and I were just passing Bob and Clara at that point. I pulled my eyes away from Cegan's and smiled at them. They were beaming, looking jubilant with happiness, wearing the same look of fulfillment that parents acquire when their child has just performed a miraculous event. How was it possible that they had become such good friends so quickly? Dad and I did not pause as we wedding marched forward, but my eyes caught the president's wink.

Then, we were only steps from Cegan, and my world narrowed to him. His eyes shone with pride, but I could read uneasiness and uncertainty in his eyes. When I stood at his side, he took my hand and studied it, then attempted to peer in through my veil. His fingers reached to lift it, but my father and the chaplain said, "Not yet, Cegan," and his hand stopped.

"Kira, say something," he ordered. I understood his disquiet then. He still feared a trick.

I whispered, "I love you." It was enough. He knew my voice. His hand holding mine squeezed gently, and I knew he was saying it back to me.

The chaplain began his sermon. He said a few words about the importance of marriage in a relationship, telling everyone that the bonds that bound us together were also the cement that kept us from breaking apart when our tempers flared or our personal interests pulled us in opposite directions.

"I misunderstood, Kira. I thought the knots were of rope, not cement," Cegan whispered.

"You're not supposed to say anything yet," I whispered.

The chaplain cleared his throat to get our attention. When he continued, it was to tell us about the customs of marriage. He explained that my white dress stood for purity and innocence.

Cegan grinned down at me. Then, he pulled me towards him slightly and kissed the top of my veil.

The chaplain looked down at us, and his eyes twinkled. "Would you two pay attention, please? We haven't gotten to the kissing part yet, young man."

Everyone laughed, but in that hushed way, as if nobody knew whether it was allowed or not, yet the feeling of happiness washed over everyone and sort of bubbled out.

"When the bride walks down the aisle on the arm of her father," the chaplain continued, "it symbolizes that she is going from the house of her father to the house of her husband, from the old life to the new. It is for this reason that I ask the question, 'Who gives this woman unto the one who would be her husband?'"

"I do," said my dad, kissing my cheek and leaving my side to sit beside Clara and Bob.

"What a pleasing gift your father has given to me," Cegan teased.

I don't think anyone saw me step on Cegan's foot except perhaps the chaplain, whose eyebrows raised at least an inch.

The man continued on with more explanations. He told us about the bridal bouquet, the rose petals, the something borrowed, the something blue, the wedding cake, and several other traditions I'd never heard of. I liked his story best about the ring being a circle of devotion that had no end. He said it was the symbol of our bond, our promise to remain true to each other in the same unending way.

The only thing that disturbed me was that so many of the Terran traditions seemed to be based on male-dominated societies. I longed to hear about the traditions of Natharan. Cegan said that they'd always had equality of the genders. I wondered what their weddings were like.

The chaplain moved on to a more normal litany. W*e are gathered here together to celebrate the union of this male and this female . . .* kind of stuff, and I relaxed. I shouldn't have, for that's when the minister jumped into another touchy subject.

"There are those who will say that this particular marriage is an offense against all those traditions . . ." he began.

Cegan's body immediately tensed up, and his grip on my hand tightened painfully.

"Trust," I whispered.

The chaplain paused to look at us. I think Cegan was giving him the "Natharan outraged stance" that usually scared everyone to death. The man didn't even blink.

"Is the bond of this couple an offense?" the chaplain asked, his eyes surveying the pews behind us.

"Look at them. They stand together closer than any other couple I've seen. Not once have they released their entwined hands. They cling to each other like one piece, like one bonded whole. I ask you, you who have come together to honor this connection of theirs, how could anyone believe that there could be a sin in such love? Perhaps we must reexamine our definition of love.

"I did not have the opportunity to speak with the couple before the wedding, as is my usual procedure. I had no chance to determine the merit of their marriage, yet I chatted with the bride's father, with President Clayborn, and with Mrs. Clayborn individually. Each of them shared with me their observations of the couple's devotion, affection, commitment, loyalty, and passion.

"Each of them used their own words: Mr. Stevens spoke of his son-in-law's attentiveness to Kira's needs. He told me how thankful he was for Cegan's protective nature of Kira. He said the two of them were besotted with each other, a word I rarely hear in today's world.

"Our first lady told me of Cegan's gentleness and sensitivity to Kira's needs. 'But what of Kira,' I asked her. She answered me without a pause, and I quote, 'Kira has such a sweet nature one might suppose that Cegan could overpower her, but she is not only full of spirit — she is resilient. She stands up to him. Her courage cannot be disputed, yet I think it is her love for Cegan that centers Kira and allows her to find that courage.'

"President Clayborn responded, in almost the same manner, and I quote, 'Cegan's and Kira's loyalty and their obvious joy and passion in each other allow us to perceive the depth of their relationship. This love and commitment of theirs, against all odds, should be an inspiration for future generations."

"Good folks, we have come together to marry this couple, but I must tell you first that I have married many couples with far less promise. Many of those couples lacked the elements of devotion, affection, commitment, loyalty, and passion. Yet it is those qualities, my friends, that give a relationship endurance. This young couple seems to possess them all. So, how could anyone question the rightness of such a union?

"Oh, I have heard the picketers who proclaim that the marriage between alien and human is a sin. Yet, this couple chose not to sin. They pledged their love lawfully before a minister who gave his full blessing to their marriage. I believe that there is no sin in this couple or in their marriage. The sin is in the eyes of those who would turn away from the love we witness here. This couple has already received the sanctity of God. man and Natharan.

"So when I must ask the words 'Is there anyone present who can give any reason why this marriage should not take place?' Let it be known that I expect only silence." The chaplain was quiet for a moment, allowing for the opportunity.

"If someone speaks, will you tramp their foot, my resilient and spirited Siren?"

"I would if they dared, Cegan."

The chaplain was looking at me sternly. He heard my words and waved his finger. "She's rather willful, son. Are you sure you want to go through with this?"

I gasped, and again, there was a ripple of chuckles in the pews. My father laughed the longest, but Cegan nodded and smiled down at me.

"Kira Stevens," the chaplain said, and Cegan's head suddenly reared up to glare at him. The chaplain held his ground before Cegan's glowering eyes. "How did you two ever get through the first ceremony?" the chaplain asked, but he didn't wait for an answer.

"Kira Stevens," he said, pointedly meeting Cegan's eyes. When Cegan said nothing, he continued, his eyes looking at me. "Do you take this man to be your lawful husband, and do you promise to love, honor, and obey him 'til death do you part?"

Cegan was watching me now with the strangest glint in his eye. I ignored him. I looked up at the chaplain and said, "I do."

"Dramsté Cegan, Caste Five of Natharan, do you take this woman to be your lawful wife, and do you promise to cherish her, care for her, and comfort her in sickness and in health 'til death do you part?"

Cegan lifted up my chin to look into my eyes, peering through the gauze of the veil. "I do," he said.

"Who has the ring?" asked the chaplain. The president pulled it from his pocket and came up to hand it to Cegan.

"Please, place the ring on her left hand. Her index finger, son," the chaplain said, watching Cegan. "Now, repeat after me, Dramsté Cegan, Caste Five: 'With this ring, I thee wed.'"

Cegan said the words. His voice, although not loud, rang out clearly in the silence, and a shiver ran down my spine. Cegan's teeth flashed at me. I said my vow, and we finally got to the best part:

"I now pronounce you husband and wife. You may kiss your bride."

Cegan lifted up the veil, tossing it over my head as if he'd longed to do that the whole ceremony. Then, his arms pulled me fully against his body, and his lips joined mine. No one had told Cegan that it was only supposed to be a token kiss. When his mouth met mine, I felt the loveliness of that long, sweet well that was the start of our journey into soul binding. I plunged down it with eagerness and desire.

I think it was the president who nudged Cegan back to our surroundings. He was standing there with his hand on Cegan's back when I became aware that we were still in the chapel and everyone was waiting for us to walk down the aisle. President Clayborn gave a gentle push, and Cegan and I started forward. However, we'd only reached about halfway down when Cegan stopped me.

"You promised to obey?" he teased.

"It was the old-fashioned phrasing of the ceremony. The chaplain shouldn't have put it that way. I think it's supposed to be cherished."

"But you didn't give your promise on the word *cherish*. You gave your promise to *obey*."

"I didn't want to stop in the middle of the wedding, Cegan, and ask him to correct it." Cegan gazed down at me with the most pleased expression in his eyes.

"Please, don't tease me, Cegan," I pleaded.

"Your wish is my desire," he said, but the smile remained in the corner of his mouth.

We continued forward to the end of the aisle, and then there was my father shaking Cegan's hand, wedding cake to cut, and champagne to sip. Cegan liked the taste of neither the cake nor the drink, but he was a good sport. I'd been afraid that he wouldn't allow us to touch anything but bottled water, but my dad told me how he'd also chatted with Cegan about trust.

The photographer took pictures of everything, even my putting cake into Cegan's mouth and his pretending to enjoy it. When it was my husband's turn to feed me, Cegan growled about having to start all over to purify my body of all its harmful Terran chemicals. I just laughed, and then he started to kiss me again. The photographer got pictures of that, too.

My father and Ben pulled us apart and insisted on taking pictures with everyone. We posed with Ben, the vice president, Mr. Chey, Clara, Ben, and then the chaplain. I took the opportunity to complain to him about the obedience thing, but he only roared with laughter, and everyone turned and looked.

"I don't use that wording often anymore, young lady, but I thought that under the circumstances, your husband being a pacifist and you a bit of a rebel, it might be a wise choice. Of course, you can always get an annulment, but watching the way you two kiss, I don't think that'll be happening."

He smiled up at Cegan and said, "I must say that there were several moments there (one was when I called your wife by her maiden name) when I wasn't sure I'd heard right about you, son. Your species hasn't always been peaceful, has it?"

Cegan shifted. You could see he was deciding how much to say. "Rev. Marsh, I found your service to be interesting and informative. I thank you for your courageous stance. For that reason, I will be equally honest. It's true, as you surmised. There was a time when Natharans were bloodier than Terrans."

The chaplain smiled and thrust forth his hand. "You give me hope for Earth, Dramsté Cegan, Caste Five, and I want to congratulate you two. You have shown great courage."

Again, he held out his hand, this time for me to shake. "Dram Kira, Caste Five, I think you are a fitting emissary to represent Earth. If this big fellow doesn't cower you, I imagine you'll stand up to anyone. You'll do Earth proud."

His compliments embarrassed me. He couldn't know how undeserving I was of them. He hadn't seen me make a mess of the treaty talks with the president. Nor had he seen how scared I felt at the thought of being an emissary. If anything, his words caused me even more anxiety. Would I be on trial as a Terran? Would everything I did be thought of as a reflection of how a Terran would act?

But I didn't tell Rev. Marsh my thoughts. I just said, "Thank you."

I had lowered my eyes, yet I could feel both the chaplain and Cegan watching me in the silence that followed. I took a deep breath and looked up.

"I agree, Rev. Marsh," Cegan said. "Kira would be an excellent diplomat, but unless she has the desire to do so, she will not carry that kind of responsibility. The Natharan government will encourage Kira to retreat to our family residence and move about without publicity. Our government understands how important it is for a new citizen to have the opportunity to feel accepted and safe among his or her new family."

"That sounds good to me. How about you, Kira? Think you'll be content to live without the excitement of the past weeks?"

"Gratefully," I said, smiling.

The photographer interrupted us then. He'd waited patiently but was itching to get pictures of us with my dad. So, there was another round of photos that included Dad with all the others.

Then, when we were finished, Clara escorted me up to the room so I could change back into my dress. "It was a beautiful wedding," she said. She took my hand and admired the new diamond ring and wedding band.

"When you come back from your travels, my husband and I may not be in the White House. Will you come to see us anyway?" Clara asked.

The fact that she cared pleased me. Of course, I said "yes."

Cegan was waiting at the door. As I joined him, he ordered the field back on, and the yellow powder surrounded us.

When we rejoined the others, Ben told us that he and Clara had a present for us. An aide brought it forward and set it down on the floor. Cegan acted suspicious about the box, especially when it moved.

"Stop it, Cegan," I said. "Whatever it is, I know we'll love it. I'll open it if you won't."

"I will open it, Kira," he insisted, and somehow, he stepped out of the field and left me inside.

The box was moving quite a bit by then. Cegan tilted his head, puzzled. His eyes flew to my dad as if asking, "What kind of tradition is this?"

The rest of us were laughing. You could hear the box meowing. It was pretty obvious what was inside. But Cegan continued with his cautious approach. He pulled at the bow and stepped back as the lid started lifting up to reveal a tiny, furry little body attempting to climb out.

"He's from our cat's first litter," Clara said. "She's a champion Blue-point Siamese."

Cegan picked up the little kitten. He held it away from his body as if he expected it to explode.

"Cegan," I cried, with my arms outstretched for the kitten.

He studied the wiggly animal a moment. Then, he spoke a word of Natharan and stepped back into the yellow haze. He handed me the bundle and shook his head as I cuddled, cooed, and allowed the kitten to lick my face.

"Perhaps this kitten will liven up that dreary spaceship you told me about," Clara said.

"Thank you," I told her, hoping Cegan hadn't heard the word "dreary." "She's adorable!"

Cegan was too much the diplomat to let the president and his wife know how he felt. He'd agreed on my having a cat on the ship, but this little wiggly kitten didn't much resemble the plump, sedate Muffin. Cegan's arm went around me, and he said formally, "Bob and Clara, you have honored us with a gift from your heart. We thank you for the baby cat and for the happiness that you have brought to my wife and her father."

"Couldn't you turn off this machine so I could hug them goodbye? Please? I want to thank them," I whispered.

"I have yielded enough, Kira," Cegan said. I sighed but didn't argue. He had been very generous with his trust.

I thanked them again, and we left the White House, throwing goodbyes in our wake. Clever Dad had an armful of newspapers. I smiled and hoped that Cegan wouldn't ask what they were for.

The vice president, Mr. Chey, accompanied us in the pilotcar, and the kitten became the center of everyone's conversation. My dad had asked for a rag when he requested the newspapers, and as we flew, the kitten chased it and waged a battle. By the time we reached SpacePort, the kitten, which had run circles around and around its tail and bounded about the pilotcar with unbelievable energy, lay sleeping in my arms.

"You don't mind dropping me off at my own house, do you, Mr. Chey?" said my dad. The V.P. shrugged.

I smiled at Dad. I noticed that he hadn't mentioned how far he lived from SpacePort.

When we reached the ship, Dad handed the newspapers to Cegan. "Kira will need these," he told my husband. "Do you mind carrying them?"

Cegan wrinkled up his brow, but he took them. He thanked Mr. Chey, said goodbye to my father, and helped me through the door of the pilotcar with my sleeping bundle.

The reporters were waiting for us. Although they'd already heard that the contract was signed, had learned the secret of the cargo, and knew all about our wedding at the White House, they still had a hundred questions to ask.

"Later," Cegan promised them, but I stopped to answer a question about the kitten in my arms. "Yes, President Clayborn and his wife gave him to us," I told them.

"And will the kitten travel into space with you?" asked another reporter.

I looked up at Cegan. His eyes met mine, and he nodded. "I came to Earth for a trade negotiation, but Earth is very generous. It has given me a beautiful wife *and* a cat."

We were all laughing when Cegan turned me around, and we walked up the ramp into the ship. But as we stepped through the entry, Cegan called out in Natharan, and a Yellow came running. Cegan gave him the newspapers. Then, when a second Yellow came bounding in, Cegan took the kitten from me and handed it to the Yellow.

I didn't really feel comfortable about that, but I rattled off instructions and tried to get Cegan to tell the crewman about putting down the papers on the floor and about how the cat needed food and water. Cegan didn't translate. "The cat will be fine," he said, turning me to go to our quarters. Cegan was being very impatient. When I stopped to look back at the Yellow, who had the little kitten, Cegan lifted me up and carried me.

I wanted to be angry. This was exactly the part of our relationship that had gotten out of hand. I tried to talk to him about it, but Cegan had other plans. He ignored my words, and then, when we entered his chamber, his lips drove me down the well of forgetfulness, and I couldn't remember anything I'd so much wanted to say.

Chapter Twenty: The Yellows

When we came back to Earth, so to speak, I crept out of our quarters, leaving Cegan asleep in bed. I wanted to check on my kitten. Leaving him with the Yellows seemed a risky thing to do. So far I hadn't noticed them being very friendly.

I thought I was learning my way around the ship. I'd been certain that I at least knew the way to the Yellow camp. But the halls were long and segmented in all directions. I think directions were written on the walls, but whatever their symbols or letters signified, I couldn't read Natharan. So, I got lost, and by then, I didn't even know how to get back to where I'd left Cegan.

The crewmen and I couldn't communicate, but it was worse than that. Whenever I saw a Yellow, he glanced at me, turned, and ran away.

I stumbled into the dining room, which was very lucky since I'd almost been to the point of sitting down on the floor and waiting for Cegan to find me. That would have been embarrassing.

But the dining room was perfect. Usually, there were Yellows there. I saw three of them sitting at a table, eating. I walked up to them and began to make gestures to indicate "cat." I groomed my face, purred, and then meowed. Maybe that's what scared them. The Yellows paled and fled, racing away, leaving their unfinished meals on the table.

I walked around a few more areas of the ship where Cegan had taken me, but every time I saw a Yellow, he ran off. Finally, I gave up, and knowing where I was then, I was able to return to Cegan.

My husband was pretending to sleep, one arm thrown casually over his eyes. I pounced on him, sitting on top of his chest and raising his arm upwards so he'd look at me.

"I can't find my kitten, Cegan, and every time I try to talk with a Yellow, he runs away from me. I think they're afraid of me. Why, Cegan? I thought you told them I wouldn't hurt them."

Cegan lifted me up into the air and placed me down on the bed beside him. Then, he stretched his arm back across his eyes. I think he thought he could ignore me and go back to sleep.

"Cegan," I said, pulling his arm away again. "I'm one of those Terrans who will *worry* a problem until it frays, remember?"

He opened one eye and looked at me. His arm sprang out and pulled me close to his side, holding me still when I struggled.

"Cegan, you might be able to hold me down, but you can't make me stop talking! I refuse to lie here without knowing what that Yellow is doing with the kitten!"

Cegan groaned and let go of me, but he didn't open his eyes.

"The first thing you showed me, Cegan, was how to get cold water," I teased him. "Have you ever had water, ice cold water, poured over you when you're trying to sleep?"

"No wonder Terran men beat their wives," Cegan said, sitting up.

"They don't. At least, most of them don't."

"I suppose we have to go find your kitten then?" Cegan asked, yawning widely.

I ignored the sight of all his teeth, but I could see how his yawn could be terrifying to someone not expecting it.

By that time, I was as concerned as a mother bird with a snake climbing up her tree. It wasn't that I didn't trust the Yellows, but had they ever seen a kitten before? Would they know how to take care of it?

My husband rose up, donned his slacks, and turned to face me. He was still yawing. I felt a moment of guilt. I was pushy, selfish, and demanding. I promised myself that I'd improve the moment I found the kitten. I'd behave more like a caring wife from that day forth. At least I'd try.

"Cegan, why are the Yellows afraid of me. Is it because they think I'm a monster? Are they xenophobic? And why are they so quiet? I've never seen them smiling or having a good time. Why don't they ever get off the ship? Why . . ."

"Kira, be silent, and I'll explain."

I stopped talking. I knew Cegan wasn't angry with me for waking him up. I'd seen the twinkle in his eyes and the hint of a smile that barely touched his lips.

"Come here and sit down," he ordered, just because I was pacing back and forth.

"You're not angry, right?" I asked, seeking reassurance that I was reading him correctly.

"No, Kira."

I sat down gingerly. Cegan swung his arm around me. "I only get angry when you put your safety in jeopardy," he told me, kissing the top of my head.

"Then will you explain? They didn't used to run. Why do they do so now?"

"Because I told them to stay away from you."

"Why?"

"That is what I need to talk to you about, he said, looking about as enthusiastic as he'd been with drinking champagne and eating cake. "I had hoped this discussion could wait until we left Earth, but in the end, you will just have to accept it, Kira."

"I can't accept it if you don't tell me what I'm supposed to be accepting."

"I am attempting to clarify the situation."

I resolved to keep quiet, but it was looking like a very long explanation.

"You have adapted to many things, my wife, but this will seem even stranger and more difficult for you to understand because there is nothing like it in your world." He paused a moment to brush the hair out of my eyes. It wasn't bothering me.

"Natharan is not Terra," he continued. "There will be many things that are dissimilar. You must be willing to shift your thinking and accept patterns of thought not compatible with what you are familiar with."

"Are you stalling?" I asked.

Cegan's smile was broad, but he continued in the same meandering way. "Natharans were not originally as we are now, Kira. We are engineered beings. Do you understand what that means?"

I shook my head.

"It means that we chose certain qualities and characteristics and altered our chromosomes to obtain them. We designed the Natharan body through genetic screening and manipulation."

I nodded my head rather skeptically. "Long ago?"

Either Cegan ignored me, or he didn't hear, but he kept on talking. "In our biological engineering, it was decided that a caste system was most logical. Caste Five, which is what my green coat represents, is the highest level. It is the intellectual, the caste with certain enhancements. Each of the castes has a different color and a different purpose.

Caste One is the Yellow. It is the lowest of the intelligences. Yellow is the caste of the servers. Their only function is to please us. They find no pleasure, Kira, in going off the ship or in entertainment such as you or I enjoy. In fact, a Yellow is afraid to leave the ship and will only do so if ordered. The Yellows on this ship know no other home, and they do not tolerate new places or people well."

"But that's awful! Doesn't anything make them happy?"

"They are happiest when they serve," Cegan told me. "They will become used to you. As you learn, Natharan, they will desire to serve you as eagerly as they serve me."

"But that's cruel. There must be something that makes them happy."

"You are thinking like a Terran. To understand what I am trying to tell you, you must envision almost a different species. Yellows are not like you. They do not think like you or act like you."

"But Natharans made them Yellow so they could never rise to a different caste. What if they wanted to? What if they wanted to be like you?"

"Does Muffin, your cat, want to read a book or become a lawyer?"

"Muffin is not a person."

"The Yellow caste has about the same level of intelligence as your cat. Trust me, Kira. They have no desire to change castes."

"Couldn't they be taught to read? Maybe they'd want to change then."

"Kira, the Yellows do not have the intelligence to read a book. If they could, they would not have the intelligence to learn from it. And if they could do both of those things, read and learn, they would still not have the inclination to do so."

"How do you know? Have you ever tried to teach them?"

"This is a futile conversation, Kira," Cegan said, swinging up off the bed.

I hadn't even started to ask questions. "Cegan, I don't understand."

"No. I know. When they get more used to you, I will let them come to you. Then, you may attempt to teach them to read or solve math problems or anything else you wish to try to teach them. Until that time, I won't discuss the Yellows with you."

I sighed. "Then, can we find the kitten now?"

Cegan didn't say anything, but he went in to use the facility. I assumed that meant "yes."

"What do you think we ought to call him?" I asked.

"The cat? According to Ben, the cat is a she."

"I didn't know that. What do you think we ought to call her?"

Cegan's eyes twinkled down at me. "First Lady?"

"Lady. OK. I like that."

It wasn't easy for Cegan to track down the kitten, either. He started speaking in Natharan, and several Yellows came to stand in front of him. They didn't look at me but kept their eyes lowered to the ground. When Cegan spoke, they answered him with short replies.

"Do they know?" I asked.

"Yes. She's with a group down in the hold."

"Is she OK?"

Cegan shook his head at me. "Kira, I told you they would not hurt her. The Yellows have no violence in them."

I had never been to the hold before. We had to take an elevator down, and when the door opened and I saw it, I froze to the floor of the elevator and stared into its enormity. The hold stretched almost across the whole bottom level of the ship. It reminded me of an underground parking lot, except it was missing all the cars.

The copper-colored top and sides of the cargo hold were dulled and slightly greenish and had a framework that looked like the inside of a whale's rib cage. Cegan called the ribs "seams" and pointed out the Natharan numbers on each. Of course, the symbols had no meaning to me. If I got lost, I could never find number one again.

We kept walking and walking. We'd probably passed thirty of the rib-like seams and had seen only boxes and crates when we heard the Yellows laughing with their high-pitched shrieks.

I began to run, and Cegan kept even with me. I didn't slow down until I saw a group of Yellows. Then, I stopped and proceeded very slowly towards them. Even so, as usual, my presence frightened them. The eyes of the Yellows bulged with fear.

There were eleven of them, all gathered in a circle around the kitten. They had been sitting on the floor, apparently watching Lady play with a wadded paper she was batting about. Our arrival made the Yellows bolt up as if they were guilty. The bobbing of their heads and the way they shifted nervously from side to side added further to the illusion.

Their eyes darted from Cegan to me and back again. They didn't dare run away with my husband there, but I could see that they wished to.

"Cegan, you were right. They weren't hurting her. I'm sorry. How do I say 'thank you'?"

"Tashtega, but it is not necessary to say anything, Kira."

I left Cegan's side and stepped closer to them. Immediately, they moved back from me. I saw their eyes fly to Cegan. He gave them an order in Natharan, and they froze.

I reached down and picked up Lady. "Tashtega," I said.

The word traveled among them. Smiles appeared on their faces. "Tashtega, tashtega," they said.

"I am afraid that you have just officially named your kitten," Cegan said. His smile was full of amusement.

"Named her? But I was just thanking them."

"Thank you is *Tashtega*, accent on the last syllable. You've named your kitten *Tashtega* accent on the second."

The Yellows were singing Tashtega over and over. It didn't look like I could do anything to correct my mistake.

"You said Natharan was easy," I reproached Cegan.

"It is," he smiled. "You now know two words: thank you and the name of your cat."

I walked closer to one of the Yellows. His eyes flew to Cegan. He didn't dare back away, but his eyes were saucers as he watched me come closer. I held out my kitten and said, "Tashtega?" The Yellow looked up at Cegan again and then at me. His voice shrieked something in Natharan, and Cegan answered him.

"What did he say?" I asked.

"He wants to know if you are dangerous."

"And, you told him . . . ?"

Cegan smiled again. "I told him the truth, of course, Kira." He was teasing me, as usual, but I was far more interested in the Yellows than responding to Cegan's bait.

"Tashtega?" I asked the Yellow again.

"Tashtega," he repeated, looking down at the purring cat. He looked over at the others. They all repeated the word. The Yellow I had spoken to put out his hand gingerly. His eyes remained on me, cautious, fearful, but he bravely stretched out his hand another inch and touched the kitten. She licked it.

"They really like her, Cegan."

"I see that."

Others began to crowd around, all reaching out to pet Tashtega. Suddenly, all eleven giant Yellows were crowding forward, coming closer and closer.

"Sopta go la manila kula," snapped Cegan, and all the Yellows dropped their hands and backed away. "Sopta go Dram Kira snept to gova."

"Dram Kira," the Yellows began to shout, bowing and saluting and then starting again.

"Sopta go napta ka selop teka," Cegan said.

"Dram Kira," they answered.

"What are you telling them? Why are they doing that?"

Cegan continued to speak in Natharan, and each time, the Yellows responded with "Dram Kira."

"Stop it, please stop it," I pleaded. "I don't want them frightened of me!"

"I am attempting to teach them manners," he said. His face was starting to look like a winter storm brewing, but I hadn't done anything to make him angry. Not yet, anyway.

"Cegan, the Yellows and I were just getting to know each other. I don't want them bowing and yelling out, 'Dram Kira.' I want to be their friend."

Cegan grimaced, gave an order in Natharan, and the Yellows all ran off.

"Cegan, I told you I wanted . . ."

"I know. I heard you. Bring your kitten, Kira. I was wrong. We do have more to discuss about the Yellows."

We returned to our quarters. I sat down on the floor with Tashtega, and Cegan started in with his lecture. "The Yellows are asexual, so they will not bother you in that manner, Kira, but they have no concept of how they might trample you if they crowd about."

"Then why did you think it was safe for Tashtega?"

"The kitten is different. They do not identify it as a person. I am drilling them on the fact that you are a Caste Five, my wife, but they do not understand your helplessness."

"I am not helpless."

Cegan shook his head and issued some kind of Natharan hissing sound. "My, sweet Siren. You would be helpless if they panicked and trampled you. Listen, Kira. It must be obvious to you that they're a great deal bigger than you."

"Cegan, if they got too close, I'd simply scream, or I'd kick them if necessary."

"The scream they would probably ignore, Kira, but it would be unwise. Strange noises frighten them even more. To kick them would be worse. They do not understand your Terran violence. If they felt pain, Kira, they wouldn't associate it with you. They would crowd closer to you, thinking you would protect them. Do you understand, Kira? They would not mean to hurt you, but they would crowd around you if frightened."

I sighed. "Then what should I do?"

"Clap your hands, palm to palm. Show me, Kira."

I did it, feeling stupid. "But what if they can't hear that?"

"Natharans hear vibration much better than Terrans. They will hear it, and they will freeze. Do not ever do anything at that point except hit your palm to palm. Understand?"

"No. Like what?"

"Do not scream, or run, or try to move away. That might alarm them. If they are confused, they can stampede. Now, show me again what to do if they crowd you."

I knocked my palms together and shot a dirty look at Cegan for making me repeat it, like a child or an idiot who couldn't remember.

He smiled. His hand brushed at my hair, and then he sat down with his legs sprawled on both sides of me, his chest up against my back. He was silent for a moment, watching me play with the kitten that was swatting at the hem of my dress.

"For a while, Kira, until I say differently, I want you to stay away from them."

"They didn't do anything to hurt me," I protested. "And you told me what to do in case they crowd me."

"You will not argue about it, Kira."

I stood up and turned to face him. "Cegan, we have to talk about this. You're doing it again. Issuing orders."

Cegan stared at me a moment. My eyes held his.

"I see," he said. He stood up and walked toward the door.

"Cegan, I want to talk about this," I said, but the door was already sliding closed behind him, and for the first time, it was locked.

I sat down on the floor and played with Tashtega. When I got hungry, the food machine issued me one of the dry bars that were supposed to be a healthful snack. I drank water, supplied Tashtega with her needs, and lay down on the bed.

I thought about the Yellows all that evening. Had Cegan not been there when they crowded around me, I would have been frightened. Sometimes, I forgot about Cegan's being a giant, but the Yellows, even though they were the same size, were so different from him.

They were like small children who'd grown enormous. I tried to imagine being calm enough to clap my palms in the way Cegan had taught me. Would I have the courage not to scream, not to try to run?

I'd once been told that if you came upon a wild bear, you were supposed to stand there and growl back at him — never to run from him. It was the same with the Yellows. Could I stand still and do what Cegan had told me? It hurt to admit it, but maybe he was right.

I fell asleep, but even with Tashtega at my side, I slept fitfully, waking often to see if Cegan had returned. In the night, I heard him come in. He sent the kitten out with one of the Yellows and lay down beside me. I didn't protest when his arms wrapped around me. I snuggled up to him and slept.

In the morning, I woke to find him watching me. I smiled, forgetting how angry we'd been with each other.

"Last night, the trade was completed, Kira," Cegan said.

I sat up. "Then we're leaving today?"

His eyes were studying me, watching my reactions. "Yes."

"Then I can't say goodbye to my father?"

A corner of Cegan's mouth twitched with the merest flick of a smile. "Kira, did you think I'd take you away without letting you see each other again?"

"He's coming?"

Cegan nodded. His hand traced my cheekbone downwards to my jaw. "He has already left the farm.

"Kira, I am sorry about yesterday. I must not have explained sufficiently."

"No. It was my fault. You were right, Cegan. I'm not ready to be alone with the Yellows. I'm sorry for being so stubborn."

As usual with our arguments, the "making up" was delightful. Later, I lay beside him, my fingers stroking the soft petals of his chest, and I felt a surge of happiness flooding my mind. I was so lucky to have his love. Cegan was always so patient with me. I promised myself I'd try harder not to argue.

Chapter Twenty-one: Good-byes

My father arrived a couple of hours later. He'd brought a box of things for me to take with me, mainly pictures of Mom, Powder, and himself, a yearbook from my senior year, a couple of videos of dancing competitions and some of me barrel racing, and the stuffed animal I'd always kept on my bed. I hugged him and thanked him for his thoughtfulness.

Cegan whistled for a Yellow. It came running in. My husband took the box and gave several sharp orders in Natharan. The Yellow immediately ran off, carrying my box. Cegan turned to my father. "Are you sure you will not come with us, Hank? I would be honored to present you to my parents."

My father kind of guffawed, but his eyes were still looking worried about the Yellows. "Maybe next time, Cegan. You're sure those men won't hurt Kira?"

"They're not dangerous, Dad. I'm going to teach them to read."

Cegan let out a strange noise, and my father and I both stared at him. His double row of teeth was flashing.

My father shuddered. "You didn't answer me, Cegan. Your crew — they're big like you, but they're different. How do you know they won't hurt her?"

"Dad," I sighed and shook my head. "Cegan says they're not violent."

My father continued to ignore me, studying Cegan.

"The crew are neuter, Hank, but Kira knows that she is not to be alone with them."

Since the Yellows had been the object of our most recent argument, I wisely fell silent.

Dad nodded, tossed a puzzled look at me, then glanced at Cegan. "Hey, that reminds me. Cegan asked me to bring your jeans to you, Kira," he said, handing me a bag.

I laughed and took them from Dad. They were my newest jeans, the ones I hadn't even had a chance to wear yet. But why had Cegan asked my father to bring something that could be formatted in the clothes machine?

I was careful not to mention Natharan technology, but I figured he'd know what I was talking about. "I don't understand, Cegan. You don't want me to wear them, so why would you ask Dad to bring them?"

Cegan's smile disappeared. His eyes darkened, and his face grew stern. "The jeans are an expression of who you are, Kira. I want you to understand that it will never be my intention to change that part of you. Let them be the symbol of your spirit. I salute them, but they are also my challenge. I think you have learned that I will not waver on those issues we have discussed, and I will remind you of our agreement."

I understood exactly what Cegan was saying. The jeans would disappear if I wore them outside our quarters, and if I challenged him on any issue that involved safety, there would be the chair or my room.

"I accept your terms, Cegan. I can't promise that I'll always remember when I lose my temper, but I'll try."

Dad was shaking his head. "Are you two arguing again?"

"No, Dad, not at all," I said.

Cegan didn't say anything, but his arm circled me, and he pulled me close.

"The pictures from the wedding are not ready," Dad told Cegan. "You'll have to wait until you return, but I did bring you this." He handed Cegan the color photo the newsman had taken on the day Cegan's ship arrived. Dad had had it enlarged, professionally mounted, and framed. It was the picture taken just after Dad said that Cegan was a mistake that could be corrected. Dad's words had angered me, so I'd flung my head up in outrage, and my eyes had been full of defiance.

Cegan took the picture. His eyes studied it. Then, he reached out his hand and shook my dad's. "I am immensely grateful for your gift, Hank. It has captured the highest essence of Kira. I thank you sincerely."

Again, a Yellow was whistled for, and the picture was taken away. My dad's eyes narrowed with distrust.

"Kira," my father said, and he took hold of my shoulders in a grip that told me a lecture was coming. "I don't have a present for you, except advice. You've rarely taken it, but I pray you'll listen now. Your husband is not the one I would have chosen for you, but he's a wise man, and he loves you. Don't get so stubborn that you don't listen to him. I've watched him examine the issues and base his actions on them. His judgment is good. You rely too much on emotion, and you let it flare up with no thought for the consequences."

My father was gripping my shoulders much too tightly. "Dad," I complained.

'No, you listen. You trust Cegan's common sense, Kira. You hear me? Where you're going, you're like a baby learning to crawl. If

Cegan says, 'Don't touch,' you mind him. Understand what I'm telling you?"

I nodded. One of Cegan's brows arched like a Halloween cat. I hoped that he wasn't treating the lecture as if it were addressed to him.

Dad repeated, "Do you understand me, Kira?" in a tone of increased intensity.

"Yes. I understand, Dad."

"I don't want to hear that you've gotten hurt out there, Kira. I want to see you come back, just like you are, whole and safe. Will you give me your word that you'll heed him?"

"I told you, I will."

Dad crushed me in an embrace so tight I couldn't breathe. "I gotta go now. I know your husband needs to lift up. I love you, baby."

"I love you, too, Dad."

He turned and walked down the ramp. Too quickly, the door was sliding shut. I barely heard the clank of its locking mechanism, the sound that had frightened me so much on my first day. All I could think about was that my father was leaving, and I wouldn't get to see him for several years.

Cegan walked over to the door and manually bolted a second security lock. He'd never done that before. He was preparing us for the blast off.

Cegan didn't look at me, but I could see the worry in his posture and the way he carried his head. Did he still believe that I might demand the door be opened so I could walk away from him? I went to my husband and wrapped my arms as far around his body as I could reach. I lay my head on his chest and breathed in the wondrous scent of him. "I love you," I told him.

At once, his lips were on mine, and he was swooping me up into his arms. "I have not yet carried my bride across the threshold," he said.

I laughed. "Where did you hear about that?"

"I have been reading more about your wedding traditions," he told me as he carried me up to the front of the ship. "I should have preferred stepping on the champagne glass rather than drinking from it," he teased. He whispered several more traditions that he especially liked. Some of them made my face heat with embarrassment.

Cegan carried me to the foreword section of what humans would call the bridge. I hadn't been there yet. Had I thought about it, I would have expected to see a group of Yellows all bent over controls and dials, but the room was empty.

Cegan held me for another moment. He watched as my eyes scanned the room. Then, he pretended to drop me. I screamed and laughed, clutching at his neck.

"Good," he said. "I want your complete attention as I carry you over the threshold."

He trumpeted like an elephant, stamped his feet, and made a grand announcement about its being the official threshold and the start of our life together.

It was all so charming. I giggled at his silliness. Next, he placed me into one of the white leather chairs. There was no seat belt, no special padding. It was simply like all the other chairs around the ship, comfortable and body-conforming.

He spoke in Natharan, and a wide screen opened in front of us — perhaps opened is the wrong word, for nothing moved. The wall just cleared so you could view SpacePort. I could see that a huge crowd had assembled in preparation for the ship's departure. Policemen were standing around, holding everyone back, and a man was stretching out orange tape to outline safety borders.

Newsmen and the camera crews were in front, just beyond where the orange tape formed the border. All the excitement, all the crowding, reminded me of the day when Cegan had landed. Had it truly been so short a time since I'd been standing there in the crowd, waiting for the husband I'd never met?

"Are you positive that you are willing to go with me, Kira?" Cegan asked, dropping to his knees. "There are no Terrans in Natharan. Everything will be strange to you. Are you sure that this is what you want?"

"I'm your wife, Cegan. Wherever you are, I'll be happy. Remember?"

"I promised you that I would ask you again, Kira, but I am so relieved that your answer remains the same." He lifted up my hand. His lips touched the warm underside, and he placed tiny kisses across the palm. "You honor me, my beautiful wife."

A voice speaking in Engspan announced that SpacePort was now ready for our departure. Cegan stood up, and his eyes stared out at the crowds below us.

He spoke a word or two in Natharan and then said, "Thank you. Goodbye, Earth."

He glanced at me. "Do you wish to say anything, Kira? It would please the newsmen if you would."

What was I supposed to say? Something historic? Cegan saw the panic in my eyes. He spoke a word in Natharan to close the system and said, "Do not *worry* it, Kira. Say what you want or say nothing."

He stood up and waited for my answer. I thought about my dad and everyone I was leaving behind. I nodded. "Yes, please. I would like to speak."

"Tonoke," Cegan said, and then he nodded for me to begin.

"Goodbye, Earth. I will miss you. Thank you to all my friends, to President and Mrs. Clayborn, and to my father. I love you, Dad." I nodded to Cegan. He flashed his teeth at me and then spoke several sentences, all in Natharan.

The view screen rippled like waves of silver water were rushing across it. "Why is it doing that? What does it mean?" I asked, a little scared.

"It means that we are lifting up, Kira."

"But are you piloting the ship all by yourself? You didn't do a countdown! Where are the controls?"

Cegan moved to stand behind me. "Relax, my Siren. Everything is fine." His hands began to massage my neck. "Remember, Kira, this is a Natharan ship. It does not need any of that."

The people in SpacePort began to grow smaller and smaller, and then we were up above them, and they were just globs of color and flashing lights. The ship began to move forward, as well as up, and I could see buildings and streets with tiny, darting pilotcars zipping about like humming birds searching for flowers.

It was day, and yet the moon hung, a pale light against a washed-out blue. I could feel no movement in the ship's shift, no bone-crushing thrust, no lack of gravity or air, yet the moon was growing closer, the sky bigger. Off to the right, the sun leered down at us. It, too, seemed large but dulled, as if the screen were coating its light with a misty fog.

Cegan spoke in Natharan, and the screen was divided in half. One part showed what I'd been watching — the sun, the moon, the darkening sky. The other looked down on our departure.

My eyes fastened to the second screen where the Earth was growing round. It was so beautiful — the blue of blue jay's wings and babies' eyes. Its brownish patches were wreathed in puffs of albino clouds. Tears filled my eyes, and I wanted to stop and re-examine what I was doing in leaving my home world.

Cegan sat down in the chair beside mine. He launched into an explanation of trajectories and how we'd be swinging off Mars' gravitational pull. His finger pointed back to the first screen, where a huge reddish planet was growing. Another word spoken in Natharan zoomed Mars in closer. I could see the settlements and farm zones, with their globes of protection surrounding them, translucent and sparkling in the sunshine.

Cegan spoke again, and then Earth was suddenly bigger, too, like a weather map from a TV news broadcast. I sighed. "Can I stand up yet?"

"At any time, Kira. Even during liftoff. I thought that this first time, you would be more comfortable sitting."

I circled the room, inspecting it, comparing it to what I'd imagined it to look like. It wasn't impressive: five chairs, an elaborate screen, a food and drink machine on one wall, and a computer terminal that could issue books or clothing or whatever you desired. The room just didn't look like a ship's bridge.

"If everything is computerized, what if there is an emergency?" I asked. "Don't you have to have a control panel for that?"

"There are no control panels, Kira. This ship has two main computers, each with an independent brain. Should both of them fail us, an emergency beacon notifies Natharan and all spacecraft in the Grid. There is only a .00001% chance of double malfunctions. Your odds of getting safely to Natharan in this ship are far greater than taking a Terran elevator to the top of a tall building."

Cegan stood up and came towards me. "If it were necessary for an organic brain to control this ship, Kira, I'd urge us to jump off."

Cegan draped his arm about me and began to tell me about Mars. That settled my uneasiness. We stood there, watching the red planet for a while. Cegan pointed out several landmarks that I'd heard of. It was fascinating, but my eyes kept veering back to Earth.

Sadness enshrouded me. It seeped into my chest until I could scarcely breathe. Then, it formed into tears and began to slip down my cheeks.

Cegan turned me away from the screen. "Kira, Earth will still be there when we return. Don't focus on what you are leaving. Turn your eyes instead towards your destination."

He spoke a word, and Earth was gone. In its place was Natharan, the Natharan we would see in three months. It was a beautiful planet, green and blue, with swirls of white. It looked peaceful and calm.

"We are a long way from your new home," Cegan told me, "and that is good. It will give you time, Kira, to learn the language and the customs. I will teach you, and the books and the computer programs I have made for you will help you learn. By the day we reach Natharan, you will be ready. In the meantime, there will be a quiet period away from others in which we can love and grow even closer together. We will be able to knot the cement of our marriage."

I laughed when he said that, understanding that he was making a joke, connecting "tie the knot" to the minister's preference for cementing relationships.

Cegan's arms, green and soft as silk and velvet mixed, pulled me closer. The beauty of his features still awed me. His eyes were alien eyes, yet how familiar they seemed now. I couldn't imagine them being any different. They were accepting eyes, eyes that loved.

My husband smiled down at me. "The future is a lovely concept, is it not, my Siren? The past has mistakes written on it — not that we error deliberately, but yet there are situations we wish we'd handled better, words we wish we hadn't said."

Cegan's eyes were soft, the diamonds clouded by his vision. He was playing with my hair, his fingers weaving among my curls. I sighed softly, contentedly.

"It is the future I prefer, Kira. The future stretches across the horizon, always in perfection."

I was listening to his words, admiring the fine tapering of the hand that was indicating the horizon of our future. The fingers, so long and slender, moved gracefully, yet I knew their strength, the power of their clasp.

"And every day, Kira," Cegan continued, we can choose what we will write about in that future and which dream we will follow." His hand reached out to enfold mine, and he brought it up to his mouth to kiss the back of it. "Together, you and I, Kira," he said, staring into my eyes. "Together, we will write that future."

He pulled me close and kissed my forehead. I realized I felt no sadness anymore. Cegan was right. The past was only whispers and remembrances. I would hold it dear. I had lovely memories: my father, my mother, playing on the farm, riding Powder, dancing in competitions, and my friends in high school and at Transtel System. All those days of the past had made me who I was.

But the future was ahead of us and filled with Cegan, strange adventures, and the life we would build together.

I smiled into my husband's eyes, and under Mars' unwinking appraisal, my lips sought his, and together we celebrated our future.

www.ingramcontent.com/pod-product-compliance
Lightning Source LLC
Chambersburg PA
CBHW070843250626
47159CB00003B/912